To Bea

Yellow Bird

a Webb Sawyer Mystery

by

Douglas Quinn

Enjoy the read!

Douglas Quinn

Books by Douglas Quinn

The Ellis Family Novels/Suspense

The Catalan Gambit
The Spanish Game
The Capablanca Variation
— The End Game

Webb Sawyer Mysteries

Blue Heron Marsh
Pelican Point
Swan's Landing
Egret's Cove
Yellow Bird

The Ancestor Series

Cornelius The Orphan
Samuel The Pioneer
Hate Evil The Nomad

Anthology

Four of a Kind: an Anthology of Mystery and Suspense

Children's Chapter Books

**Charles of Colshire Castle
Charles & Hero (Fantasy)**

The Purple Dragon
Isle of Mists
The Dreadmen

The Adventures of Quinn Higgins Boy Detective The Case of . . .

The Missing Homework
Bigfoot on the Loose
The Haunted House
Blackbeard's Treasure
The Lost U-Boat
The Gray Ghost's Belt Buckle
The Secret of Crater Lake

The Adventures of Summer McPhee of Ocracoke Island

The Midnight Skulker
Kilroy Was Here
The Pink Lady
The Mystery Club

Little Books for Little Readers

Gracie The Undercover Beagle — The Egg Thief

Solstice The Determined Beagle — Long Journey Home

Gracie The Undercover Beagle — Little Miss Stinky

Gracie The Undercover Beagle — Ghost of the Forest

Egret's Cove
a novel by Douglas Quinn

This is a work of fiction. All of the characters, organizations, and events portrayed in this novel are either products of the author's imagination or are used fictitiously.

No part of this publication may be reproduced in whole or in part, or stored in a retrieval system, or transmitted in any form or by any means, electronic, mechanical, photocopying, recording, or otherwise, without written permission of the publisher. For information regarding permission, write to AAS White Heron Press, 1623 Soundneck Road, Elizabeth City, NC 27909, USA.

ISBN 13: 978-1545038116 / EAN 10: 1545038112

Text copyright © 2017 by Douglas Quinn
Cover art copyright © 2017 by Donna Higgins Colson
All rights reserved
Published by AAS White Heron Press
1623 Soundneck Road, Elizabeth City, NC 27909
White Heron Press and associated logos are trademarks
and/or
registered trademarks of American Artists' Studios

Printed in the U.S.A.

Cover Design by Kim Colson

Once again, thanks to

Donna Higgins Colson
for the manuscript readings
and good advice

and to

James Fletcher
for spending time with me
and providing valuable information
about flying and maintaining a
crop duster, including how to
sabotage one for the sake of my story

This one

for Donna Marie

the one for me

Vengeance has no foresight.

—Napoleon

Prologue

ERSKINE WEEKS HAD a dental appointment at one that afternoon, so he'd only booked two of James Nixon's fields for spraying, a total of 200 acres. Truth was, the tooth was aching and he'd wished he'd put the jobs off until tomorrow. Too late for that now. He'd committed. Besides. It was a perfect day to fly. And he needed the extra money if, for nothing else, to pay for the new filling and cap. Even though their plan was very expensive, it didn't include dental.

Always something.

He went through his routine. It began with coffee, black, a banana and an Entenmann's chocolate covered donut. Just enough to keep him going without setting too heavy on his stomach. Betty had been on his ass about his gut. She'd thrown out the last box of Entenmann's he'd bought. This time he found a hiding place. And he didn't have to worry about her catching him with them. She was up and out of there early every morning for a workout with her trainer at the Elizabeth City YMCA. She'd been on this working out kick for the past three months. One day, she just got up and said, "I'm gonna get my body looking good again. Hell, he'd been satisfied with it how it was. She had lost about twenty pounds though. He'd give her that.

Once Erskine was finished with his breakfast, he collected his aerial maps, which he'd already marked. A farmer may have several fields, but may only want a certain field or fields sprayed. Sometimes, he just wanted a particular section of a field.

Erskine studied the maps, then folded them up and headed out to the hanger, which was really just a open-faced metal building with an office and connecting storage room. He had a four-wheeler parked near the side door, but he didn't bother using it much anymore. Erskine preferred a leisurely walk up the field road out to the shed.

Five minutes later he was unlocking the office door. Once inside, he stood there and collected his thoughts. He went through his morning, step by step, one, two, three . . . .

Once the schedule was organized in his mind, he stepped into the storage room next to the office and went straight to the mixer, where he filled it with water in preparation for adding the Asana, the insecticide.

The Asana AX, a Dupont product with an emulsive concentrate of .66 pounds of active ingredient per gallon was delivered to him in 30-gallon drums. Erskine connected the pump to one of the drums, which he used to pump and meter the insecticide into the mixer. As he added it, the mixer kept the water moving, agitating the 50 gallons of Asana into the plain water. For the 200 acres he needed to do this morning, he needed two loads, which used about six ounces per acre.

Before he loaded up with insecticide and fuel, Erskine did his pre-flight walk-around. His yellow crop duster with black cowl and side stripes, and a closed cockpit was an Air Tractor, designed and manufactured in Texas by a man named Leland Snow. Erskine gave it a name. He called it Yellow Bird. As part of pre-flight routine, he checked the oil and gas tank, the prop for nicks, as well as the rest of the plane for anything loose. Once that was done, he hit the fuel drain, bleeding some fuel into a plastic cup to check for water. Once he was sure there was no water in the fuel tank, he filled both 84-gallon tanks with 170 gallons each of Jet-A fuel—a fancy name for kerosene—from his 2,000 gallon storage tank. Finally, he filled the spray tanks with the insecticide from the mixer.

Once Yellow Bird was ready, Erskine got his ear plugs, his ag pilot's helmet, given to him by his father before he'd died, his Ray-Ban sunglasses, because his daughter said he had to be cool when he was flying, and his maps, then crawled into the Air Tractor. Once in, he set the maps in the open glove compartment, then did a quick look at the gauges, including the torque meter, alternator and temperature gage. Everything looked normal. Even though the land was actually about twelve feet above sea level, there were enough topographic fluctuations that it worked best to set it at zero, which he did.

Everything was a go. He flipped the ignitor switch, hit the starter, introduced fuel into the carburetor, and cranked up the Lycoming Radial 9-cycle piston engine. He listened closely to the whine to be sure it was running smooth. It was.

He taxied out onto the air strip, which was a two-hundred-yard mowed area cut into the crop field, rolled down to the west end, closest to the hangar, then turned the plane around. He rotated the props from level to a slight pitch. This assured oil was moving to them. He then feathered them as flat as possible so the engine could get more horsepower for take off.

Since he didn't have a heavy load, he set the flaps at ten degrees, then powered up and began rolling down the runway. While he monitored the torque and heat gage, he pushed the speed for take off up to 2,500 rpms. On a hot day Erskine's take-off speed was about 90 mph; on a cool day, between 70 and 80 mph. Today was somewhere in between and he lifted off at about 85 mph. Once he was off the ground, he pulled back to about 2,000 rpms.

Like his father, who taught him how to fly, Erskine was old school. He'd flown without communications in the plane for many years. Finally, he broke down and got his first radio in the cockpit. That said, he refused to use it unless there was an emergency. If he was going to be flying near the Coast Guard Station or over the Pasquotank River, he'd call the base air control tower before take-off and let them know his schedule, but this day he wasn't doing either.

James Nixon's farm was right next to John and Tabby Markham's place on Tyler Swamp Road. When John was still alive, he and Erskine's dad, Clayton, had been best friends. Erskine liked Tabby but, while she was a kind-hearted woman, she was also a non-stop gabber and he avoided her when possible.

Erskine flew straight to Nixon's fields. Even though he was very familiar with them, he double-checked his maps to be sure he sprayed the correct sections. Once he was sure, he began his passes over the spray sites. As a precaution, he always did three passes to be sure there were no new obstructions that would hinder or endanger his runs. Once he was satisfied that all was well, he began his run, although if something didn't "feel" right, he would abort and make another pass.

This morning was particularly calm. Even so, that could quickly change. His first pass was to check the wind drift. There were two reasons for this. One, he didn't want to fly back into the spray on the next pass. Two, he wanted to avoid having the spray drift into the owners or his neighbor's house and yard. To do this safely, he engaged his smokers by flipping the switch to inject Corus oil, a paraffin-based substance, close to the end of the exhaust pipe where it is extremely hot. This creates smoke, which is expelled out the rear of the plane, mimicking the actual insecticide spray run.

From above, Erskine watched the smoke settle pretty much straight down. That was good. If the breeze had been blowing right to left, on his first run he would have had to release the spray over Tabby's side yard to let it drift onto that edge of the field of soybeans. If that happened, he knew he'd get a call. Not that she would bust his chops for it, but there would be an excuse for her to say, "I saw you flying over my yard this morning," and on and on it would go. If he let the call go to voice mail, she would fill up the space, then call back later anyway. Even Betty had mixed feelings about Tabby. Betty always checked caller ID, never picked up when it was Tabby, and always acted as if she didn't get or hear her messages.

He remembered the time, not long after he'd taken over the business from his father, when he'd either misjudged his tailwind, or an unexpected gust had come up—he never had determined exactly what had happened—and caught him at the end of a pass, just as he was beginning to pull up. His heart almost blew up when he saw the oak tree at the back of Tabby's yard looming in front of him. On pure reflex, he'd yanked the stick all the way back and just made it over the top of the tree, but not without several terrifying seconds of bumping and scrapping as he passed over. Later, he had to call her and ask if she minded him coming over and looking for the expensive nozzles that had been torn off the end of the booms. It had not only been a frightening ordeal, but embarrassing as hell.

With his right hand on the stick and his left hand working what crop-dusters called the money handle, which opened and closed the valve under the plane to move the spray from the pump to the booms and out the nozzles, he began his first pass. With no appreciable wind, he didn't have to worry about kicking the rudder to keep level.

On the first pass, he used his GPS system to mark the A/B line, which is the set-up for the rest of the run, then set the GPS at three feet for the vertical. Each pass he would check the light bar in front of him on the outside of the cockpit, which had three red vertical lights with a horizontal amber light on each end. This was to be sure the plane remained as level as possible during the passes.

At the end of the first pass, he pulled up and turned to his right, being sure to go around the north end of Tabby's house and yard. If she was home, she'd make it a point to come out on her front porch while he was spraying and wave at him as he came in for his runs. This, of course, would also prompt a phone call later. When he came around for the second pass, sure enough, there she was, hand in the air, waving away. As always, he groaned and waved back.

Sometimes, by the third pass, she'd have returned inside, but she was still there. As he pulled out of his fourth pass, Erskine Weeks was thinking ahead to the coming ordeal in the dentist chair. He was at the top of his climb and had just turned to the right when he heard a distinct POP. "What the—" The words died in his mouth as the stick went dead in his right hand. Erskine wasn't a man who used profanity, but the words, "Son of a bitch, this isn't fuckin' good," came roiling out like water over a falls.

The Air Tractor continued up and forward for a short period of time while Erskine tried to think of something he could do. Radio? Too late for that. His frantic thoughts were useless. The last thing that went through his mind was something his father once told him when Erskine was first leaning how to fly. "If the stick goes, you'll lose total control of the plane and you will come down like a shot turkey buzzard."

Fortunately, Erskine Weeks had passed out before he hit the ground.

Chapter 1

EXCEPT FOR THE man in the far back corner, The Java Hut was quiet. Basil was draped over on my right shoulder, causing the usual reaction and chatter from the baristas behind the counter. Basil is a gray, tiger-stripped cat with emerald green eyes and a perpetual smile who thinks he's a dog. I call him my watch cat. He'd been given to me a while back by my long-time friend, Blythe Parsons, the well-known fantasy writer who lives in Ocracoke Village at the southern end of the Outer Banks. She thought I needed company. I don't know about that, but I do know that Basil once saved my life. But that's another story.

I ordered my usual, a large snickerdoodle, a pound of the same with an espresso grind to take with me to Aunt Tabby's, and a saucer for Basil. I'm a coffee snob and if it isn't snickerdoodle, it isn't my cuppa jo.

My thought was to head straight out to Weeksville. But, since I was running early, I decided to sit down and read the local paper. I found a copy lying on the table next to the corner man.

Things in Elizabeth City hadn't changed much. Members of the city council fighting with each other over some procedural matter as if the world was going to end if some agenda item wasn't voted on within the next seventy-two hours. Over on Winston Street somebody had shot somebody else in a domestic argument, apparently over laundry. A new fast-food place had just opened up on Ehringhaus. I figured that fast-food places open for business inside the city limits were running neck-in-neck with the number of churches.

On the whole, not much changed; just got larger and more.

Too many people.

Whatever happened to sex for fun?

"The world is a funny place," the corner man said, interrupting my musings. He didn't say anything about Basil, who was lapping up the last of the cream laced with a few drops of coffee

"Yep, sure is," I said, knowing that there was nothing funny about it at all. To avoid further conversation, I wished the corner man a good day, put Basil back on my shoulder, got up and departed.

The road out to Weeksville took me past the turn-of the-twentieth-century house where Amanda Eure had lived. Soon I would be crossing the bridge where she'd died. It made me think of Benjamin Wilson, Jr., the man who I knew killed her, but could never prove—nor did I ever want to. That, too, was another story.

I probably could have taken my hands off the wheel of Trusty Rusty, who I was sure knew the way. Trusty Rusty is the 1986 Ford Ranger pickup I'd inherited from my dad. I could afford a new vehicle, but why bother. I seldom drive the old girl, except for errands around Nags Head, over to Nan's restaurant in Manteo, or an occasional trip to Ocracoke or to Weeksville.

Every time I fire up the old powder blue rust bucket I think of Dad, driving around the narrow, winding Weeksville country roads, checking on his crops and workers. My theory is, if a car—or in this case, a truck—starts up and gets me where I'm going and back home, it's a good vehicle, no matter what it looks like.

As I came over the Newbegun Creek and past the Weeksville Ginning Company I heard sirens. There was a fire station on Peach Tree Road and I presumed the sound was coming from there. I took a left on Mill Creek Road that cut behind the Weeksville Grocery and rolled up to the stop sign at Union Church Road. That's when I saw two fire trucks and an emergency medical vehicle blowing through the caution light at the crossroads in front of the store, and were coming my way.

Basil, who had been asleep on the passenger side of the front seat was up on his hind legs, peering out the window. He howled as the three vehicles wailed past us, then made an immediate right onto Tyler Swamp Road.

My immediate thought was, *This will give Aunt Tabby something to talk about besides the flying turtles and red, hopping rabbits.*

Since I didn't own a telephone of any kind, she'd called Brant Cloninger at the Whalebone Junction Bait and Tackle Shop on the Nags Head Causeway. Brant then sent his son Rudy, who took a skiff out to my stilt home in the marsh. He found me on the upper deck, the one facing the marsh. If my house sat ten feet higher, I could see the Atlantic Ocean.

I had been reading an Ed McBain crime novel titled *Give the Boys a Great Big Hand*! Basil had already alerted me to someone's arrival, so I'd taken a look and saw it was Rudy. Brant never sent Rudy out unless it was something important enough to bother me. Those were my standing instructions.

It turned out it was a message from my Aunt Tabby. Rudy said she was babbling about flying painted turtles and giant red bunnies that could hop as high as the house. Aunt Tabby had always been an excitable woman, but had she suddenly gone bananas? I'd never known her to touch even a glass of wine. Had she started drinking? I'd calmed her down and promised that I would come out the next morning and see what was going on. She'd asked me to stay for a few days and visit. Since I hadn't seen her in months, and Nan Ftorek, my friend with benefits and more, was up north visiting a long lost relative, I'd packed for a week; actually, I hoped to only stay a couple of days, then take a drive over to Troy, North Carolina to do some fishing with my friend Ben Straker.

As it turned out . . . .

I followed the fire brigade down Tyler Swamp, hoping they'd continue past Aunt Tabby's so I wouldn't get tied up in their important business. I wasn't one of those who enjoyed watching or rubbernecking fires, accidents or the like. In fact, those who did annoyed me to no end.

Once, on Interstate 64, I got stuck in heavy traffic that had slowed to a creeping stop when gawkers just had to see what happened to a large, black Nissan Armada with tinted windows. The Armada had been stopped by two police cars— maybe chased down for all I knew. They had pulled completely off the highway and weren't blocking traffic, so there was no need for a traffic jam.

Ridiculous! It turned my three-hour trip to Richmond into five hours. From that day on, I became a blue-highway traveler.

As I broke from the tree line, ahead I could see a narrow plume of smoke rising from the ground. I wasn't sure, because the road curved to the right and there was a house and outbuildings blocking my view, but it seemed very close to Aunt Tabby's. Once I'd rounded the curve I saw that it, in fact, was Tabby's property. Not her house, thank goodness, but something in her front yard.

There were police cars already on the road in front of her place and the fire trucks were pulling up, one of them into the yard, the other about a hundred yards further down at the tree line on the other side of Tabby's property, where the hydrant was located. Tabby was always bragging how her insurance premiums for the house were a lot less because the hydrant was so close.

I had to do a double-take. I couldn't believe what I was seeing.

Just before I got to Tabby's, I pulled into James Nixon's field lane. I told Basil to stay put—I wasn't sure he would, because it was warm and the windows were halfway down; not to mention that he thrived on excitement—I got out of Trusty Rusty and headed up the road.

What I saw was Erskine Weeks' bright yellow crop duster—or what was left of it—buried nose-first in Aunt Tabby's front yard. The canopy had blown off and was lying top down in the first several rows of the soy bean field. I could see Aunt Tabby on the front porch, hands to her mouth, being steadied by a sheriff's deputy. She had yet to see me. Her eyes were riveted on the wrecked plane. That was probably a good thing. Tabby going into hysterics, which is what she'd probably do, wouldn't be helpful.

The one fire truck had already began hosing down the burning wreck with the limited supply of water they carried in the truck, while the firemen from the other truck had hooked up their hose to the hydrant and were rushing it to the scene. Through the smoke and wreckage I could see an arm extending out of the cockpit area, on the ground.

"Crap!" I muttered. If that was in fact Erskine's arm, and I had no reason to doubt that it was, he was not walking away from this one. My next thought went to Betty, his wife. I looked around to see if she was anywhere around, but if she was I didn't see her.

My dad and Erskine and Betty had all grown up together, had all gone to the original Weeksville School when it was first through the twelfth grade. I remember Erskine began flying Yellow Bird—the name he'd given his Air Tractor—when he was spraying Dad's crops. He used to wave at me from his cockpit as he came in to start a run. Once Erskine even flew under the power lines next to the road because he knew I was watching. I was a kid and it had both scared the crap out of me and thrilled me at the same time. He was not only a good pilot, but a good person with a fun sense of humor. Knowing I would never see him again made me sad.

Finally, the firemen got the blaze out and the EMTs moved in. I knew many of the men who were working that day, both firemen and the med-techs. I knew many of them knew Erskine, too. It was a hard thing to watch, but as much as I hate to admit it, I'd seen worse in Bosnia — much worse.

Cops were everywhere taking pictures. I saw two of them take Aunt Tabby back inside, presumably to interview her as to what she might have seen. I was happy she wasn't there to see them extract Erskine's body from the wreckage and place the charred remains in a body bag. One of the deputies, Aubrey Meads, a man I'd known all my life, saw me standing there and waved me into the yard.

When I walked over to him, we shook hands. "Been a while since I've seen you," Aubrey said. Then, "Looks like you got here at a good time for your aunt. I'm sure she'll need your comfort and support."

I'd always liked Aubrey. He was a good guy with a nice family and a sense of fairness in dealing with the people of the community where he'd grown up. Not all of the deputies for the county were like that. Packing a sidearm with the law on your side to use it corrupted some people. I didn't tell him what brought me to Tabby's house at that inauspicious moment.

"It's a shock for me, too," I said. "Our families were close."

"Yeah, I know," Aubrey said.

"He was a skilled pilot," I said. "Must have had a malfunction of some kind."

"Yeah. Had to of been. They've already called the NTSB. They'll have somebody out here pretty quick to check it out." Then, "I feel bad for the family."

"Anybody been in touch with Betty?" I asked, looking around to see if she'd shown up while we were talking. All I saw was a blond-haired kid next to the road standing next to a bike. Another gawker. Starting young.

"Sheriff Grimes got their daughter, who called her mother. I think she was supposed to be at the YMCA when this happened. I understand she's on her way." Then Aubrey said, "Maybe you ought to go see about Miss Tabby."

"I will in a minute. Two officers took her inside, I guess to get a statement. I don't want to disturb them. Soon as she sees me, she'll get all worked up and they'll never find out anything."

Aubrey just nodded.

It was about a half hour before I was able to go inside to console Aunt Tabby. Betty Weeks had shown up just as I went up onto the porch. There was nothing I could do or say to her right then. Anyway, it wouldn't have been appropriate, so I went on into the house. As I suspected, when Tabby saw me, she jumped up from her chair, ran to me and flung her arms around my arms pinning them to my side. She was a five-foot-three, sixty-two year old gray-haired woman with a pudgy countenance. I didn't really know what to do or say, so I just stood there letting her hug me.

Then I noticed a neighbor lady from down the other side of the road, coming out of the kitchen with a cup of something hot in her hand—tea, I guessed,

"Oh!" she said when she saw me.

If I remembered correct, her name was Sarah Aycock, but I wasn't totally sure. As far as I knew, she and Aunt Tabby weren't all that close. I took a chance and said, "Hello, Miss Sarah."

She scrunched her eyebrows, then said, "You're her nephew, right? Jenson Sawyer's boy."

"Yes ma'am. Webb Sawyer."

She nodded and pursed her lips as if she knew something else about me and wanted to say so. Instead she said, "I brought hot tea for Miss Tabby. You want me to make you some?"

"No thank you, ma'am." Then, "Thank you for coming in to help. I'll take it from here." I thought that would do it, but she ignored me and sat down on the couch, dead center in the middle of it, I suppose hoping Tabby would sit on one side and I'd be forced to either sit in one of the other two chairs or sit next to her. Some people just don't have a lick of sense.

Suddenly, Aunt Tabby pulled away from me, put her hands on my shoulders and said, "Oh, Webb. Thank God you're here. It was terrible! Terrible!"

"She told the deputies all about it," Sarah Aycock butt in.

"I'm sure she did, Miss Sarah. I'm sure she did." I was trying to find a way to get rid of the neighbor without offending her. Tabby might need someone to keep an eye on her for the next few weeks, maybe even look in on her. Tabby had a tendency to put off some of her church-lady friends with her well-meaning but sometimes intrusive ways. I wondered if Sarah Aycock went to Tabby's church. I guessed probably not. Turns out I was wrong.

Tabby interrupted my thoughts with, "First the flying turtles and rabbits and now this."

I got a quizzical look from Sarah Aycock and said to her, "This is why she needs to rest." Then to Aunt Tabby, "Everything will be just fine once you drink the tea Miss Sarah made for you, then lay down and take a nap. Then we can talk about it all."

To Sarah Aycock I said, smoothly, "I'll be here to look after her for the next couple of days, but it would be appreciated, Miss Sarah, if you could keep an eye on her after I leave. Maybe stop by from time to time."

She said okay, that she would, but when she didn't move her ass off the couch, I just grabbed the cup of tea off the coffee table, put my arm around Aunt Tabby and led her back toward her room, telling her I'd stay inside until things quieted down.

I got her in her bed on top of the covers with the pillows propped up behind her so she could drink her tea. I was about to say something comforting to her like, "Just lie here a while and . . ." or whatever when, from out of nowhere, there was Basil on the end of the bed.

"Oh!" Tabby gasped.

I figured he'd jumped out of the truck and followed me up to the house. Probably slipped through the door when I came inside and hid until now.

"Hope you don't mind that I brought him. He'll keep you good company while I check on how things are going outside." In the meantime, Basil had strolled up the bed and snuggled into Aunt Tabby's ample flesh.

"I thought you were going to stay inside," Tabby said, going into her whiny mode. I can't say how much I hate it when women do that.

"I just need to get my stuff out of the truck and I'll be right back," I assured her. "Basil's here now, so that's almost as good as me," I joked.

Aunt Tabby just frowned.

Chapter 2

WHEN I CAME into the front room to head outside, Sarah Aycock had gone. Thank goodness for that. Maybe that's when Basil had slipped inside.

Outside things had settled down. The fire department had left the scene and the EMTs had hauled away Erskine Weeks' body. Betty Weeks wasn't there, so she'd followed them to wherever they'd carried her husband — to the Albemarle Hospital, I presumed. Sheriff Grimes and two deputies were still there, setting crime scene tape around the crash site, even though it wasn't actually a crime scene. I didn't see Aubrey Meads around.

I asked the sheriff if it was okay to pull the truck into the yard, and he said it was as long as I parked it far enough away from the crash site. I asked him, "Any idea what might have happened?"

I didn't know Grimes all that well, so didn't expect an answer, but was surprised when he said,

"According to your aunt, she'd been looking out the window and had seen him fly in to do the run on Nixon's fields," gesturing toward the soy bean field next door, "and came outside to watch him. Something she usually does."

"She likes to wave at him when he makes his runs," I said.

"Yep. That's what she said. Anyway, Mr. Weeks made several passes." He paused for a moment, then, "I'd have to check the deputies' notes, but I think she said he had just completed his fourth pass and was curling around—that's how she said it, 'curling around'—up over the house when all of a sudden he just started coming down. Poor woman thought he was going to come right into her house. 'Scared the devil out of me,' she said."

Just then one of the deputies came up to them and said to the sheriff, "Amy says the NTSB will have someone out here in about two hours. You want Daryl and me to sit on it 'til they get here?"

"Yeah, I do. Sorry, but you're going to miss lunch."

I cut in, saying, "I'll fix some sandwiches for them, sheriff. I'm sure Tabby has something inside I can rustle up."

"That'd be right nice of you . . . ah . . . Sawyer, isn't it?"

"Webb Sawyer," I said. I'm Tabby's nephew.

"Oh, right. The guy who was in the Army."

I knew he wanted to say the guy who got booted out of the Army after he'd shot that Serbian guy. Maybe he'd even thought *Serbian bastard*, which was what Radovan Tadić was.

"Yep," was my reply.

"Well, I'm off." Then, to the deputies, whose name tags said, William Terryberry and Daryl Perkins, "Call Amy if anything new comes up."

"We can go when the NTSB gets here?" Perkins asked.

"Sorry, boys. You gotta stay here with them until they're done." They didn't look any too happy with that news.

"You think they'll get the wreckage out of here today?" I asked.

"I expect so, but can't be sure."

What can yah do? I thought.

Before Grimes left, he motioned me over to the side and said, "You know, Sawyer, you might want to have a doctor check out your aunt."

"I think she'll recover from this," I replied.

"I don't mean this. I mean those flying turtles and red bunnies she called us about."

I kinda chuckled. "Haven't had time to talk to her about it yet, sheriff, but I'm sure it's just bad dreams."

Sheriff Grimes shrugged. "Yeah, maybe so." Then, "Gotta go. Hope your aunt is all right."

After Grimes drove off, the deputies thanked me for offering to fix them lunch. I said sure. That I was hungry myself and I'd fix something for all of us once I pulled my truck into the yard and got my stuff inside.

It wasn't until 3:30 pm (actually 3:33 pm, to be precise) that the investigators from the National Transportation Safety Board took Yellow Bird away on a flatbed to wherever they take that kind of thing. Poor Aunt Tabby was distraught the whole time, even after they departed. All she kept saying was, "Poor Erskine. Poor Erskine." I couldn't blame her but, being the practical man I am, I really wanted to find out about the turtles and the rabbits. In the meantime, I'd help her with some yard chores and replace the brakes on Trusty Rusty's front wheels. They'd needed replacement for longer than I'd like to admit and now they were making funny noises. I didn't want to drive down to the Sandhills with suspicious brakes.

I decided to salvage the day and mow the lawn. Early tomorrow I'd head on into town to the auto supply store and pick up new brake parts for Trusty Rusty. They said they had them in stock. I'd replace them in the afternoon. It was a good plan. But we all know about plans. We have ours and the Gods of the Universe have theirs.

Mowing Aunt Tabby's lawn turned out to be a non-starter. The engine wouldn't kick over. When I asked Tabby when was the last time she cleaned the air filter, she asked, "What part is that?" I showed her. It was so bad that simply cleaning it was a non-option. That wasn't the only problem. I decided while I was in town getting the brake parts, I would replace everything on the lawn tractor: air filter, spark plug, battery, and fuel filter. Also, when I checked the oil it was so dirty that I added 4-cycle engine oil to the list.

With mowing out of the picture, the place where I wanted to change the brakes on Trusty Rusty was the equipment shed. But when I checked it out, it was so full of junk that, like it or not, I'd have to clean it out before I could use it. I decided, unilaterally, that there was stuff in there that needed to go; some to the recycle center, some to the dump, and there were a number of items I could take by the guy who bought metal and the like. I could use that little bit of money to buy what I needed to get the lawn tractor back in mowing order. I just had to keep Tabby busy while I was "helping her out." Having her make my favorite something or other sounded like a plan. Something that took a lot of prep time and required keeping an eye on the stove top and oven.

Beef Wellington and baked Alaska? Or maybe *Coq au vin*?

It wasn't until early that evening that Tabby finally settled down. She made fried chicken, mashers and fresh-picked corn-on-the-cob, rounded out with peach cobbler. Typical country fare that, as Dad used to say was, "Fittin' for your mouth." After we filled our bellies, Tabby finally got around to telling me about the flying painted turtles and giant red bunny rabbits with Olympic hopping skills.

"Webb, they come at night," she said.

"Every night?" I wanted to go along with it. Try to assess whether or not she needed medical or psychiatric attention . . . or both.

"Almost every night."

"How about last night?" I asked.

"Uh-huh."

"Turtles and bunnies almost every night?"

"Yes."

"Are you sure you're not . . . ," I wanted to say hallucinating but instead I asked, "dreaming?"

Tabby began to tear up. "You don't believe me, do you?"

How to handle this? "I believe you saw something." I really didn't. "So let's try to figure out just what."

"Okay," wiping her cheeks and the corner of her eyes.

"Okay. So, tell me what you see exactly and where and when you see it."

We sat across from each other in her kitchen at the small 1950s vintage dinette she'd had ever since I remembered. She pushed her chair back and said, "I'll show you."

I followed her into the front room, then down the hall to her bedroom. Of course. If she saw it at night, it was probably from in there. She went to one of the two windows at the south side of the bedroom nearest the head of her bed. She pulled aside the drapes and said, "Out there," pointing.

"In the yard?" I asked. She nodded. "Don't you keep your drapes closed when you come to bed?" I knew she was paranoid about someone looking in at her at night." Again she nodded. "Then how do you see anything outside? Or even know it's there?" I really didn't want to think she'd gone bonkers, so now I was leaning toward a recurring dream.

"It's like a light coming through the drapes."

"So it's always dark when it happens?"

"Yes."

"Hmm. Then what?"

"Then I see them?"

"Both at the same time?"

"No," she said. "It's usually the flying painted turtles first. Then the rabbits."

"Huh. So, run through it for me," I said.

"What do you mean?"

"I mean, from the time you see the light coming through the drapes to everything that happens after that. Don't leave anything out." I have to admit. It was very curious. She really believed she saw turtles and rabbits. It had to be a recurring dream. What else could it be? Nothing I could think of.

She told me that she'd first see the light. Then she'd go to the window and just peek out between the drapes. The first time it happened, it was only the flying painted turtles. "It seems like they're coming from up on the roof. It had to be from there, because they come from somewhere above the window, then fly across the yard toward the soy bean field behind the house. Then they come back and go up to the roof out of sight. Then back down again toward the field."

"How many of them are they and how many times do they do it?" I asked.

"There's like three of them I think." she thought for a moment. "Yes, I'm sure. It's three every time."

"And they never fly toward the road."

Tabby shook here head. "No. Always toward the field."

"Hmm. How can you see them? Your yard light is on the other side of the house and shines toward the driveway and the street."

"Remember, I said there was a light on the drapes. And there's like a light on them."

"A light?" I asked. She nodded. "What kind of light?"

"Like a . . . like a hazy kind of light. Like . . . like the kind you used to see in the movie theaters. You know, when you'd look up toward the ceiling and see that hazy looking light coming from the projection booth going toward the screen."

"Hmm. Okay. Then what happens next?"

"Then they go away, so I go back to bed."

"And go to sleep?"

"Oh no. You know me, Webb. I may go to bed early, but I sit up and read, sometimes for hours if it's a really good book." She likes romances. She buys them by the box loads from a local used book store. Reading material for a lonesome widowed woman.

"And then?" I prompted

"And then, the light comes through the drapes again."

"How soon?"

She shrugged. Sometimes just a few minutes. Sometimes it's longer."

"What's the longest between the first time and the next time?"

"Um. Maybe ten or fifteen minutes, but usually it's shorter."

"Then come the rabbits?" I had a new thought. Someone was messing with her. If that was true, that pissed me off to no end.

"Yes," she said, then ran through what happened with the rabbits. They were large and red and hopped across the soybean field toward her house, hopping really high into the air. As soon they reached the house, they hopped up over it. Then nothing happened for a few seconds, and it would start all over again.

"How many rabbits?" I asked.

"Like with the turtles. Three."

"Every time?"

"Yes." Then, "It's kinda scary, Webb?"

I thought it over for a moment. "And it's always after dark, right?" She said it was. When I talked to her on the phone, she'd said she'd called the sheriff's office about it, but all they said was they would have a deputy drive past the house to check it out." The standard line. After my talk with Grimes, I knew for sure he hadn't taken her call seriously.

"I'll be back in a few," I said.

"Where are you going, Webb."

"Just to look around outside while it's still light. I won't be long." I knew she'd watch me from the window, but that was all right.

I went outside and around the house to her bedroom window, which was on the first floor. When Uncle John had been alive, they slept upstairs, but she moved downstairs after he'd passed. I looked out across the yard and the soy bean field between her property line and the tree line and got a bead on a dead oak that stood out between the surrounding trees. Then I walked out to the street and walked down to the tree line, walked through the drainage ditch, which was bone dry, then walked up the tree line next to the edge of the soy bean field.

When I reached the dead oak, I studied the ground. It looked as if someone had been messing around. There were a lot of broken branches and trampled down brush. When I looked toward Aunt Tabby's house, I could see where somebody had cut across the rows of soybeans and wasn't too careful about it. I followed the trail in until I was about halfway between the trees and the house.

Not being much of a technoweenie, I wasn't quite sure yet what was happening but I had an idea. I wished I'd brought my HP laptop—also a gift—which I use for one thing: research. Tabby didn't have a computer I could use, so I'd have to resort to the old-fashioned stake-out method.

When I got back to the house, Aunt Tabby asked me what I was doing in the field. "Just looking around," I said, then asked, "What's the latest at night you've seen the turtles and the rabbits."

Tabby shrugged. "I don't know. Maybe eleven or so. Why?"

"Just sorting it all out," I replied.

I knew what I would be doing later, after dark.

Chapter 3

EARLIER, I'D PULLED Trusty Rusty around the house, backed it up to the equipment shed and loaded it for the morning trip into town. Uncle John used to have an open-air metal carport on that side of the house, but over the years it had gotten rusty. weather-beaten and generally beat-up looking so, after he died, Aunt Tabby had it taken down and, although she had good intentions, never replaced it.

Now, about an hour before dusk, I'd plunked myself down on Tabby's front porch with a cup of snickerdoodle and the morning paper, this one the *Hampton Roads News*. She subscribed to it for the horoscopes and the entertainment pages. She liked to keep up with the overpaid, over-made up and self-absorbed celebrities of the world.

After I promised Basil a saucer of cream laced with coffee, he joined me. I tried to get Tabby to join me, too, but she said she wouldn't be able to keep her eyes off burned grass and the hole in the ground where Erskine had made his unscheduled one-point landing. I told her I'd add filling the hole to tomorrow's chores. Wasn't much I could do about the burned grass.

According to the paper, several of the sixteen announced Republican candidates for the GOP nomination for president were coming through Hampton Roads looking to create some interest and excitement, while the two up for the Democrats, a grandma and a grandpa, watched with amusement from afar. It was the season not to have a newspaper subscription or a television. I qualified on both counts. The newspaper reading I'd done today reinforced my thoughts on that.

As the sun started to go down and the mosquitoes came out, I went back inside, changed into some darker clothing—I hadn't brought much of a selection, so a pair of army green cargo pants and a black t-shirt would have to do. I headed down the road, crossed the ditch and up the tree line to take up my post. Tabby had asked me if I wanted to take a flashlight, but I told her no. There was a three-quarter moon and figured I could see just fine.

"Watch out for snakes, Webb," Tabby said. "You know there are moccasins back in those woods."

When I told her the only things I needed to look out for were flying turtles and giant bunnies, she wasn't amused. She still didn't have a clue what was going on and I didn't bother sharing my thoughts on it. I didn't want to get her hopes up that I could solve the problem that night. I told her as soon as it got dark to shut off the porch and inside house lights, except for the one in her bedroom, like she was in bed reading. That if she saw a light from the drapes, she should open them and look outside.

I found a place in the trees where I could see but not be seen and hunkered down for the wait.

I don't wear a watch, but I figured it was only about a half hour before I heard something from the road. Soon I heard someone coming up the tree line, As they got closer I could see the beam from a flashlight, pointed toward the ground.

It was a clear, moonlight night, so when the person got to the dead oak I could see the outline of what looked like a young boy. The kid had on a backpack. He stood there for several minutes looking toward Aunt Tabby's before he moved into the soybean field. I had to make a quick decision. Should I follow him in now, or wait until he was set up and concentrating on his show. It was less likely he'd hear me if he was moving himself. I decided to follow him in.

I kept low, moving carefully over the rows so as not to alert him. About half way to his "spot," he suddenly stopped. I thought he'd either heard me or sensed someone was behind him. The soybeans were only about fourteen inches high, so I flattened myself out between a row of plants. But when I peeked up, he was looking toward the road. Then, I heard a vehicle coming. The kid dowsed the flashlight and stooped down.

Soon, the vehicle came and went and the kid was back up heading toward his spot in the middle of the field. I got up and continued to follow until he stopped. Again, I flattened out in a row and peeked up over the top of the beans. He turned off his flashlight, then took off his backpack and laid it on the ground.

I watched the little bastard taking things out of the backpack and assembling them. I wondered if his parents knew what he was up to . . . or even knew where he was . . . or even cared. It looked as if he was ready to start his show when another vehicle came down the road and the kid hunkered down until it passed. Then I saw a light pop on in front of him and soon I could see images of something colorful against Tabby's window. I saw the drapes open several inches and the outline of Aunt Tabby standing there, peering outside.

I rose to my knees and watched him. The kid did just what Tabby described. First he ran the image up toward her roof line. Then drew it back down as if the "flying painted turtles" were flying off the roof and swooping toward the ground. Then he moved them toward the soybean field that ran behind her house. When he started bringing the images back into her yard, I got up and moved toward him, at first slowly until I was within ten fee of him. Then I rushed him.

With the palms of my hands I hit him high on his back, knocking him forward onto his equipment. The kid let out a yelp, then rolled over onto his back and look up at me. I stood there looming over him, glaring down.

"The fun's over, kid."

I could see his long blond hair reflected in the moonlight. *The kid watching the firemen and police from the edge of Tabby's yard.* I was about to tell him to get up and come with me when, suddenly, he jumped to his feet and bolted past me to my right. As he went by I reached out and grabbed him under the arm by the t-shirt, but he ripped right out of it and ran, stumbling, for the trees.

"I'm coming for you!" I shouted, although I had no intention of trying to run him down. I watched him reach the edge of the field and the tree line, and expected he would run toward the road for his bike, but he didn't. Instead, he tore right into the forest. "That should be interesting for him," I said to myself, then turned to see what he'd left behind.

The toe of my right sneaker hit something. I bent down and found the kid's flashlight. I could see well enough, so I decided not to turn it on, lest he'd know I wasn't following him. I gathered up the equipment, which looked like a hand held projector mounted on top of a small tripod, and headed back toward the tree line.

When I reached the dead oak I stopped and hollered into the trees, "I'll find you! You can't hide in there for long!" I heard him trying to find his way through the trees and bushes. He wasn't all that quiet about it."

I shook my head. "Little shit."

I headed down to the road. I knew the wooded land was only about fifty yards from one side to the other, but I saw no reason to go down the street and wait for him there. Once I described him, I was sure Aunt Tabby would know who he was and where he lived. I found his bike lying in the ditch. I pulled it up and rolled it on back to the house, where I took it back to the equipment shed.

I guess Aunt Tabby was still back in the bedroom, because as soon as I came inside, she came hustling down the hallway, breathing heavily as if she was out of breath. "What happened, Webb? You're okay, aren't you? Did you find what was happening?" Then, "What's that in your hand?"

I held up the equipment. "This is your flying turtles and hopping bunnies."

Tabby frowned. "I . . . I don't understand."

"Let me call the sheriff first, then I'll explain."

It was about twenty minutes before a cruiser pulled into Tabby's front yard. Tabby had put on the porch light and I went outside to greet the deputy, who I soon found out was Aubrey Meads.

"Aubrey. Are you working 24/7 these days?"

"Hey, Webb. No, I'm covering another guy's shift. Vacation time, you know. So what going on? They said you called about someone trespassing and making threats against Miss Tabby."

I chuckled. "Well, I might have embellished it a little, but it is something serious. Come on inside and I'll tell you what's going on."

Inside, Aunt Tabby started in on Aubrey, saying how terrible and frightening it had been and that kids these days needed a good behind-whipping to set them straight. Aubrey listened patiently then turned to me and said, "So give me the story, Webb."

I did. From the time she'd talked to me on the phone until my stake out and about the kid who'd got away from me and ran into the woods. I showed Aubrey the equipment. "Now I don't know much about this kind of technology but, obviously, from how I saw it work it's a digital laser projector. And here is one of the chips. Like the ones you put in digital cameras to store photos. This is the one for the turtles. I figure he had the one for the rabbits in his pocket."

Aubrey listened, then asked Tabby. "And you say you think you know who this kid is?"

"Yes, sir, Deputy Aubrey. Webb saw him the other day watching when . . . when, you know."

"Oh, yeah. I remember seeing him," Aubrey said. Then, to me, "And you're sure it was the same kid?"

"Sure as I'm standing here," I said.

"I don't know his name, but he's Jeb Renner's kid," Tabby said. "They live down the end of the road on the left, just before it crosses Triple Bridge Road. In that old trailer back in the trees."

"Yeah, I know them," Aubrey nodded. "It figures. That Jeb, he ain't got the good sense God gave a goose. Nothin' but trouble. In fact, I arrested the man six months ago when he put three rounds of 22-250 45 grain bullets in a man's house over on Fairfield Road. You hear about the big to-do over dogs huntin' on the guy's property and he shot two of 'em?" I said I hadn't. "Had to arrest him, too."

I shrugged. "Don't keep up much with the goings on around here. I live down on the Outer Banks now."

"Oh, yeah. I heard so. Well anyway, back to business," Aubrey said. "I wonder if the boy made his way home by now?"

"One way to find out," I said.

We left the bike in the shed and the projector with Aunt Tabby and I rode down the street with Deputy Meads. We had a very brief conversation

44

about my deceased parents and their stilt house at Blue Heron Marsh, before we pulled into the dirt entrance that led back through a small stand of trees. It opened up into a yard with a single-wide trailer sitting about fifty feet back. There were lights on inside. Off to the right, the cruiser's headlights caught a mud splattered pickup of unsure date and make with a dog crate taking up most of the bed. When Aubrey turned off the headlights and we climbed out of the cruiser, curtains were pulled aside at the front window next to the door and a face peered out. When we came up to the stoop, the door opened and a woman stood there looking out at us.

She looked familiar, but I wasn't sure until she said, "Is that you Webb? Webb Sawyer?" Her voice was high-pitched and nasally. Just as I remembered it.

Aubrey looked at me, then at the woman. "Hi Jenine. You know Mr. Sawyer."

"Yeah. Way back. From school."

"I'll tell you later," I said to Aubrey.

"K." Then, "What's your son's name, Jenine?"

"My son? Why?" But when Aubrey didn't answer, she said, "Andrew. Like the Duke of York. Greece and Denmark, too. I call him Andy, though. Why'ya want to know?"

"Uh, is Andy here?"

"Yeah. He's in his room."

"Can we talk to him?" Aubrey asked.

"Uh...."

"We think he might have seen something that will be helpful to us," I cut in.

"Oh, uh... I didn't know you were a policeman, Webb?"

I smiled."I'm not. I'm just helping Deputy Meads with something."

"Oh. Okay." Jenine turned and shouted for her son.

Shortly, he came out of a door at the end of the room. Right size, long blond hair, but a change of clothes. His face and arms were laced with abrasions and minor lacerations.

"Well, Andy," Aubrey said in his Mr. Friendly voice. "Nice duds you got on their, son. You always put on new clothes at 10:30 at night?"

The boy stood there, eyes big, with a frightened look on his face. His mother answered for him, saying, 'Oh, he had an accident with his bike and got his clothes dirty. Even tore his shirt."

The kid had that "I've been busted" look on his face.

"Had an accident on your bike, did you?" Aubrey asked. Andy nodded. "Could I see your bike, son?"

"I... ah... lost it," he sputtered.

"Lost it!" his mother said. "You didn't tell me you lost it. Oh, your father's gonna to be mad about that. He spent four-hundred bucks on that bike."

"Did his father buy him a digital projector, too," Aubrey asked. "Maybe even a tripod to set it on?"

"Oh, sure," Jenine said. "Last month. For his birthday. Spent almost five-hundred on that, too. Now he wants to buy him a four-wheeler. He's only ten, for Christ's sake."

From the tone of her voice, it was obvious she got the short end of the stick in the family. "Bet you need a new washer and dryer, though, right Jenine," I said it in a joking way, but I wanted to needle her just to see what would happen. Aubrey gave me a frown.

"Yeah. I wish I even had an old washer and dryer. Have to go to the laundromat all the way in town. He don't get me—"

"Can you show us your laser projector and tripod?" Aubrey asked Andy, cutting off the beginning of Jenine's rant.

Andy did a little foot-to-foot dance and said. "Uh . . . I lost that, too."

Aubrey let out a long sigh, then asked Jenine, "Where is Mr. Renner?"

Frowning, she said, "He's out on a run. He's a truck driver. He'll be back tomorrow afternoon. Why?"

"Because, Jenine, we know Andy here has been terrorizing Webb's aunt. You know, Miss Tabby, up the road. Mr. Sawyer here caught him, but he got away. We have both his bike and projector outfit and are holding them as evidence. This is serious business, Jenine."

"Andy! Did you do what he says?" screaming like a banshee.

"I didn't do nothin;" Andy said.

"'Cause if you did, your father is going to beat your ass!" Jenine started toward her son, but Aubrey stopped her. "Jenine, where are the t-shirt and pants he took off?"

Jenine glared at her son, then stormed across the room, down a narrow hall, and into a bathroom. Andy stood there looking as if he wanted to crawl under the trailer. She came back out holding up a pair of pants and t-shirt. The shirt was ripped open under the right arm. The pants were dirty with burrs still clinging to the material below the knees.

"Could I see the pants?" I asked, holding out my hand.

Sheepishly, Jenine handed them to me. I went through the pockets until I came up with a computer chip, just like the one Andy had left behind in the projector. I held it up and said, "Giant, red, high-hopping bunnies, I presume."

* * *

On the way back to Tabby's, Aubrey asked, "Wasn't Jenine in the fifth grade when you were in high school?"

Aubrey had told Jenine that he could have arrested young Andy, but that he was holding off until he could talk with her and Mr. Renner. That her husband best call him when he returned from his run. He left her his business card.

I laughed. "Yeah, but sometimes I hung around with her older brother Johnny and she was always there bugging us. I think she had a crush on me."

"You think she's on the phone with Jeb right now?" Aubrey asked.

"Probably not. Personally, I think she's happy he's away trucking."

"Yeah. I got that sense, too. I hear she dropped out of school in the tenth grade. No wonder she ended up with a loser like Jeb Renner."

"Some people are destined for the low-life," I said.

Chapter 4

I WANTED TO sleep late, but Aunt Tabby knocked on my door at 7:00 am, saying she had a man-sized mug of my favorite in hand and that breakfast would be ready in ten minutes. Just enough time for me to throw something on, pad down the hall and throw water on my face. Basil had spent the night with Tabby. He knew who put the food in his dish while he was here.

By eight-thirty I headed into town, and by nine-thirty I'd unloaded the stuff I'd cleaned out of Tabby's equipment shed and made my purchase of brake shoes and pads. I'd decided that the little bit of metal I had wasn't worth the hassle to sell, so I just recycled it. I had a half hour to kill before the Sears store opened, so I drove over to the Java Hut for another brew. Corner man was there. We waved and greeted each other as I came and went, as if we were long lost buddies. By 10:00 am I was the first customer in the Sears door.

Most people think of Sears as this gigantic two or three story operation in a suburban mall. In Elizabeth City, and most rural towns, it is no different than walking into an auto parts store. The difference is, the people in the rural stores are friendly and helpful and, if you do business on a regular basis, they know and greet you by name. I don't, so they didn't. But they were helpful, and soon I was out of there and on my way back to Tabby's.

The first thing I did was change out the front wheel brakes. Tools weren't a problem. I carried a few in the lock box in the truck bed behind the cab but, just for old-times sake, decided to use Uncle John's. Although they were all old and some of them dirty and a bit rusty, Uncle John had almost every tool imaginable. When he farmed, he did almost all his own repair work on the farm equipment. Although automotive repairs weren't my favorite thing to do, when growing up, Dad had taught me well, so I knew the basics. Basil explored the shed while I worked.

Once that was done, I was ready to fill and patch the hole in the front yard when Tabby called me in for lunch, or as she called it, dinner. She called the evening meal supper. It's a country thing. After about forty-five minutes of listening to Tabby talk about the goings on at church and in the community, I extracted myself and headed back outside.

Just before he'd died, Uncle John had sand delivered, for what reason I wasn't sure. At any rate, the pile was still there next to the equipment shed, so I loaded up one of his wheelbarrows and, three trips later, I'd filled the hole. I found a bag of grass seed on a shelf. I didn't know how old it was, but I sprinkled it liberally on the sand and raked it in, threw down some pine straw and watered it. If it didn't rain soon, all that trouble wouldn't make a difference.

Next I attacked the lawn tractor. It was a Craftsman. He'd always been a John Deere man, but when it finally bit the dust, Sears had a sale on a Pro-series, 26 HP V-twin Kohler with a 54" cutting deck, and he changed his loyalty. The Craftsman also had an extreme tight-turning radius, which he really never needed as there aren't that many trees and other obstructions in the yard to mow around. It took me about an hour and twenty minutes to finish the refurb and I was ready to go.

Tabby had a two-acre lot and I was about halfway through the mow, thinking about taking an ice coffee break (I'd made up a batch at lunch/dinner), when a pickup truck appeared roaring up Tyler Swamp. Mud splatters, dog kennel—I knew who it was.

Great! Just what I need.

Jeb Renner's pickup ripped into Tabby's yard so fast I thought he was going to roll it into the street ditch. He slid to a stop right over the top of the hole I'd just filled. When he leaped out of the truck he had a rifle in his hand. I turned the mower so it was facing him, disengaged the blades and shut off the engine. I figured I could start it up and take a run at him if I had to.

Red faced and angry, he came storming across the lawn with the gun barrel pointed down; at least not at me — not yet.

He came up, stopped in front of the mower and growled, "I want the bike and the other stuff you stole from Bubba."

"Bubba? I thought his name was Andy. Is there a Bubba that's a Duke of York, Greece and Denmark?"

"What the fuck are you talking about, Sawyer?"

I gave him a non-committal head nod, thinking, the dumb kid doesn't have a chance with an ignorant, indulgent and anger-driven father, and a uneducated wimp for a mother.

"Yeah, I know who you are. You're Jenson's Sawyer's kid who got thrown out of the Army."

"That's me," I said, grinning.

"Don't be a smart ass with me, Sawyer. I want that stuff back and I want it back now, or I'll have you arrested for theft. In fact, I might just have you arrested for assault on a minor, too, just 'cause I don't like you people who think you own this part of the county."

I ignored his rant. "Your son, Andrew," using that name just to annoy him, "was terrorizing my Aunt, not to mention trespassing." Then, "I take it you haven't called Deputy Meads yet. You know, he's the one who's got Andrew's bike and projector."

"I ain't calling that Meads son-of-a-bitch for nothin'," Renner said. "And just so you know, Sawyer, he weren't trespassin' on her land. He was on Nixon's property."

I snorted, "So, you admit he was terrorizing her."

"I ain't admittin' nothin', mister. "You stole his flashlight, too. You got that?"

I'd forgotten about his flashlight. I didn't remember if I'd given it to Aubrey or if it was in the house. I'd seen Tabby at the front window and hoped she'd called 911. I decided to stall him and play along. "I might still have that in the house. I'll check," I said, getting off the mower.

That's when he brought up the rifle, pointing it at me, "You stay right where you are, Sawyer." It was a Weatherby Vanguard Series 2 Stainless Synthetic bolt-action deer rifle with locks for a scope. I'd only seen one like it before and that was a guy I knew at Ft. Bragg.

I got back onto the mower and said, "Now how am I supposed to check on the flashlight if I don't go up to the house?"

"You know, Sawyer, for two cents I'd shoot you where you're sittin'."

"Those Weatherbys come with a scope don't they?" trying to lighten it up. "You hunt with a scope, Jeb?"

"I don't need no scope to put one right between your eyes if I want," he said, the left side of his lip curling up. As he said it, he pushed the barrel of the rifle forward.

I moved my right hand to the starter, thinking it was time for Plan B. Act as if I was shouting at someone on the front porch and, when he looked, start up the mower and run over his sorry ass. Then I saw the cruiser come around the corner down Tyler Swamp. It was running silent. Jeb was too locked on to me to hear it.

I pulled my hand away from the starter and said, "We got company, Jeb. It's your old friend, that son-of-a-bitch Deputy Meads."

Renner scowled and looked over his shoulder. When he saw Meads' cruiser, he lowered the rifle to his side, then looked back at me and said, "Maybe he can do somethin' right this time, 'cause I'm gonna have him arrest you for theft and assault."

"Right. You told me that already," I said.

"That's right, Sawyer. You're goin' down for this one."

The man was not only delusional, he'd been watching too many cop shows on TV.

Deputy Aubrey Meads pulled into the yard right behind Renner's truck. Aubrey got out of the cruiser his weapon drawn, and came toward us. "Drop that rifle, Jeb!" he shouted at Renner.

Renner turned toward him. "What? I ain't done nothin'. I'm just holdin' Sawyer here so's you can arrest him."

"Drop the gun, Renner. Now!"

Jeb stooped down and put the rifle on the ground, then stood back up, muttering, "Damn cops are all alike."

Aubrey holstered his handgun and said, "What are you doing up here, Renner? You were supposed to call me about your boy when you got back and I haven't heard peep one from you."

Ignoring why he hadn't called, Jeb said, "I come up here to get Bubba's stuff back that Sawyer done stole. And I want him arrested for it, too."

"That so," Aubrey said. "Well, I hate to tell you, Renner, but the only one who might get himself arrested . . . again! . . . is you. Now, unless you want that to happen, I suggest we go down to your place and talk with you and your son about this business of troubling Miss Tabby." Then Aubrey looked at me and asked, "Unless you want to press charges of threatening with a deadly weapon. 'Cause if you do, I'll take him into town and deal with the boy later."

I looked at Jeb Renner and asked, "Which one would you prefer, Jeb? Door number one or door number two?"

Renner gave me a look that said, "I'd shoot you right here and now if this son-of-a-bitch cop wasn't standin' here to protect you." He didn't answer. Instead, he stooped to pick up his rifle.

Aubrey stopped him, ordering him to leave it on the ground. "I'll bring it down and give it to you when we get to your place."

Renner gave the deputy an unfriendly glare, then stormed off towards his truck.

Aubrey picked up the gun, checked the chamber, popped out the bullet, saying, "The son-of-a– I can't believe he had one ready to go. I oughta—"

I held up my hand. "Just put the fear of God in him, Aubrey. In fact, put the fear of God in all that bunch down there. Then we'll talk about charges against the kid when you get back."

Aubrey nodded, then said, "Good, because there's something else I want to talk to you about when I'm done with them." Then, Jeb's Weatherby in hand, headed across the lawn to his cruiser. Renner had already pulled around and peeled out of the yard. On the way by, he yelled an obscenity and gave me the finger.

Classy guy.

* * *

After they departed I decided I'd better go inside and talk to Tabby . . . get a glass of ice coffee. As I suspected, when she saw Jeb Renner with his weapon she'd called 911. She was a mess, blubbering and babbling. I couldn't blame her. She'd had a rough couple of days. A rough week if you counted the time before I got there, her dealing with the idiot kid.

I soft-peddled the encounter with Renner, telling her that he was just mad that I'd taken his kid's bike and that I'd talked him down. I also told her she'd done the right thing by calling it in."

"He had a gun, Webb. I was afraid."

I got back on the mower knowing that I'd have to call Ben Straker later. Explain the situation and tell him I needed to postpone my trip for a couple of days. I had just started mowing again when I saw another cruiser coming down from Union Church Road, flying by silent but with its lights going.

Oh brother.

About a half hour later, up the road came the two cruisers, Aubrey's behind the other one. The first deputy went on past. I could see Jeb Renner in the back seat, his face pressed up against the window, mouthing something at me. Aubrey, however, pulled into the yard.

It seemed the turtles and the rabbits had turned into more than we all bargained for.

Aunt Tabby and Basil had come out onto the front porch as Aubrey exited the cruiser. She waved at him and he waved back. "Would you like some ice coffee?" she shouted.

"No thanks," he called back. "Just need to talk to Webb for a minute."

By then, I'd shut down the mower and had walked over to the cruiser. We both turned to look at Tabby and I guess she got the hint because she went back inside. Basil bounded off the porch and headed around the house on an important mission.

"What was that all about?" I asked, nodding toward the road.

"The man is a complete jackass, Webb. I'd given him back the rifle but kept the bullets. He was none to happy about that. I tried to explain how he was lucky you hadn't asked me to arrest him, and he gave me some guff on that, too. For the moment, I'd decided to ignore his attitude. Jenine and the kid were standing there and I wasn't looking for another confrontation, so I started in about the kid, Andy. Funny how he calls him Bubba and she calls him Andrew."

"Probably the only thing he lets her get away with. Then again, maybe not. The son may be named for a duke, but Jeb's a real prince."

Aubrey laughed. "To make a long story short, once again the kid denied everything. Then, when I told him I didn't believe him and if he didn't come up here and apologize to Miss Tabby, I'd have to take him in and bring him before a Juvenile Judge. Well, when I said that, Renner went berserk, cussing me and telling me to get out of his effing house and don't come back unless I had a warrant."

"Cop show talk," I said.

Aubrey snorted. "That's when I asked him to turn around and put his hands behind his back. That I was arresting him for obstruction of justice. So, he pushes me and I had to take him to the ground and cuff him. He may be bigger than me, but I was an All State wrestling champ in high school, so ... ," shrugging.

"I'll bet he was surprised," I chuckled.

Aubrey shook his head. "I hated to do it in front of his family, but I had no choice. I hauled him outside, put him in the back of my car and called for backup."

"After you already had things under control?" I asked, curious.

I thought he was going to say because he was going to take in the kid, too, but he said, "Because I wanted to talk to Jenine and the kid alone. Also, I had something I needed to talk to you about, private like."

"Okay."

"About the crash. One of the detectives told me that the sheriff had him and a NTSB investigator go down and talk to Miss Betty Weeks."

I waited.

"The NTSB guy said the preliminary investigation showed it was some kind of rod that connects the stick to the elevator. That it came loose during the stress of the high turn and Erskine lost control. Nothing he could do at that point."

"Jesus! Knowing what's coming and nothing you can do about it." I shook my head. "Jesus!"

"So anyway, Miss Betty told them that Erskine didn't check the connection all that often because you had to take apart too much stuff to get to it, and it took a lot of time."

"Did she say how often?"

"The detective didn't say, but I'll tell you this, Webb. I used to talk to Erskine about flying and all that. How cool it must be and all. You know, just chit-chat. Anyway, I remember asking him once if he was ever afraid of crashing, and he told me he had a near miss with a tree once. Matter of fact, it was that big oak in Miss Tabby's back yard," gesturing in that general direction. "Clipped the top of it and lost some of his spray nozzles. You hear about that?"

I shook my head. "I must have been in Europe when that happened. If Dad or Mom told me about it, I don't remember."

"Well, here's the thing. Even though it was pilot error, it scared him. Got him thinking more about other things that could go wrong. Worn or faulty parts and the like. I mean, he always did routine checks, but after that he got to checking all those hard-to-get-to control lines, rods and connection a lot more often, even if it added a half hour or so to his schedule."

"I guess that included the rod the NTSB guy was talking about."

"You would think, right?"

I nodded. "I would. As they say, 'Better safe than sorry.'"

"See, that's the problem. She knew he was adamant about checking those lines on a regular basis."

"She's under a lot of stress right now," I said. "She probably just figured he forgot. You know how you can get complacent and let things slide."

Aubrey shrugged. "Maybe, but that isn't all. And, Webb. This is strictly between you and me, okay."

"Sure, Aubrey."

"You know I told you how I arrested Jeb Renner for shooting the guy's house up? The one on Fairfield Road?" I nodded. "And that I arrested the guy who owned the house for killing two hunting dogs?"

Again I nodded. "Were they Renner's dogs?"

"No. A friend of his." Then, "Anyway, I patrol out that way all the time and—" he looked up toward the house to be sure Tabby hadn't come back outside. "And on several occasions I've seen Miss Betty's car turning down this guy's lane." I waited. "I thought, maybe there was a good reason for it, so once, just casual like, I asked Erskine what days Miss Betty went to the YMCA. He told me she went there regularly, usually in the mornings. Anyway, I belong to the Y, too, and said I hadn't run into her."

I suppose there was a point to all this, but I had yet to hear it.

Aubrey shook his head and took a deep breath. "It turns out that a lot of the times she's supposed to be there are the same times I've seen her going into Perry Adams' property. "

"That's the dog killer's name?"

"Yes it is. And I'm not sure, Webb, but I'll bet she wasn't at the Y when Erskine's plane went down either, 'cause she came here from the Triple Bridge Road end of Tyler Swamp. That wouldn't be the fastest way to get here from in town at the Y." When I didn't respond, he said, "Just saying . . . ."

"I take it you haven't talked to Sheriff Grimes about it."

Aubrey shook his head. "No way. He's known Miss Betty all his life. In fact, his sister married one of her cousins, so they're kinda kin that way."

"Why are you telling me this?" I asked, even though I really knew why.

"Look, Webb. I've read the papers. About how you tracked down those kidnappers at Pelican Point in Camden. How you hunted down that serial killer in Hertford. And just last month how you rescued your writer friend in Ocracoke from that psycho fan. You're the only one I know can see if there's anything funny going on here. He paused for a minute. "Thing is, Webb. I really liked Erskine, and he didn't deserve what happened to him. And if it wasn't actually an accident . . . ." Aubrey let the words hang out there.

I knew when I made that call to Ben Straker it would be more than just telling him I'd be a few days late for our fishing trip.

Chapter 5

BEN MADE ME feel guilty for not making it out to the Sandhills for what he called some "deep creek fishing." I knew he was just giving me a hard time, but what can you do? That's a rhetorical question, of course. What I could do was take care of my Aunt Tabby's mental well-being, take a quick look into Deputy Mead's concerns, give him a report, then head back to Blue Heron Marsh in time for Nan's return.

I had just hung up, contemplating what had transpired over the last two days, when the doorbell rang. Basil ran over to the front window to look out. Tabby was in the kitchen fixing "something special" for supper. I'd tried to talk her into going into Elizabeth City for an evening out, my treat, but she would have none of it. We compromised on breakfast in the morning at her and Uncle John's favorite cholesterol hit, the sausage-gravy-over-buttermilk-biscuits place called Esther's, out on Highway 17

South. Their place used to be the Water Street Café, downtown at the waterfront, until it closed. The café, not the waterfront.

I told Tabby I'd get the door. She had a peek hole, but I didn't bother. I figured it was Sarah Aycock from down the street, but to my surprise, standing there was Jenine Renner and her son, Andrew. Jenine had an embarrassed look on her face. Andrew/Andy/Bubba looked as if he'd rather be sitting in the principal's office at school (a place I guessed he'd been many times) — anywhere but here. Basil had moved from the window to the couch, sitting there, glaring at the boy. He sensed hostility and I heard a low, almost indiscernible growl in his throat.

"Who's there, Webb?" from Tabby.

"Guests," was all I said.

The kid gave me a look of disdain. A chip off the old Renner block.

Tabby came out of the kitchen, wiping her hands on her apron. She reminded me of Aunt Bee from the old Andy Griffith show. Even her voice. "Oh, my!" throwing a hand to her mouth in a dramatic gesture.

I stepped back to watch the show.

Jenine said, "Andrew has something to say to you, Miss Tabby." She placed a hand on Andrew's back and moved him forward. The kid shook her off and just stood there. "Well," his mother said.

"Sorry," was all that came out of his mouth.

Tabby started to say something when Jenine said, "Andrew, we talked about this before we came down here and again on the way over," her voice rising as she spoke."

The kid frowned and said, "I'm sorry I scared you with the laser projector." And that was it.

Aunt Tabby gave the kid the benefit of the doubt because she was a kind person and, as she told me later, it was the Christian thing to do. She told him she accepted his apology. Jenine then went on with her own apologies for what her son had done, as if somehow it was all her fault. Tabby listened and just said, "All is forgiven and forgotten." I believed the forgiven part, but I doubted she'd forget it any time soon. I could picture her peeking out the bedroom window every night before she got into bed to be sure there were no or rabbits or turtles jumping or flying around her yard.

I walked out onto the porch with them when they left. Jenine was still apologizing to me, both for the kid and the way Jeb had come at me with his rifle. I told her there would be no problems as long as he minded his own business and let me mind mine.

Like his father had, when Jenine backed out of the yard, the kid glared at me from the car window. At least he didn't flip me the finger. Even though, as

69

my father used to say, she'd made her bed and had to lie in it, I felt sorry for her.

The next morning, I woke up unrested. I couldn't get to sleep thinking about how I was going to investigate Aubrey Meads' suspicious death claim about Erskine Weeks. I hadn't come up with much and decided to, as they say, play it by ear . . . or sight . . . or whatever.

It was while I was in the kitchen having coffee, waiting for Tabby to get ready to head out, when something she'd said last night gave me an idea. She'd been wondering when would be the right time to take some food over to Betty Weeks, something people felt compelled to do when a friend or relative had a death in the family.

When Tabby finally arrived in her going-out-for-breakfast attire, I mentioned we should get something in town and go by Miss Betty's house on the way home.

"Oh, no. We can't just buy something. I have to make it. Besides, I don't think I'm ready to face her after . . . well, you know."

I'd thought it would be a good way to talk to Betty Weeks and make my own assessment, and that having Tabby there, any inquisitions I might make would seem innocent. I should have felt guilty using Tabby in that manner, but I didn't. So much for that idea. By the time Tabby came around to feeling like a visit, I hoped to be sitting in my skiff in the marsh, fishing.

I'd think about it on the way into town.

It was a Saturday morning and Esther's was packed. We had to wait about fifteen minutes for a table. It was like old home week for many longtime friends of my parents and those who knew Aunt Tabby. They all wanted to talk about the crash and what Tabby saw and what I saw and how I was doing and did I really kill that terrorist in Iraq—actually, it was Bosnia and he was a right-wing militia asshole. All in all, the meal was uncomfortable for both of us, and I was happy to pay the bill and get the hell out of there.

When I pulled into a small bakery a few blocks from the restaurant, Aunt Tabby wanted to know why. "I can bake anything they can and much better, too," she told me, huffing and frowning.

I told her I was getting it for Miss Betty. That I knew Tabby wasn't up to seeing her and I wanted to go by and offer our condolences. Tabby didn't mind my going to see Miss Betty without her, but she wasn't going to let me bring along something she hadn't made. When I told Tabby I wanted to go by before midday so I could take care of a few more yard chores in the afternoon, she wouldn't accept that.

"No," Tabby said. "You do the yard chores when we get home and I'll make something you can take to her later."

It was no use arguing. Not all ideas are good ones. Reluctantly, I pulled out of the lot and we went back home.

I still had some work to do straightening up the shed. I found a box of really old tools on a back shelf. Antiques, but still usable. Trouble was, there was no one there to use them. Even so, I didn't have the heart to suggest that Tabby sell or donate them, so I took them out of the box, cleaned them up as best I could, and hung them on the wall, hammering in new nails where needed.

Before I knew it, Tabby was calling me in for lunch. When I got inside I said, "Lunch? I thought you called it dinner," teasing her. When she told me it was only sandwiches she'd made, so it didn't count for dinner. "You've been away from home too long, Webb," she chided.

She was correct. I had. But I didn't consider that a bad thing. Before I enlisted in the Army, I'd helped my father and uncle with farming. I could drive a John Deere tractor, combine or potato harvester with the best of them—I'd learned to use them all by the time I was twelve. But, to my father's disappointment, farming wasn't what I wanted to do for the rest of my life. After he passed,

I leased the land to other farmers to work. Technically, I was still responsible for the lease arrangements, collection of lease fees and the like, but I'd hired an attorney who knew the ag business to do that for me. He had all the fun and I just made decisions and collected my cut, less his fee.

"I made a nice chicken pot pie for Betty," Tabby said. She always said she liked my chicken pot pies, so I think she'll be pleased to have this one. You know, Webb, people in grieving shouldn't have to cook their own meals for at least a week."

I didn't know there were rules about that, but since there were rules about everything else, why not.

Since I'd left Basil home earlier, I brought him with me. I thought he might be a comforting distraction. Besides, unlike most cats, he liked to ride in the car. Betty Weeks lived on the south end of Estercliff Road. To avoid going past the Renner place—I wasn't looking for any more trouble with them and didn't want to take any chances—I went up Tyler Swamp to Simpson Road, which was a one-mile cut through over to Estercliff. The Weeks lived about two miles down on the right.

It was a nice frame house, built new in the 1960s. It had a detached two-car garage and a work and equipment shed in the back right rear, connected by a breezeway.

There were three vehicles in the yard. Two, a late model Ford F-150 and a newish ultra-blue Toyota four-door sedan, were pulled off to the right in front of the garage. The car in the driveway was a brand new Lexus SUV. Based on Aubrey Meads' info, none of them belonged to Perry Adams, the dog killer who lived on Fairfield Road.

I pulled off the driveway besides the Lexus, got out of Trusty Rusty, put Basil on my right shoulder, went up to the side door by the breezeway, and knocked. Shortly, a familiar face opened the door.

At first, she just stood there, mouth hanging open. Finally, she said, "Oh my gosh, it's you."

"It's me," I replied. I hadn't seen Erskine and Betty's daughter, Patty, in a long time, but I would have known her anywhere. She'd had a page boy haircut ever since she was a teenager. The only thing that had changed was the auburn hair, starting to show some gray. She was several years younger than me, but when I was a kid and we came to visit, Patty and I always had a good time playing in the yard. She'd married a fella named Bobby Nixon. Bobby was my age, but was more a friend of my good buddy, Randy Fearing. Randy is the District Attorney for Elizabeth City and several of the surrounding counties, including Pasquotank. Anyway, Patty and Bobby lived in Edenton, where he had a successful investment and financial planning business. I heard they'd had two kids, who must be grown up by now.

"Oh, and look what's on your shoulder," putting a hand out. I guess it spooked Basil, because he leaped from my shoulder and ran toward the driveway.

"Oh, I'm sorry," Patty said. "I didn't mean to frighten him." I told her I probably should have left him in the truck and that he'd be fine in the yard. She watched Basil until he disappeared around the front of the house, then said, "My gosh, Webb. I haven't seen you in years. Been reading about you though. You sure lead an exciting life."

Under the circumstances, I wasn't sure what to say, so I shrugged and held out Aunt Tabby's dish. "Aunt Tabby sent this with me for your mother. I sure am sorry what happed with your dad."

She took the dish from me, thanked me, and said, "It was a terrible thing, and so unexpected, but I suppose God took him for some reason we don't understand."

I admit, much to my family's chagrin, I'm not a religious person, but I try to be open-minded and tolerant of other's beliefs—or disbeliefs—no matter what religion they espouse—or not. But for some reason, the idea that God plans for someone's death just rubs me wrong. Does He plan how they die, too? When that Serb bastard Radovan Tadić destroyed the Musa family, was that part of some grand scheme? When I shot the bastard in the face, was that part of the plan, too?

Just asking.

I followed Patty inside to the front room. "Look who's here," Patty said. She was a little too upbeat for the situation, but what do I know. Bobby Nixon was there. I hadn't seen him in a while. While Patty had kept a pretty good figure, Bobby had gained weight where all married good-ole-boys put it on—in the gut. Good cooking at home and business luncheons with the boys will do it to you. Miss Betty was sitting across the room in an easy chair, sipping on a glass of ice tea. She had a grim look on her face.

Betty nodded and said, "Hello, Webb. I appreciate your coming by."

Bobby got up from the sofa, came toward me and extended a hand, "Nice to see you, Webb." It was something to say.

"Good to see you too, Bobby." Then, to Betty, said, "Aunt Tabby wasn't up to coming over yet, but she sent along some of her world's famous chicken pot pie."

"Oh, yes," Patty said, holding up the dish. "I'll put it in the kitchen."

She turned and headed back out of the room and her mother said. "Tell Tabby I appreciate her thoughts and prayers." I hadn't said anything about thoughts and prayers, but I guessed that was understood. I said I would.

"Please sit down, Webb," Betty said. I took the one empty chair.

"Ah, we were just discussing the, ah, arrangements," Bobby said.

"Oh, well," I said. "I can come back another time. I know it's important to get that taken care of."

"We don't mind if you stay," Betty said.

I was uncomfortable with the situation. I couldn't very well ask anything about Erskine and his flying habits with Patty and Bobby there talking about funeral arrangements. I was about to get up, tell Miss Betty how sorry I was about Erskine, which I was, and excuse myself, when Bobby asked, "Are you back in Weeksville now?" I told him I wasn't. That I still lived at the old vacation house on the marsh.

"Oh, that's nice," he said. Then asked, "I take it your staying with your aunt while she's dealing with what happened," glancing at his mother-in-law, I guess to be sure he didn't upset her with the question.

"For a few more days," I said. There was no reason to go into the episode with the Renners. Patty came back into the room and sat down next to Bobby. Silence settled into the room, so I got up and said to Bobby, "If you don't mind, let Tabby know about the arrangements." Then, to Betty, "Again, Betty, I'm so sorry about Erskine. I know we will all miss him very much." Platitudes, but well meant.

"Well, that was a bust," I said to myself as I backed into the pull off and rolled to the end of the Weeks' driveway. Basil was already back in the truck. He's usually pretty sociable, but who knows. I promised him a special treat when we got back to Tabby's — I'd brought along several cans of some overpriced fancy feast mixture that he liked.

However, before I went back to Tabby's, there was one other place I wanted to go. Just to, as some seventeenth century Brit was supposed to have put forth, get the lay of the land.

I drove back the way I'd come, took a left on to Triple Bridge where it T'd into Estercliff, three miles down to Little River Road, out Old Nixonton Road to Summer's Creek Road all the way to and across Route 17, where the name changed to Fairfield Road. As the crow flies, six minutes; on country roads, fifteen. I wanted to see where this character, the dog killer, Perry Adams, lived. Or, at least the driveway leading into where he lived.

There was a mailbox with his house number on it about a mile and a half from 17. The mailbox was on the left, the driveway on the right. I went past, then turned around and pulled over in front of the mailbox where I could see down the driveway.

Aubrey said there was a chain across the entrance, about a hundred feet down, and there it was.

I thought about it for a moment, then decided to pull ahead and park on the grass shoulder. I rolled the windows up just high enough so if Basil got it in his mind to follow along, he couldn't. I didn't want him roaming around out here and trying to find him in a place where I didn't know any of the residents. The temperature was in the mid eighties, so I left Trusty Rusty running with the air on, which still worked, but just barely.

I walked across the road and down the lane, hoping to get a glimpse of the house where the dog killer lived. When I reached the chain, held by two metal posts, I peered down the rest of the driveway. The trees were mostly pine, but there was a lot of new growth that made it unable to see through. In addition, further down, the gravel lane turned off to the left, so there was nothing to see. Aubrey said Renner had shot up the guy's house. He must have actually come into the property to do it, unless he got a couple of lucky shots through the trees.

I was contemplating stepping over the chain when a voice from somewhere growled. "Who is it and what do you want?"

I had thought up some bullshit answer in case I was discovered, but was startled by the unseen person on a hidden speaker. "Sorry, but I'm lost. I'm looking for the, ah, Glendale family residence.

They said they lived down a long driveway in the trees.

"Well, this isn't the Glendale residence, so I'd appreciate it if you'd get off my property now. I have a weapon," he added.

Nice fellow.

"Sorry," I said. "I'm leaving now."

He didn't reply.

On the way back to Tabby's I thought, *Now that was bizarre.*

By the time I reached Tabby's I'd decided I'd have to call Aubrey and tell him I didn't think there was much I could do to help him with his suspicions. It wasn't that I was giving up. I didn't have anything to give up on.

Besides, Betty Weeks was a family friend, and even if she'd been slipping out on Erskine, which I had a hard time believing, I surely didn't believe she had anything to do with her husband's death.

Chapter 6

ACCORDING TO TABBY'S back deck thermometer it had warmed up to 93 degrees, so I decided to put off the weed-wacking until evening. The shed still needed some cleaning and straightening up, so, a tall glass of ice snickerdoodle in hand, I went back out there to play in the shed—Tabby's words.

I'd spent about three hours and was pleased with my work. I stood there, hands on hips, admiring the now functional shed, when I heard Tabby's call for supper. It reminded me why I lived alone at Blue Heron Marsh. I'd had enough regimentation in the military. On the marsh I could eat—or not—when I felt like it; go fishing when and where I felt like it; even read a book and drink a Jack Daniels Black Label at ten in the morning if I felt like it.

However, I was hungry, so I took one last look at my handiwork and headed in for another one of Tabby's full-blown meals. She wasn't a big fan of fish. I'd already decided since I'd missed out on the fishing expedition with Ben, I'd get up early tomorrow morning, go over to Big Flatty Creek and try my luck on some big mouth bass, or even catfish. It had been a while since I'd gone after catfish.

The only trouble I could foresee was that tomorrow was a Sunday, and I knew Tabby would lobby for me to take her to church. It wasn't that she couldn't drive there by herself, because she did all the time. However, I knew she'd play the "This whole business with Erskine has left me shaken and I'm not sure I can go anywhere alone just yet" card. I'd have to think about how to handle that. Maybe I could get the Aycock woman to take her. She had to be useful for something.

Supper was leftover fried chicken with mashers and green beans. I felt as if I needed a two-hour workout just to get back to where I was two hours earlier. I didn't want to become addicted to her fare. But I'll admit, it *was* pretty darned good. After the meal, Tabby asked me if I wanted to watch the news on TV with her. I wanted to say "Hell no! Why would I want to spend the next hour getting an update from talking heads on all the latest abductions, assaults, rapes, robberies and murders; not to mention there was an election year coming, and the hot air, inane remarks and absurd promises were sticking to the walls like you know what. I begged off, saying I needed to go back outside and weed-wack the yard.

"I tell you about what's going on," Tabby said, as if I really wanted to know.

I gassed up the weed eater and started at the north side of the yard, along the edge of Nixon's soy bean field, right next to where Erskine crashed. After that, I cleaned up around the shed, then around the house. In the middle of the back yard there was what Tabby called her Flower Boat. I called it a mowing obstruction.

Uncle John had inherited an old wooden skiff with two planks for seats. When he purchased a new fiberglass fishing boat, which he used to haul out to Newbegun and Big Flatty Creek, Aunt Tabby refused to let him scrap the old one. Instead, she made him turn it into a flower garden—right in the middle of the back yard. She'd also had him put up a section of wood rail fence behind it to, as she'd said, "Fancy it up." She'd fancied it up with snap dragons, marigolds and zinnias; back to front rows of yellows, oranges and reds. In a pique of asserting his own aesthetic into the structure, Uncle John had placed an old hand plow on the south side of the boat garden.

Basil must have been following me around, because suddenly he was there, hopping up into the flower bed, sniffing around. I wasn't watching what I was doing and accidently wrapped the plastic string from the spool around something, shutting off the machine.

"Damn!"

I had just stooped down to look at it when I heard the sound of a rifle shot and a millisecond later the ping of bullet striking the metal plow.

"What the—"

The sound of a second shot reverberated in the heavy evening air, the bullet tearing a chunk of the top of the boat's gunwale, just above and to the right of my head.

"Son-of-a-bitch!"

Fucking Renner!

Out of the corner of my eye I saw the blur of Basil bounding out of the boat garden and streaking toward the back porch. I wasn't sure what to do, so I belly-crawled to the front end of the boat and peeked around the end. I was too low to see anything but the soy beans, but it was obvious the shots had come from the trees across the field.

I looked over toward the house and saw two things. Basil had jumped back off the porch and was tearing across the yard toward the field. The other thing was Tabby standing at the kitchen window looking out at me. I put my thumb to my ear and my little finger to my mouth, hoping she'd get the message.

I stayed down until a deputy arrived.

* * *

I was hoping it would be Aubrey Meads. Instead it was the other two guys who'd showed up at the crash; the two I'd gotten sandwiches for, Deputies Terryberry and Perkins, I presumed they'd come in two separate cruisers.

Tentatively I got up and, looking warily across the soy beans, walked toward them. Pointing, I said, "Some son-of-a-bitch took two shots at me from the trees."

Deputy William Terryberry looked at Deputy Perkins and said, "Daryl, go check it out. I'll get Mr. Sawyer's statement." Then, to me, "You okay?"

Tabby was at the back door, watching, a hand over her mouth.

"A little unnerved is all."

I could hear Deputy Perkins tearing down the road toward the tree line. I told Terryberry what happened and added, "You want my two cents worth, I'd go down and check out Jeb Renner, post haste."

"I'll do that right now," Terryberry said, "Go inside and stay put." Then he turned and ran back around the house for his cruiser.

I went inside more for Tabby's benefit than mine. I wanted to kill Jeb Renner and his stupid kid for the terror they'd rained on my family. Well, maybe I wouldn't kill the kid. Just slap him silly.

I was doing my best to calm down poor Aunt Tabby when I heard another vehicle pull into the driveway. I looked out the front window. It was Aubrey Meads. He got out of his cruiser, looked down the road, hitched up his belt and walked toward the house. He was still looking toward the tree line when I came out onto the porch.

Aubrey looked at me and asked, "That bastard Renner actually shoot at you?"

"Didn't see the shooter but who else? If you're asking, I presume he's out on bond."

"Oh, yeah. Yesterday, Five grand. Jenine put up the truck as collateral."

"Perkins is checking out the trees. Terryberry went down to Renner's."

"Yeah. He just called in. Nobody at the house. Everyone is lookin' for him."

"Why the hell would he do this?" I asked. "Doesn't he know he'd be the suspect?"

"Suspect, my ass," Aubrey said. "That's words for the lawyers. "Who the hell else would want to put one in you?"

"He would have, too, if the damn string on the weed eater hadn't hung up on something. I'd just stooped down to check it when 'ping,' a bullet hit the plow."

"Plow?"

"Follow me. I'll show you."

I took Aubrey around the house, into the back yard and over to Tabby's boat garden. I picked up the weed eater, which was still lying where I'd dropped it, showed him where I'd been standing, then went through the motions of what happened, second by second.

"Jesus!" looking at the top of the boat's gunwale where the second bullet had ripped through the wood. Then he walked around to the other side of the garden and inspected the plow. "Yep. Can see where it clipped the edge of this piece of metal," showing me where.

"I'm pretty sure the guy was using a scope."

"Yeah," looking back toward the trees. "Could be."

"Reason I say that is, if you remember, Renner had a scope mount on his rifle. Second reason is, Basil ran up onto the porch after the shots—"

"Basil? The cat?"

"Yeah. He was sniffing around in the flower bed when it happened. He ran across the yard and up onto the back porch. He was looking toward the trees. Then he jumped off the porch and ran like a bat into the soy beans, heading across toward the tree line. I think it was because he saw a glint of light off something. Most likely a scope."

"Hmm. Makes sense . . . both things. Renner and the reflection, I mean."

"I figure Perkins is in the trees looking for casings, but, you know, those two bullets had to go somewhere. Maybe we can find one of them.

"Good thought," from Aubrey. "I'm thinkin' the one that ricocheted off the plow could have gone anywhere. But the one here," running his finger over the boat's gunwale, might be the easier one to figure. Plus, it hit pretty deep, so it must have slowed it down considerable, don't you think?"

I agreed. We eyeballed a possible trajectory, then started walking a grid on the outside edges of where we figured it might have gone, me on the right, Aubrey on the left. We had gone about twenty feet when Deputy Perkins pulled back into the yard. When he got out of the cruiser, Basil bounded out with him and ran over to me, meowing, telling me everything that happened.

Perkins came up to us and asked us what we were doing. We told him.

"This cat of yours was already at the scene of the shooter when I got there. Pretty smart cat. He led me right to one of the casings under some leaves and pine straw. Figured the shooter couldn't find it before he high-tailed it out of there. I didn't find the other one. Shooter must have picked it up."

"Good boy, Basil," I said, bending over and scooping him up. But he was having none of that. He twisted out of my arm and leaped to the ground, where he began sniffing around.

"I wonder if he's sniffing out the bullet," Aubrey said.

"He's like a dog in a cat's body," Deputy Perkins said.

We all stood there watching. "I'm glad the sheriff ain't here to see us lettin' a cat do our job," Perkins said.

Aubrey laughed. I would have, too, if someone hadn't just tried to kill me.

"Speak of the devil," Aubrey said. Sheriff Grimes had just pulled into the yard. "Not that he's really the devil. Just a saying," giving a nervous laugh, afraid Daryl Perkins might repeat it to Grimes.

Grimes walked up, looked at us for a moment, then said, "What's everybody standing around for. Wasn't there a shooting here?"

To avoid either deputy having to sound stupid, I said, "We're waiting for Basil to find one of the bullets."

Grimes looked at the cat, then at me, then at the deputies. "Is this some kinda joke?"

"No joke," Aubrey said.

"Yeah," from Deputy Perkins. "This cat found a spent casing at the site of the shooter."

"That so." Grimes looked down at Basil, who was pawing at the ground. "Maybe I should put him on the payroll," deadpan.

I squatted down and used my fingers to dig in the dirt where Basil was pawing. It wasn't long before my fingernail touched something metallic. I pulled off my t-shirt, wrapped part of it around my hand so as to not mess up any possible prints, dug out the object, then stood up and held out a slightly damaged bullet. "I guess maybe you should, sheriff." Then, "You coulda been digging this sucker out of my head."

"Guess we need to get the casing and the bullet to the lab people." By lab people, I knew he meant a man named Clyde Henderson, who did all the routine stuff for the city and county, including some of the surrounding counties. Anything beyond routine had to be sent to the SBI, the State Bureau of Investigation, in Raleigh.

"Let me see that casing," I asked Deputy Perkins. He pulled out a plastic bag with the casing inside. I took it, held it side by side with the bullet and studied them. "In my not so expert, but knowledgeable opinion, this is NATO standard issue 7.62 by 51 millimeter ammunition."

"What the hell does that mean?" from Sheriff Grimes.

I shrugged. "It means that unless Jeb Renner has another rifle you don't know about, it might not of been him."

Who else have you pissed off lately?" Grimes asked.

The dog killer out on Fairfield Road flashed into my mind, but I didn't really do anything to piss him off except for standing in his driveway. Even so, I thought it might be worth looking into. On my own. I'd think about it. "No one I know of," I said.

"What kind of rifle shoots them kind?"

"Anything that would shoot .308 Winchester ammo," I said. What I didn't say was, the last time I'd seen that ammunition they were being shot out of a Russian bolt-action rifle called the Izhmash SV-98. It was something I'd have to think about before I sent ill-equipped and unknowledgeable rural law enforcement officers on a wild goose chase.

Chapter 7

SHERIFF GRIMES CALLED later that evening, saying they had caught up with Jeb Renner, and that Renner had an alibi, which they confirmed. When I was being shot at, he and his wife and kid were at the El Camino Mexican Restaurant eating fajitas and fried beans. Grimes also told me that he and Clyde Henderson had been out to the shooter's nest, as he called it, and taken a cast of several footprints, some of which he was sure was the Renner kid's and one set looked like it was probably mine. There was also a third set they were looking at. He'd let me know what they came up with. Other than that, there was nothing new. He asked me once again if I'd thought of anyone else who might enjoy putting a bullet in my head. Again, I told him no, but that I'd let him know if I came up with another name. He just grunted, told me to keep my head down, and hung up.

Of course, Tabby wanted to know everything, Including whether or not they'd arrested "That awful Jeb Renner." I told her that they'd already talked to him and the investigation was under way. "Now he knows they're watching him, I don't think we'll have any more trouble from him," I said, which was true, unless he'd hired someone to do his dirty work for him, but in my gut I knew the shooting had nothing to do with him.

"But he tried to kill you," Tabby said, tears streaming down her chubby cheeks.

I gave her a hug and said, "He was shooting over my head. Just trying to scare me," I lied. Why upset her any more than she already was. "He's just a bully. Don't worry about it. The sheriff will take care of it." What I really thought was, I need to get myself a gun so I can protect myself.

Then she started in on me about church. I had one big problem. Well, two if you counted I really didn't want to sit through sermons from Deuteronomy 10 or Romans 5, or whatever else the pick-of-the-week was. The main problem, however, was a more practical one. I didn't want to leave the house empty, then come home to a surprise when we opened the door. "Hello Mr. Sawyer, you son-of-a-bitch."

BOOM!

I didn't want to be paranoid, but I didn't want to be careless, either. If it wasn't Jeb Renner who'd tried to shoot me, then who? Whoever it was must be watching me. I wished Nan was back in town. I'd have her come out with my rifle and my mother's .32 special, which I'd kept. Then again, maybe it would be best just to go back to Blue Heron Marsh and let them follow me there, where I could deal with them on my own turf and my own terms.

" . . . feel like driving there by myself," Aunt Taby was finishing up when I came out of my thoughts.

I didn't feel like a long drawn out discussion about how church was not more than a mile and a half away, and on and on, so I replied, "You'll just have to call Sarah Aycock and have her take you. I have some personal business to take care of here."

"But can't you take care of it after church?" she whined.

"No. I can't." I stood firm and she pouted. I thought she might break out again in tears and I was prepared to hold my ground, when she hung her head and said, "Okay. I just thought . . . ," letting the words trail off.

About then I felt more like dealing with someone trying to kill me than Aunt Tabby getting all pouty on me.

She was clattering around in the kitchen when the phone rang. The jangling sound always set my nerves on edge, which is why I refused to have one, land line or cell. Phones were necessary evils only when necessary.

The call was for me. It was Bobby Nixon.

UNNECESSARY!

Tabby, a pout still on her face, handed me the receiver. I took a deep breath, sighed, and said, "Hello, Bobby."

"Hey, Webb. Sorry we didn't get to talk more at Miss Betty's but it wasn't a good time."

I wondered what he was getting at. We didn't have anything to talk about. Then, I thought, he's not going to try and sell me insurance or an offer to handle my financial planning, is he? Without responding to his opening, I said, "I hope you were able to work out the funeral arrangements," realizing that was probably what he was calling about.

But no . . . .

"Yeah, well. We're still working on it. I'll let you know by tomorrow. Maybe at church. Patty and I are going to stay with Miss Betty. They're doing a little memorial for Erskine. Maybe you'd like to say something at the service."

"Ah," caught off guard. "I'll think about it, Bobby," letting him assume I'd be there.

"Well, good. If you'd like." Then, "There's something else I really wanted to talk to you about."

Uh-oh. Here it comes.

When I didn't respond, he said, "It's something personal, Webb. May I call you Webb?" The old salesman's buddy-up-to-you trick.

"Sure."

"Something I'd rather not discuss by phone," Bobby said.

"So we're not talking about insurance or investments, I take it."

"Ah, not really. Not unless you want to. This is something . . . something private. A family matter."

Hmmm. "About Erskine?" I asked.

Bobby cleared his throat. "Ah, best we talk in person. After church. Patty's going back to her mother's and I can drop her off, then say I need to meet a client in Elizabeth City."

What to do, what to do?

"Call me back here at Aunt Tabby's in about an hour," I said.

Bobby hesitated, then said, "Sure, Webb. "About an hour," and he hung up.

"What did Bobby want?" from Aunt Tabby, still in a funk.

"Want's to get together and talk about financial matters," I lied.

"Oh." She went back to shuffling dishes, saying, "I guess I should clean up the kitchen."

I told her I'd take care of it for her. I needed to make a call and I'd do it while I talked. She didn't argue about it, telling me she was going to watch some television. I wondered if she would actually call Sarah Aycock, but I didn't want to get that going again. If she didn't, would she pressure me in the morning, or just forget.

I hated this kind of drama.

I dug out the micro-sized address and contact book I carried around in my wallet and looked up Nan's cell number. I felt the urge to hear to her voice. She didn't answer and her automated message service kicked in.

While I rinsed the dishes and cookware from supper and put them in the dishwasher (at home I washed mine by hand and put them in a drainer by the sink—real low tech stuff) I though about Bobby Nixon's call. When I'd asked him if he wanted to talk about Erskine, he'd hesitated and avoided my question. Did he know something about the accident? Or about Betty and Erskine's relationship? Was Aubrey really on to something about seeing her car going into the dog killer's driveway? Maybe I should see Aubrey, but this whole business about someone wanting me done in was unnerving because I didn't know who it was—or why. And I didn't want to put Tabby in the middle. Hell, I didn't even want her to know any more about it than she already thought she did. She'd believed what I'd told her and I wanted to keep it that way.

The phone rang.

"I'll get it, Tabby," and picked up. It was Nan.

"Saw you'd called, but was just getting done with a late dinner and didn't want to be rude taking a call. So, how's things at Aunt Tabby's?"

I didn't tell her about Erskine's accident or about Aubrey's concerns. I'd talk to her about that later when Tabby wasn't within earshot, or maybe after I got back to Blue Heron Marsh.

I did tell her about the flying turtles and giant red bunnies, but not about the confrontation with Jeb Renner or the two bullets someone tried to put in me.

"What a little shit," she said about the Renner kid.

"Pretty much what I said. So, when are you due back?"

"Leaving early next Saturday morning. Flight is due into Norfolk midday. Can you pick me up?"

"I hope so," I said, disappointed that it wasn't in the next day or so. I'd hoped to get her to bring up my weapons.

"By the way, I thought you were going down to the Sandhills to go fishing with your Bass Ale buddy."

I gave a half laugh. "I cancelled." Speaking lower, I said, "Aunt Tabby is still shook up about everything," not saying what everything was, "so I decided to hang in here for a while longer," telling the truth without telling all the truth.

* * *

Bobby Nixon called back. It was exactly an hour later, as he'd said. He was a man of exactness. A good trait for someone in his line of work. I still hadn't worked out the timing, so I gave myself some cushion saying, "I can meet you in town tomorrow, but maybe not until, say, one-thirty. How about at the Java Hut? You know, the coffee house on Main and Road Streets."

"Ah, okay. I'll make that work." Then, "Will I see you at church?" I told him no, that he wouldn't.

For some reason, I decided to take the initiative and just call Sara Aycock myself. As my mother used to say, "My nose is itching to get this done." I found the Aycock number in the phone book, which Tabby kept in one of the kitchen drawers. I was in luck. Sarah answered the phone on the second ring. I asked her if she would mind taking Aunt Tabby to church with her in the morning, to which she said she would, as long as Tabby didn't mind coming straight home, as Sarah had company that afternoon and had food to prepare. I wanted to kiss the woman.

I called Bobby Nixon right back and told him that I could make it by noon if that would work better for him. He said it would.

I was making the damn phone work for me for a change. That said, it didn't change my mind about having one in my house. Been there, done that. Not again.

When I went into the living room, Aunt Tabby asked, "Who was that who called earlier?"

"Good news,' I said, glibly. "It was Sarah Aycock. She said she'd be happy to pick you up for church tomorrow morning, but that she'd have to bring you straight home. She's having company." Tabby would find out tomorrow that it was me who'd called Sarah, but it would be too late to complain.

"Oh. It was nice of her to offer," still pouting. Okay then," resolved that was how it was going to be.

Two minutes later, the phone rang again. "Geeze," I muttered.

"Could you get it, Webb," Tabby whined. "I just don't feel like talking to anybody right now." That was a first.

It was Aubrey Meads. He wanted to know if I'd had any thoughts about what he'd told me about Miss Betty and Perry Adams. "I know with all this other stuff going on, you haven't had time to think about it," he said. "so's I don't mean to bother you, but I was just wondering." I lied to him, too, saying I had and was working something over in my mind. That I'd have to get back to him about it. I didn't say anything about Bobby Nixon.

I was lying up a storm to everyone.

Maybe tomorrow, after I talked to Bobby Nixon, I'd have something to grab hold of. Then again, maybe not.

The shooting incident was still forefront in my mind. I had to work that business out first. It was a matter of life and death.

Mine.

Chapter 8

AFTER MUCH SEARCHING, Aunt Tabby found a pair of Uncle John's binoculars in the back of the linen closet. What they were doing there, she didn't know. When you can't find things, that's when you know one of two things: you have too much stuff, or you never put things back where they're supposed to go. It would have been nice if they were infrared. Too much to ask. I settled for the fact that she didn't ask why I wanted them.

I'd determined that after Tabby got back from church and after I'd met with Bobby Nixon, I'd go by Billy Jackson's house to see if I could get him to open up the little gun shop next to his house and sell me something I could use to protect myself. I suppose I could have driven all the way back to Blue Heron Marsh and got my own, but I'm a stubborn person, sometimes to a fault. A lot of shit was falling on my head in my old neck of the woods and I decided I'd deal with it here.

I had a plan for while Tabby was at church. After Sally Aycock picked her up, I went upstairs, sat on the floor in front of each window so as not present a nice target for anyone out there headhunting. Using Uncle John's binoculars, I swept the area within the parameters of the window for anything that didn't seem right, movement or otherwise.

Once that was done, and I'd set basic traps at all the windows and both the front and back door, Basil and I got into Trusty Rusty and drove down Tyler Swamp to the tree line, where I did a Uey and pulled off between the road and the ditch. The traps I'd set were simple one-inch lengths of fishing line strategically placed to fall out of their placement if anyone opened the doors or windows.

Basil followed me along the tree line to the place where the shooter had set up, which was by the same dead tree where I'd waited for the Renner kid. Even with the three cops who'd been mucking around back there, It didn't take me long to find the odd footprint that wasn't theirs, the kid's or mine. I'd brought a roll-out tape measure with me and measured the length and front and back widths. With that I could get the shoe size and maybe a general idea of the size of the person. It was hard to read because the ground was dry, but it looked as if the person had been wearing tennis shoes. I hoped Henderson, the makeshift forensics guy for the sheriff's office, might be able to tell what brand from the cast of the faint print he'd taken earlier.

At first guess, I suspected it might be a woman, which surprised me. What woman did I know who might want to shoot me? Unless Elizabeth Traynor, who'd just been sent to a guarded mental health facility, had escaped. She was the one who'd kidnapped my friend Blythe Parsons. That had only been a couple of months earlier. It seemed like years ago. At any rate, if Traynor had escaped, I would have been notified or heard about it. I'd check that out. Besides her, I couldn't think of anyone else.

While I was at that, Basil sniffed around. After some searching, I found two other sets of prints of the same size, one set heading into the site and another heading out. The one heading out was clearer, indicating to me that the person had moved fast, exerting more pressure on the balls of their feet. I'd have to ask the sheriff if he or Henderson had found that one, as it gave a clearer indication of the tread design. I marked where it was with a teepee of sticks, then counted how many steps it was the dead oak.

The next thing I did was continue through the trees to the field on the other side. Along the way I didn't find any other tracks. I'd never been much of a hunter, and tracking in the woods wasn't my forte. I walked up and down the tree line on that side, but found nothing of interest. I went back to where I'd exited the trees and looked across the field—more soybeans. Suddenly, Basil jumped over the first row of beans and raced into the field. My instinct said, follow the boy.

There were a number of places where someone had gone straight through there, stepping on the plants along the way. About half way across was a lane that ran right up the middle of the field, dividing it into two sections. I hadn't noticed it when we'd gone to and from the Renner house. Basil headed down the lane toward the road. I followed.

About thirty feet in from the road, Basil stopped, sniffing the ground. I saw fresh marks where tires had dug into the ground when it peeled out. A quick getaway? I walked out to the road, Basil following, but there was no indication of which direction the vehicle went. Most likely toward Triple Bridge. I picked up Basil and walked back up the tree line to Trusty Rusty, then we headed back to the house.

I checked all the traps before I went inside. All was safe. I took out the ones from the front and back door, put the lines on the top of the dresser in my bedroom, then called the sheriff's office. It was Sunday, so I presumed I wouldn't get anyone I needed. I didn't. I'd call them tomorrow morning—Monday.

About a half hour later, Sarah pulled into the yard and let out Aunt Tabby, who came trudging up to the front porch. I opened the door for her. She had a sad look on her face. Once inside, I heard a long story about the eulogy for poor Erskine Weeks and how she wished I would have been there to say something. When I asked if she'd gotten up to speak, she said, "Oh heavens no. I couldn't do that in front of all those people." I asked her if Miss Betty and Patty and Bobby were there, and she said they were.

When she said, "As soon as I change I'll fix you something to eat," I told her I'd already had something (really only a cup of coffee and an English muffin with butter and jam), and that I had an appointment to see an old friend in town. When she asked who, I lied and said it was Randy Fearing. "He's a nice man," she said. I agreed that he was.

I told her not to let anyone in the house she didn't know. Much to his displeasure, I left Basil behind as a guard cat, then headed into Elizabeth City. I knew I'd be about a half hour early, so, instead of waiting until after my meeting with Bobby, I drove by Billy Jackson's place to see if he was around. He was. I told him what I wanted and he was ready to go down and open up right then. I told him I had an appointment in town and asked it I could meet him at his gun shop between 2:00 and

2:30 pm. He said that would be fine. We shot the breeze for about fifteen minutes. Like everyone else in the Weeksville area, he wanted to know all the gory details about the incident at Swan's Landing in Perquimans and what had recently happened down at Ocracoke Village, but I told him there was wasn't much to tell other than what he'd read in the papers. When he asked if I'd really shot that Russian guy in the face (he was Serbian, but I didn't correct him), I told him I had. "Fucker deserved it," was all Billy said.

I arrived at the Java Hut about five minutes before Bobby showed up. I'd already gotten a large snickerdoodle and offered to get him something, but he declined. I suggested we go outside. There was a table with two chairs at the front of the building facing Main Street and, while it was noisy with intermittent traffic, it was away from listening ears.
When we sat down, I thought he might want to talk about the church service first, which I'd already heard about from Tabby, so I got right to it. "What's up Bobby?"
Bobby Nixon used to be a outside linebacker on the high school football team. He'd played for two years at State before he blew out a knee. He also used to be lean and muscular. That had been a couple of decades ago. He'd since gone to seed with

the usual beer belly, round face and rapidly receding widow's peak. That said, he'd always been a pretty nice guy and still was.

He leaned in as if we were in a noisy, crowded bar and he needed to get close for me to hear him. "It's about this business with Miss Betty," he said furtively.

"Miss Betty?" wondering if I was about to hear the same thing Aubrey had told me. As it turned out, it was, only from Bobby's perspective.

"I don't know quite how to say this, Webb. And the only reason I'm telling you is because I really liked Mr. Weeks. We did things together. Went hunting and fishing, even took a trip together down to Charlotte to see a Panthers football game once. He was a real nice man. Real nice."

Before he continued, I asked, "What about your relationship with Miss Betty?"

I guess that caught him a little off guard, because he paused, then looked up over my head, which is what someone does when they are trying to decided what to say. "I . . . ah . . . it's been good. We're not as close as I was with Erskine."

"But she's close with Patty, right?" I knew that originally Bobby had met Patty at church and had immediately had a thing for her, but Betty hadn't cottoned up to him as quick as Erskine, who seemed to get on with Bobby right away.

"Oh, she and Patty are tight. Always have been." Then, "You knew she had a child before Patty, a daughter named Caroline who she lost to leukemia when the girl was six years old. Patty was just a baby when her older sister died. Betty never seemed to get over that. It's a hard thing to have a child die."

"It's a hard thing to have anyone you love die," I said.

"Yes, I suppose. My parents are still with us, praise the Lord."

"But you and Betty got along after you and Patty married, I guess." All of a sudden I was reverting back to my soft interrogation days in the Army. Gathering information. Figuring out later if it fit in and, if so, where. Most of the time it was just garbage, but you never knew what might be important.

Bobby shrugged. "We've always been pleasant with each other, but she never confided in me with anything really important. That was all channeled through Patty."

"Miss Betty and Erskine have a close relationship?" I asked. They'd always seemed that way to me, but I hadn't been around much the last twenty years.

"Yeah, I guess. Just the usual nit-picky stuff. Although Patty said her mother said something about Erskine not understanding her needs."

"Emotional? Sexual?"

"No, no . . . well maybe emotional. It had something to do with Caroline, but Miss Betty wouldn't say anything else about it to Patty."

"Caroline? You mean the dead daughter?"

"Yeah. Weird, huh?"

I wasn't sure what to make of it. "So, back to where we started, Bobby. What's up?"

"Ah, here's the thing. I don't want to cause any trouble, but I found out something that's been bothering me and I needed to tell somebody."

I waited.

"See, I have a good client who lives out on the south side of Fairfield Road. The guy, I don't want to say his name, because he knows the family. I mean both mine and the Weeks. Anyway, he know's Miss Betty's car and he tells me one day, just a couple of weeks ago, that he saw her going into a driveway across the road."

"He lives right across the road from the driveway?" Even though I knew where this was going, I wanted more details.

"Well, it's across the road, one house down before you get to the driveway he was talking about."

"And?"

"And, she was there for about an hour and a half before she came back out."

It made me happy I didn't live around here any longer. This was two people, three if you count Bobby, who knew something about Miss Betty's personal business, whatever it was.

"Maybe she was just visiting a good friend," I said, seeing how much more he'd say.

"I can tell you this, Webb. I don't think she's friends with this person, cause it's Perry Adams, the guy who was arrested for killing hunting dogs on his own property."

"Ah, Perry Adams. I think I read something about him," I slid out there. Then, "But why do you think this is some concern and why are you telling me about it?"

Again, he leaned in. "Because Patty said her mother and Erskine had been having arguments about something recently and Miss Betty wasn't too happy with him. After Benson . . . uh, after I was told about this, and then Erskine had this unfortunate accident, I got to wondering if she was having an affair. And maybe he found out about it and . . . well, you know. Killed himself."

Now that was something I hadn't expected. "You mean flew the plane into the ground? Committed suicide."

"That's what I'm wondering, Webb."

I frowned. "But, Bobby. If that is true, There are any number of places he could have done that without endangering anyone else. why would he fly it right into Tabby's front yard?"

"Geeze, Webb. I hadn't thought about that."

Chapter 9

ON THE WAY back to Weeksville, I contemplated the way Bobby and I left it. Even though it didn't make any sense, he still had it in his head that Erskine might have flown his plane into the ground on purpose. What did he want me to do? He asked if there was any way I could find out without upsetting Patty or Miss Betty. I told him that unless someone came up with a suicide note or someone else knew of his plans, which was doubtful, there probably wasn't any way to determine if that was true. But Bobby Nixon wasn't a man who just let things go. Otherwise, he wouldn't be as successful as he was in business.

He asked if I'd at least look into it the best I could, being discrete, of course. I told him I'd try my best. I didn't tell him it was because he wanted me to. What bothered me was that now, two different people had asked me to look into Erskine's death, although for different reasons. Just what I needed to get involved with when someone was out there trying to knock me off. I wondered if there was some connection, but for the life of me I couldn't see how.

Billy Jackson was waiting for me at his little gun shop. The first thing he said was, "You said you wanted a rifle with a scope and a handgun, but you didn't say why. You want something for deer season when it opens up?" meaning the rifle.

Here's the thing about Billy Jackson. He wasn't a bad guy, just mildly annoying. Back in high school he was one of these guys who liked to hang around, hoping to be one of the crowd, whatever crowd it was. He never had anything to contribute but wanted to please. He did that by saying things he thought you wanted to hear. The best way to deal with him back then as well as now was just to humor him . . . agree with whatever he said.

"That's right, Billy. A good rifle for deer hunting." Before he asked I said, "And the handgun just for personal protection."

"Yeah, yeah. I know what you mean. Lot a losers around trying to steal your stuff for money to buy drugs."

"Exactly."

Fortunately, he took credit cards. I left his shop with a Weatherby Vanguard Series 2 and a box of .308 ammunition. New, they sell for around $550.00.

Since this one was a trade-in, I paid him $350. He also sold me a little pocket Springfield XDS with three .45 ammo clips for $150, which was a really good buy. Billy reminded me to get a carry permit if I was going to lug it around with me. I told him I'd take care of it first thing Monday morning.

On the way back to Tabby's I stopped at the Weeksville Junction Grocery. I'd meant to stock up on some more cat food for Basil while in town but forgot. I hoped they had something he was willing to eat. I settled on a dozen cans of a salmon/beef mix. It wasn't fancy feast, but he'd have to live with it.

At the one and only check out counter, the woman looked at me and smiled. "I thought that was you when you came in. You remember me, Webb?"

I did. It was Margorie Englestadt. The last time I'd seen her was about fifty pounds ago. "Hey, Margie. Been a while."

She rang me up and we chatted for a while. When I was ready to leave, she said, "Some girl was in here asking about you a couple of days ago."

"Girl?"

"Well, not a girl-girl. She looked in her late twenties."

Huh! "What'd she want to know?"

"Like where she could find you and like that. I told her you didn't live around here no more, but I heard you was visiting your aunt on Tyler Swamp. Oh, and that was somethin' about what happened in her yard. You know, Mr. Weeks and all that. Real tragic."

I agreed. It was a real tragedy. "What'd she look like?" I asked.

"Right pretty. Good figure," wiggling her eyebrows. "She done had shiny black hair. Real black. And long. And had a funny accent, too."

"Like what?"

"Like . . . I don't know. Maybe it was Latino, but . . . I don't know. Just funny."

"Do you remember what she was driving?"

"Yeah. A black Jeep Wrangler. Pretty new. Soft top."

"You see the license plate?" Margie hadn't, but said when she left she headed down Union Church.

"I figured she was going to look you up," smiling. "But if you're asking questions about her, I guess she didn't find you."

Maybe she did, was my thought.

I decided to ride by Aubrey Meads place and see if he was home.

Aubrey lived on Union Church Road, on the left, just before the road did a ninety degree turn to the right heading down to Sound Point. He was out mowing the lawn. I pulled into his driveway. When he saw me he pulled the mower up beside my driver's side window and turned off the engine.

"Hey. No more problems, I hope." from Aubrey.

"Not yet. But I have a sneaky feeling this isn't the last of it."

"Where's your little buddy?"

I laughed. "He's home guarding Aunt Tabby."

Aubrey laughed back. "He's one smart little cat." Then, "You know, I still think Jeb Renner has something to do with it, but unless we can prove it, it doesn't matter."

"Got something to ask you about that, but first want to get some advice, maybe a favor."

"K. Anything I can do, I will."

"It's about Perry Adams, the dog killer."

"You found out something?"

"Not yet." I started to tell him about my meeting with Bobby Nixon when Aubrey suggested we get out of the heat and go inside. I agreed and pulled further into his driveway and followed him in through a side door.

Aubrey told me his wife KiKi had taken their two kids, Aaron, age 12 and Brianna, age 10, into town to do some clothes shopping for the upcoming school year. They lived in a frame, three-bedroom rambler that was neat and tidy, but not particularly homey. At least not my vision of homey. But I'm a bachelor, so what do I know?

Aubrey wasn't a drinker, so we agreed on some ice tea from the fridge. It was sweetened and I prefer unsweetened, but I was the intruder, so who was I to complain?

We sat in his living room. It was furnished with what looked like second-hand or hand-me-down stuff. I had no problem with that. Except for the bed and dresser in my place, everything else was inherited from my parents. Never made any sense to me to run out and spend your savings or put yourself thousands of dollars in debt for new, cheaply made stuff when you already had old, well made free stuff available.

"So you started to tell me about talking with Bobby Nixon," Aubrey said.

I told him about Bobby's and my conversation and Bobby's supposition about Erskine's death being a suicide.

"Yeah, that makes no sense," Aubrey said. "The suicide, I mean. But it is interesting that he knows about her seeing that Perry guy."

"It is troublesome," I said. I then told him about my encounter with Perry Adams . . . well, with his camera and speaker system.

"Sorry, Webb. I meant to tell you about that. So much else going on with you that I forgot."

I gave him a half laugh. "Sometimes trouble finds me when I'm not looking for it," Then I said,

"I have an idea I want to run by you, though." I told him what I had in mind regarding Perry Adams.

"Huh," Aubrey said. "Actually, not a bad idea. Might be the only way you can get to speak with him, although I wouldn't count on it. As you found out, he's not very friendly. I know someone at the Y. 'I'll check it out and give you a call."

"You know if he's married?" I asked.

"Good question," Aubrey said. "I went by the clerk of court's office and Miss Brenda there checked online for the deed for his property. It only showed his name, but I asked to see the hard copy file, because sometimes there's other papers in there. This time there was a hand-written sticky-note that said, 'See will for disposition of property.' It was initialed P.A. So I checked the will he had on file and it listed a person by the name of Bogdana Nicolescu as the sole heir to his property. But I don't know if she's a wife or who she is. Odd name. I guess it's a woman. When I asked around, no one has ever seen him with any woman, so who knows. Could be someone who staked him for the house and property. Name sounds foreign, don't it."

"It's a female's name. Definitely Romanian," I said.

"Huh. If they're related, it's a long way from Nicolescu to Adams."

"Could be her maiden name. Or maybe he changed his name. What's his background? Is he from around here?" I asked.

"I heard he was a retired accountant from New York, but I don't know if that's the Big Apple or somewhere else in the state."

"Hmm. If I had a computer I could run a search on him, but my laptop is back home and Tabby doesn't have one."

Aubrey laughed.

"What?"

"I was about to ask if you had a cell phone that was connected to the internet, but I know from talking to your buddy, Randy Fearing, that you're somewhat of a technophobe." He scrunched his forehead. "But you have a laptop at home?"

"My son talked me into it. I use it for research. Don't have time for social media, emails or any of that crap."

"You have a son?"

"Was married briefly. He lives in New Zealand now." I didn't go into the details of either, and Aubrey didn't ask.

"What kind of research? If you don't mind me asking."

"Mostly Negro League baseball cards and memorabilia," I said. "My only hobby, and lately haven't done much of that either. But I'd use it for gathering info on someone if I had to. Like this Perry Adams guy."

"Hold on a sec." Aubrey got up and went into another room, then came back with an iPad. "KiKi's," he said. "I don't have much time for online stuff either."

I told him to find a site called National Search. Once he had that, I told him to punch in Perry Adams' name and address.

"Okay," setting the iPad on the coffee table and turning the screen toward me.

I reached into my back pocket and pulled out my wallet. "I'm going to have to pay for the service. Do you mind?" fishing out my credit card and holding it up. Aubrey said he didn't. I opted for the full report, which cost $59.00.

We sat side by side and scrolled through the report. "Huh," I said. "No criminal record or problems until after he came here. Born in New York City. Queens, to parents named Adams, but later lived at a few different addresses in Riverhead. That's out on Long Island. Does have the Bogdana Nicolescu woman associated with his name, but no information on the relationship. Says they're both 57, so it's not an aunt or something. Could be a sister, though. Can you run a discrete check on her?" I asked.

"Ehhh, I don't know, Webb. The detectives usually do that stuff and I don't know what reason I'd give. You want to run it here?"

I shrugged. "Not sure I want to drop another sixty bucks just yet. Maybe I can find out on my own. Oh, I know this is supposed to be the paperless society, but is there anyway you can print this out?"

Aubrey laughed, "Paperless. Yeah, right. Then how come they're buried in it at the office?" eyes rolling. "Anyway, KiKi has a bubblejet. I'll see if I can get her to print it out for me when she gets back. If so, I'll run a copy by Tabby's for you. If not, I'll figure out a way to run by the office and do it there."

"That'll work," I said. "If you bring it by Tabby's and I'm not there, be sure it's in a sealed, plain brown envelope." Aubrey chuckled. "There are a couple of other things I wanted to tell you about."

I told him about Basil's and my investigation in the trees and the soy bean field and about the field lane with the vehicle tracks. "I'm a little worried that Grimes or Henderson won't be too happy about me tromping around their crime scene, even though I was the damn victim."

"Tell you what," Aubrey said. "You tell them you contacted me and I went there with you. In fact, I'll go ahead and report it all for you."

That's when I told him about my buying the two weapons from Billy Jackson. "I have to go in and fill out the paperwork for a carry permit, anyway," I said. "Maybe you call Grimes and tell him what 'we' did and that I'm dropping by for the permit and would give them the info and locations on it myself. Tell him Basil's part in it, too."

"Grimes will love that," Aubrey said. "Maybe he'll make him an official detective. Wouldn't that be something. The cat making detective before me."

"Make a good headline," I said.

Aubrey looked at his watch. "The Y is still open. Let me try them before you leave." He got out his cell and asked for a woman named Kelly Murray, but found out she wouldn't be in again until tomorrow morning. "Since you'll already be in town, I'll get her in the morning and leave the info with Jenny Taggert at the Sheriff's Office."

"Sounds like a plan, Aubrey." I got up and he followed suit. Outside, I said, "I'm sorry I interrupted your mowing, but appreciate your time."

"Grass isn't going anywhere," he said. "Besides, I'm the one who asked for the favor."

I waved as I pulled out of the driveway and headed back toward Tyler Swamp Road. I hadn't told him about the girl who was asking about me at the store. I didn't see where, if at all, it fit in with the shooting or anything else.

In the meantime, I'd keep an eye peeled for a black Jeep Wrangler with a pretty black-haired girl driving.

Chapter 10

I WAS UP and out early Monday morning, telling Aunt Tabby that I was meeting an old Army buddy in town for breakfast. Of course she wanted to know who. I made up a name. Said he was just in town for the day. Thanks goodness she didn't ask how we'd connected. After a while, there are so many lies thrown out there (all little and white, but nevertheless . . .), one is bound to catch up with you.

"You sure have a lot of friends, Webb," she said.

If she only knew how few people I actually put into that category.

I walked in the door to the county sheriff's office at two minutes after nine and asked if Sheriff Grimes was in. He wasn't. But Clyde Henderson was.

"Might you be Jenny Taggert? I asked the woman at the front desk.

"I might. Who's asking and why?" smiling. She had a Down East North Carolina brogue. My guess she was raised somewhere along the Bogue Banks.

"My name is Webb Sawyer, and I ask because you don't have a name tag on your blouse or a nameplate on your desk."

"Maybe you should be on our detective squad," she joked. "In fact, I am Jennie Taggert and here," picking up a manilla envelope from her desk, "is something Deputy Meads left for you. He dropped it off about twenty minutes ago."

"Thanks, may I see Mr. Henderson?" I asked.

"I'll check." She punched in a couple of numbers. Apparently Henderson picked up because when she told him who was here, he must have told her to send me back, which she did.

Before I went in back to see him, I asked Jenny Taggert for the forms to fill out for a carry permit. I didn't tell her I already had the handgun, along with the rifle, locked in the carry box behind the back cab window in the truck bed.

Clyde Henderson was a tall drink of water with an ungainly manner. He had the odd combination of a spongy handshake, but a forceful voice. He got to it right away.

"Since Grimes isn't around, Aubrey told me about your revisit to the woods. Guess I'll have to drive back out there and do a recheck. Told me your cat led you to the tire tracks. That's some cat."

"He's my buddy and my bodyguard," I replied. Henderson let out an odd sound that I took as a chuckle, not knowing I wasn't kidding about the bodyguard part.

"You want to drive me out, we can go over it together," he said. "I can get a deputy to pick me up from your aunt's place and give me a ride home afterwards."

I really didn't want him coming by Tabby's place, otherwise there'd be a thousand questions from her I didn't want to answer. On the other hand, it was a way to get him prioritizing my stuff, so I said, "Hmm. Can't right now, but I can in a couple of hours."

"Grab lunch on the way out maybe," he said. "A burger at that Weeksville Junction Grocery. I hear they make 'em nice and greasy," his face deadpan.

I snorted. "Sure. Though I think I'm gonna need a Roto-Rooter on my arteries after I leave town."

"Unless someone shoots you first," again deadpan. Then, "Oh, that shell casing and the bullet. You were right. I looked it up in NAFAR, the National Firearms and Ammunition Registry, and they were NATO standard issue 7.62 by .51 millimeter ammo. Don't know anybody around here who uses it. Wouldn't even know where to buy any."

I shrugged. "Have to get one of the detectives to do some calling around."

For the first time Henderson gave a hint of a smile and said, "One's on vacation and the other one is out tracking down something important, like a missing dining room table some woman told the landlord she didn't want when she moved. Then a week later changed her mind and went back to get it and it wasn't there. The dumb woman claimed the landlord stole it. Unbelievable."

"Takes all kinds," I remarked.

"Yeah, well, I'll see you in a couple of hours," Henderson said, dismissing me.

Maybe he'll be more fun out of the office, I thought.

On the way out of the Sheriff's Office, Jenny said, "Oh, Mr. Sawyer. Deputy Meads called while you were back with Clyde. He said to tell you usually ten to ten-thirty, whatever that means." I told her thanks without offering an explanation.

Since I wasn't going to show up at the YMCA until a little after 10:00 am, I decided to go by the Java Hut, fortify myself with a coffee and fill out the forms.

One coffee and the filled-out forms later, I headed over to the Y. It was only about a six minute drive. When I walked in I had to sign in as a guest and pay a $5.00 fee. If I had someone to reimburse me, I would have asked for a receipt. Maybe I should start charging for my private investigative services. The only trouble was, I was on the friends and family handout plan.

When I asked the front desk check-in person if my friend Perry Adams had come in yet, she said, "I think he went upstairs to use the treads." She pointed me to the stairs. I thanked her and headed up.

Armed with Aubrey's description, I had no trouble I spotting the dog killer. There were four rows of bikes, most of the treadmill variety where you walk, or run, at the speed of your choice. The place wasn't very busy. He was in the third row back, in the middle, as far away from everyone else he could get.

Perfect!

I really wasn't dressed for a workout, but since treading the mill was only a byproduct of why I was there, I didn't care what anyone might think. I wandered down by the window that overlooked the pool below. On the left was a column blocking me from his view, although he didn't seem to be paying attention to anything or anybody. I walked in behind him and took the treadmill to his right. I hadn't used one in a while. Ignoring him, I stepped on and I spent a minute looking at the controls. I noticed a quick glance from Adams, but that was all, probably wondering why I was getting on a piece of equipment right next to him when practically the whole goddamn place was available.

I'd just got the tread moving on low speed when Perry Adams said, in an unfriendly tone, "You're that guy who was in my driveway."

"Yep, that's me."

"Why are you bothering me? What do you want, anyway?"

Perry Adams was not only short in stature, but on looks. Ill-proportioned was the kindest way of describing him. Maybe it was just the permanent scowl that had frozen on his face. He had sparse graying hair, once brown. His computer file said he was 58, and he looked every year of it.

I kept my slow walk while I talked. "I have one simple question. You answer it and I won't bother you again." I wasn't going to say that somebody else might. Like one of the detectives from the Sheriff's Office. At least the one who's not on vacation.

"What?" confrontational.

"I'm a long time friend of Erskine and Betty Weeks and their family and I want to know why Betty was visiting your house when she was supposed to be coming here to the Y?"

Adams turned off his treadmill, turned toward me and said, "It's a personal matter. Why don't you ask her?"

"Because, Mr. Adams, her husband died in a terrible accident and he isn't even in the ground yet." Then I lied and said, "And his death is under investigation. So it might be better if you tell me than have some detective knocking on your door asking you. Right now, I'm the only one who knows something was up, even though I don't know what," probing with half-truths. I was becoming a pro. We were both talking in hushed tones now.

"I don't want to talk here," he said, looking around. "There's a sitting area over by the elevator. "I looked over that way. No one was there. I shut off my machine and we headed that way.

We found two easy chairs near the plate glass window and sat down. The first thing he said was, "I don't feel real comfortable talking about someone else's business." Then, "What did you say your relationship with her was." I told him how our two families grew up together and were close friends. That was good enough for him. He didn't need to hear all the gory details of my life. I figured he was ready to talk anyway, otherwise we wouldn't be sitting there.

"She didn't come to my place to see me, if that's what you're thinking. She came to see my . . . my friend."

"I took a chance and said, "Bogdana Nicolescu?"

Adams looked at me, a frown on his face. "You some kind of private detective or something?"

I chuffed. "Hardly. I told you, I am just a good friend of the family. In case you wonder why I know about the investigation of Erskine's death, it's because he crashed in my aunt's front yard and the sheriff is a personal friend of mine."

Suddenly, Perry Adams went from angry to pale.

"Just tell me what's going on and we can close this thing out . . . unless it's something to be concerned about."

He leaned in and whispered. "It's nothing sinister, God damn it. Look, I don't know how you know about Danna, but I suppose with the goddamned internet, nothing is private these days." He took a deep breath. "Mrs. Weeks and I weren't having an affair, if that's what you think. She was coming over to see Danna. She's a psychic. Danna is, I mean. I wasn't even there, except for the first time." He contemplated for a few moments. "I just don't feel comfortable talking about Mrs. Weeks personal business. The only thing I'll say is it was about a family matter."

What ran through my mind was, what would Miss Betty be doing with a psychic about a family matter? Tarot cards? Reading of the palms? You will have a happy life and all that shit? Or, something terrible would soon happen. If that was it, would the dog killer make something happen to prove the psychic's bad omen. Probably farfetched, but . . . .

"Unlike Danna, I'm no psychic, but I can read your mind . . . what you're thinking," Adams said. "Goddamnit, this really pisses me off." I could see his jaw working his teeth. "It was about her dead child, Caroline." When I wrinkled my brow, he said, "Mrs. Weeks wanted to make contact with her in the afterlife."

Oh, geeze!

On the way to pick up Clyde Henderson I wondered how much money they'd bilked out of Miss Betty. And where it came from. And if Erskine was on to it. Maybe that's what Bobby was talking about when he said there was some dispute between them that Miss Betty wouldn't even tell Patty about.

Maybe Erskine didn't want her to spend her time and money on such foolishness. Maybe it was time to check the connections on the plane's control lines and rods and his mind was elsewhere and he let it go or forgot.

I stopped at the Java Hut and got Clyde a cup of snickerdoodle and another one for myself. I had to wait twenty minutes for him at the Sheriff's Office while he finished up something. In the meantime, I handed Jenny Taggert the completed paperwork for my permit and asked if there was anyway they could be expedited. She said she'd do her best. While I waited, Sheriff Grimes came in. I told him what Henderson and I were going to do, then gave him a brief version of why. "I believe Deputy Meads left a message for you about it," I said. Grimes looked at Jenny, who confirmed that Aubrey had called earlier and left a message. Grimes nodded, asked me if Henderson had anything new on the casing and bullet. I told him that Henderson had confirmed my supposition. I also told him what I'd suggested about having a detective call around to see where that caliber could be purchased locally, and if there'd been any recent customers. Grimes said he'd take care of it, then headed back to his office, saying, "That tire track might be our best lead."

Shortly, Henderson appeared and we were on our way.

Clyde—we'd decided on first names—thanked me for the coffee and I briefed him on my conversation with Grimes. We were at the Weeksville Junction Grocery before we knew it.

In back there was a small kitchen where basic fare: burgers, dogs, pulled pork, fries and the like were made and served up at the counter. There were tables with plastic two-seater benches, booth style, but no real booths. Clyde and I ate our cheeseburgers — they weren't as greasy as either of us expected. We split a large order of fries.

We were still negotiating our way to the bottom of our large coffees when, suddenly, Margie the clerk was standing at our table.

"Hey, Margie," I said. "I didn't see you when we came in."

She gave me a big old country-girl grin and said, "I'm just coming on at noon." I started to reply, when she said, "But I wanted to tell you that I saw that Jeep Wrangler just a bit ago."

I hadn't said anything to anyone about it, so Clyde didn't know what she was talking about. "When? Where?"

"Just a few minutes ago, actually. On my way into work. Coming up Old Nixonton Road. I mean, I was coming up Old Nixonton Road. She was coming toward me, you know, going toward the turnoff at Little River."

"Same girl driving?"

"Looked like her to me," Margie said.

"Did you see if she went straight or turned?"

"You mean did I look in my rearview mirror?"

Duh. "Yep, that's what I mean," smiling to cover a wave of angst that stampeded through my brain.

"Yep. She turned down Little River."

"Shit!" I spat out. "Come on, Clyde. Let's go," and I jumped up and ran toward the front door, leaving Margie standing there, watching us, her mouth hanging open.

I jumped into Trusty Rusty with Clyde right behind, climbing into the passenger side. I tore out of the parking lot like a volunteer fireman heading to a church fire.

"This girl must be something else," he said. Raised eyebrows were the only expression on his face.

"Hang on to your lunch!" I shouted. Instead of heading down Old Nixonton Road, I went left on Union Church, then hung a quick right on Tyler Swamp. I hoped Trusty Rusty would forgive me for having my foot to the floor. Then, as I came around the bend where the road curved to the right, there she was, coming toward me on the curve. All I saw was long, jet-black hair as she swerved away from the center line, then gunned it, shooting past me toward Union Church.

I slammed on the brakes, skidded, laying rubber but staying on the road. I did as fast a Uey as I could manage and floored it again, but by the time I got to Union Church there was no sign of the black Wrangler.

"Shit!"

"That sure was exciting. What was that all about?" from Clyde.

"Shit!" again. "Maybe nothing. Let's go check that tire track first. If it turns out to belong to a late model Jeep Wrangler, then maybe it's something."

Chapter 11

FORTUNATELY, DEPUTY TERRYBERRY came by while Clyde Henderson was taking a cast of the tire track Basil and I had found on the field road. So, when we were finished, Henderson didn't come by Aunt Tabby's house, avoiding unwanted questions.

Actually, Clyde, odd as he was, was a man I enjoyed being around, and that's not something I can say for most people I just meet—or, for that matter, anyone. He was both careful and professional in the way he approached his job. He didn't ask stupid questions and, when I had questions of my own gave good, understandable feedback. It pisses me off when professionals, be they doctors, dentists, lawyers, law enforcement people, bureauweenies or whoever like to be smart-asses and show off by throwing around acronyms and jargon that only their fellow travelers understand.

I'd asked Clyde if he liked to fish. To my surprise, he said he did, although he hadn't been in several months. I told him once I got the issues about people trying to kill me sorted out, I'd be in touch, thinking maybe I could salvage something for of my time in Weeksville.

I was at Aunt Tabby's contemplating these matters, when the phone rang. Tabby was outside, so I took the call.

A female voice said, "Is this Webb?" When I said it was, she said, "I thought you were my friend."

I was caught off guard. "If I knew who this was, I could respond."

"It's me," angry. "Betty Weeks." Then, "As if it isn't bad enough losing my beloved Erskine, now you of all people have turned against me."

I took a deep breath. "Miss Betty, you know I am terribly sorry about Erskine, but I don't know what you're talking about," although I had a guess.

"You . . . you went snooping into my private business and now it's cost me my daughter." She was hyperventilating.

"Patty?"

"No," crying now. "Caroline."

Ah. The dog killer. "I take it you heard from Perry Adams."

"Yes, I heard from Perry," angry again. "He was helping me and now he said he can't continue and it's your fault. You ruined everything."

"I'm sorry, Miss Betty but—"

"Don't you but me, Webb Sawyer," crying again. "And please don't bother coming to the funeral. You're not welcomed."

I started to sputter out something else, but she'd already hung up.

"Well isn't that a kick in the ass," I said to myself. Not only was someone hunting me, but I had also become a pariah in my own childhood community.

What to do next? Should I call Bobby Nixon? Probably not. However, I did need to tell Aubrey. I felt like an ass. He'd probably feel like an ass, too. We could wallow in it together. I thought about calling him, but realized I didn't have his phone number. I looked in Tabby's phone book, but it wasn't there. Makes sense. Deputy Sheriffs don't like to have their home phones out there for every nut to use and abuse.

I figured Aubrey was working, but I'd decided to drive over to his house and leave a message with his wife, or a note in the door if she wasn't home. As it turned out, no one was home at the Meads' residence, so I left a note on the door to have Aubrey give me a call.

It was late in the afternoon and I found myself puttering around Tabby's shed. Random thoughts bounced around like snooker balls after a bad cue ball break where nothing fell into the pockets.

Events of the past several days were confusing. Nothing fit together. Nothing made any sense. It was frustrating. I picked up a wrench and thought, *I'd like to put this right in the middle of some asshole's face. Whose? I wish I knew.* What do I do when I'm annoyed, frustrated and aggravated? If I was home, Basil and I would go downstairs and take the skiff out into the marsh behind my stilt home and fish.

What the hell!

I had plenty of lures with my fishing gear stored in the truck's lock box. Even so, I wanted to try something different. Since my friend Randy Fearing had always touted the virtues of bloodworms for creek fishing, I decided to try the juicy *lumbricus terrestris*. I took Basil with me and drove up to the Weeksville Junction Grocery. Basil wanted to ride in the truck bed, but I wouldn't let him.

Margie wasn't working, so I wasn't able to get any possible updates on whether or not she'd had any more black-Wrangler sightings. A kid by the name of Bucky intercepted me, led me over to the fishing gear section and spent several minutes acting like he knew everything about fishing. The only thing he knew about bloodworms were that they were expensive. "I just dig up my own worms," he said.

He was right about one thing. At ten bucks a dozen bloodworms aren't cheap. That's because they are primarily harvested up in Canada and the

New England area, mostly Maine. So with all the packaging to keep them alive and fresh, and shipping costs, they run ten bucks a dozen. Not only that, but demand is high. But largemouth bass like them and that's what I was going after. It's probably cheaper to go out and buy the fish someone else has already caught, but that isn't the point.

Peace and quiet and lowering my stress level was the point.

Back at Tabby's I hooked up Uncle John's A&E Fiberglass, Lagoon flat-bottom sport boat to the hitch on the back of Trusty Rusty. Tabby had been invited over to Sarah Aycock's for coffee and chit-chat so, with the exception of her insistence that she prepare sandwiches and a thermos of snickerdoodle, she made no comment on my fishing excursion. However, she said that if I was still hungry when I returned, she'd be home and could fix me something. I thought about reminding her that I lived alone and wasn't helpless. Instead I thanked her for her thoughtfulness.

I'd checked the oil and filled Uncle John's 30hp, 4-stroke outboard with gas, making sure it started up and ran properly before installing it on the back of the boat. Big Flatty Creek is a fresh-water inlet and creek that empties into the Albemarle Sound. Clyde Henderson had told me that Jenny Taggert's husband had been recently successful at Big Flatty going after the largemouth. Besides, ever since I was a kid, I've always enjoyed fishing Big Flatty. Uncle John's Lagoon boat was fourteen feet, eleven inches in length with a six foot, four inch beam, drawing only six to seven inches of draft. It was the perfect boat for creek and other shallow-water fishing.

Usually, at Big Flatty I go to the back of the inlet where it narrows into the actual creek. When I did that, I didn't go too far up as the water loses its oxygen content and the bass won't stay there. But here's the thing about creek-fishing for largemouth. They like to move out of water with higher salt levels into the freshwater creeks. When enough of them come in, they tend to congregate in areas that make them easy to see and fish. I knew just where to look and drifted over to some fallen trees along the northern bank.

I knew the best way to get the largemouth's attention was to bounce crank baits off the logs, then once they were stirred up from the sound, cast into the water. However, since I was using the blood-worms, that wouldn't work. Besides, I wasn't good at the bouncing bait technique. Before, when I've tried that, I've either hooked a broken branch, or overshot and got the hook caught behind the log. So, before I put the boat in the water, I collected a couple dozen small rocks I could hurl at the logs, accomplishing the same purpose.

I laid up about twenty feet out from my targets, set my bait and pitched my rocks. Basil sat up on the hull at the prow of the boat—his usual perch—staring at the water. As soon as I saw activity, I cast out my line. The moment it hit the water I had a strike. As the saying goes, it was like shooting fish in a barrel. In fifteen minutes I brought in five largemouth bass, only throwing two back.

I decided to back off and go across to the other side of the inlet and do some less frenzied fishing. I had just rebated my hook and cast the line when I heard an outboard. It sounded as if it was coming in off the Albemarle Sound. The entrance that led into Big Flatty wasn't a straight-in affair. There is a small opening from the sound that almost immediately bends to the left, then again to the right. Not fifty feet after that, it opens up into a hundred foot expanse. The west side of the largest area of the inlet, where I was moored, was hidden by trees so I couldn't see who it was, nor could they see me.

Suddenly, I realized I should have taken one of the weapons out of the lock box and brought it with me. There were oars in the boat, so I quickly hauled in the line, slipped the oars into the oar locks and rowed backwards into the narrow opening of the creek where, if I had to, I could jump out of the boat onto dry land and lose myself in the trees.

Soon the other boat came into view. He was looking at the truck and had yet to see me. I breathed a sigh of relief. His uniform gave him away as the game warden. I whistled to get his attention. When he turned and saw me, he waved, then headed over my way. I got out my license, which I always carry with me, so he wouldn't have to ask.

"How's it going today?" he called as he neared.

"Not bad," I said. "Got three largemouth, all over fourteen inches. Threw back two under fourteen."

"Yeah? You know you coulda kept up to two under fourteen. The only length restriction around here is out on the Pasquotank."

I nodded. "Just wanted to give those guys a chance to make it to fourteen. Almost wish I had someone else along. Over by those logs," pointing to the other side of the inlet, "two of us could've got our limit and still have two of the bloodworms left over."

As the warden pulled up next to me, Basil jumped over into his boat to say hello. Apparently, the fellow was cat friendly. He encouraged the boy and Basil was all over him. "Nice cat.' Then, "You using bloodworms? They're not cheap." Then he glanced at my license, got a surprised look on his face, and said, "You're Webb Sawyer."

"Last time I looked in the mirror."

"Well I'll be darned. I bet you don't recognize me, do you?"

I laughed. "No. But I'll bet I should."

The wildlife officer laughed back. "Probably not. It's been a long time since we saw each other, and I was much younger . . . I mean younger than you. I'm Wiley Parker's son, Eddie."

I thought for a moment. Then, "Oh, yeah. I remember you. Your dad did some business with my dad, and sometimes you'd be in the truck with him. How's your dad and mom doing?" Eddie told me fine. Then we had a conversation about our families and the community in general. Not once did he bring up my Army business, for which I was thankful.

"Want to see my catch?" I asked. He said sure and I showed him. We both agreed there was good eatin' ahead. Basil had jumped back into my boat and was licking his chops. "If you're getting off duty soon you can join me if you want," I offered, but he said he'd actually just come on an hour earlier and this was his first stop.

"By the way, that was something about Erskine Weeks wasn't it?" he said. I agreed that it was and told him about arriving just after it happened, to which he replied, "So that was your aunt's property where he crashed."

I started to answer when we both turned toward the sound of a vehicle approaching on the dirt lane that led down to the concrete slab they called a boat ramp. When it got closer, I saw it was a police cruiser.

So much for peace and quiet.

"Looks like everyone's after you," Eddie joked.

He didn't realize how true that was.

Basil was back on the prow, on point, glaring at the intruder. The cruiser pulled in next to Trusty Rusty and Aubrey Meads got out. He was wearing civvies. I waved and said to Eddie, "My friend Aubrey Meads." I didn't want to explain why he might be there, so I just said, "Told him he could join me if he had time."

"Well, there's your bloodworm partner," Eddie said.

We started up our boats; I headed across the inlet to the boat ramp and Eddie chugged past it, waved to Aubrey, said something to me about nice seeing me again, then headed back out toward the sound to continue his patrol.

"He bust you?" Aubrey said, smiling.

"You got your license, 'cause he said he was going to sneak back when you least expected him and check for yours."

Aubrey snorted. "And I need one, why?"

"Because we're gonna do some fishing and talking and, besides, I don't want to waste the rest of my bloodworms. Hop in. I'll get another rod."

"Bloodworms. Aren't they kinda expensive?"

It wasn't a well kept secret.

Aubrey told me that after he gone off duty and got home, KiKi gave him my note. He'd called Tabby's, but there was no answer and he'd left a message. "But I had to know what was going on, so I decided to ride over anyway," he said. When he pulled into her yard he'd noticed my truck wasn't there. Even so, he'd decided to knock on her door. "When I got out of the cruiser, from behind, I heard this high-pitched 'Yoo-hoo'!" chuckling. It was Tabby, who'd seen him drive by Sarah Aycock's. "Long story shorter," he said. "She told me where you were."

We talked while we fished. I told Aubrey about my conversation with Perry Adams. After a lot of back and forth and suppositions from both of us, I said, "I'm not sure I'm satisfied that all is kosher with Adams and this Bogdana woman, the one he calls Danna."

"So you're not of the idea that Erskine's death was . . . you know . . . ," letting it hang.

I shrugged. "Not sure. Let's look at this Bogdana first. Run a report. See where it leads us." Then I asked, "Any chance we can do that after we're done here?"

"Sure," Aubrey said. KiKi is home, so we can even print it on her bubble-jet. Save you a trip by the office."

"Speaking of which . . . ." While we shared Tabby's sandwiches and coffee, I told him about my adventure with Henderson, or more accurately, Henderson's adventure with me. I also told him about how I'd got on to the black Wrangler to begin with.

"At first, I didn't think all that much about it, but after this afternoon, I'm not so sure there's not some connection."

"With the shooting, you mean?"

"Yeah. But I can't figure out the who or why of it."

"We can put out a watch for the vehicle. If we see it, we can get a tag number and run a check. See who it belongs to. See if it rings any bells. Hell, Webb. If you want, we can use some pretense to pull her over and get more personal info from the get-go. Long black-haired, mid-twentyish female, you say?"

"That's what Margie said, and just the quick glimpse I got confirmed it."

"Got any pissed off ex-girlfriends you want to tell me about?" Aubrey kidding, but the cop in him was covering all the bases.

"Not really."

"Well, we'll see what we can do on that Wrangler," Aubrey said.

I held back on telling him about the call from Miss Betty. I wasn't sure how I was going to handle that problem.

We finished our fishing bonanza, using up all the bloodworms, including the two that were stolen from Aubrey's hook. "I'd arrest them for theft if I could," he'd said. I told him his best revenge would be to catch them next time and grill 'em for dinner. We each brought home five largemouth bass. One of Aubrey's was under fourteen inches, but he couldn't find it in him to release it. "We're a hungry family," he said.

Once we were out of the water and loaded up, we headed over to his place to get a handle on Bogdana Nicolescu. Another fifty-nine bucks less in my account. Based on an item in the file we did a Google search and found a news account of a reported misadventure. Bogdana Nicolescu was definitely an interesting and colorful character.

After going through Bogdana's file, which was more interesting than I'd anticipated, Aubrey and I discussed it without any definitive conclusions. I told him I'd think on it and see if I had any inspirations.

I was going to head back to Tabby's but Aubrey convinced me to hang around for some ice tea while we cleaned, gutted and fileted the our catches on his backyard cleaning table. Probably a good idea. Tabby had given away Uncle John's cleaning table and I didn't want to mess up her kitchen if I didn't have to.

When we started in on the bass, I was surprised that his daughter Brianna wanted to help. Aaron, his son, wasn't the least bit interested.

"She's gonna be every local boy's dream," I said.

Brianna blushed, but she had a knowing smile on her face.

"I don't even want to think about it," Aubrey replied.

Chapter 12

I WAITED UNTIL Aunt Tabby went to bed, then sat in the living room in Uncle John's easy chair then took another run through Bogdana Nicolescu's file from the National Search Website. It read:

Name: Bogdana Nicolescu
Born: September 30th, 1959 (*making her a couple of months shy of 58 – no spring chicken*)
Place of Birth: Prahova, Romania
Father: Unknown
Mother: Ileana Nicolescu
Immigration: 1970 from Romania to New York City (Bogdana, age 11)
Resided: 1970-2000 at 3321 4th Avenue, Brooklyn, NY in the Romanian community known as Ploesti
Resided: 2000-2008 in the New York Correctional Institution for Women, Bedford Heights, NY

Resided: 2008 at 518 Anderson Road, Apt 3B, Riverside, NY

Resided: 2009-2012 at 1412 Spring Hills Road, Riverside, NY

Resident: 2012-Present at 1126 Fairfield Road, Elizabeth City, NC

Criminal Record: Charge — Murder in the Third Degree (Plead down from Murder in the Second Degree); Plead Guilty; Sentence 7-10 years; Served 8 years, 3 months; Released on parole through May 2010

The newspaper account found in the *New York Post* dated Friday, May 19, 2000 gave a brief but interesting account of the murder, the charges and trial as follows:

PSYCHIC FORESEES JURY DECISION AND PLEADS TO A LESSER CHARGE

Yesterday afternoon, Bogdana Nicolescu, self-proclaimed psychic and palm reader, changed her not guilty plea mid-trial and plead guilty to a lesser charge of murder in the third degree, more commonly referred to as a crime of passion.

On February 28th of 2000, Miss Nicolescu was arrested for shooting to death her live-in boyfriend, Sorin Kohlrus, after she caught him in their apartment over her place of business PSYCHIC REALMS with another woman. Nicolescu claimed Kohlrus, who was found dead at the scene, had reached for his gun on the night stand, but she got there first mortally wounded him with one shot to the chest. She had claimed self defense; however, she was charged with second degree murder. The other woman, a neighbor from down the block named Madalina Zuharie, who later witnessed against Nicolescu, escaped from the room unharmed.

It was reported that yesterday, two hours into the trial, the defense called for a recess, which Judge Ames granted, and a backroom deal was struck with the prosecution for murder in the third degree with a seven to ten year sentence agreed to by both parties.

As an attorney in the hallway said, "It was as if Nicolescu used her psychic powers to determine the jury was going to find her guilty of second degree murder and she decided to cut her losses."

Nicolescu was taken away in handcuffs to begin her term at the New York Correctional Institution for Women at Bedford Heights.

Crime of Passion, I thought. Interesting. The only thing the file and the article didn't tell me was how she hooked up with Perry Adams which, according to her file was by 2009 when her address was the same one as I'd seen on the Adams' file. Adams had moved from the city to Long Island, settling in Riverhead in 2002 (because of 9/11?), first into one apartment, then another, before finally landing at a single family residence at 1412 Spring Hills Road.

I'd have to digest this information and see where, if anywhere, it led me. In the meantime, in the morning there was something else I had to take care of, especially if I was going to continue looking into Erskine's untimely death—which I definitely had decided to do. There were just too many unanswered questions.

The next morning, after a hearty breakfast of three eggs, easy over, three pieces of toast, one for each egg, link sausages, orange juice and two cups of snickerdoodle, I took a deep breath and headed out the door to go see Miss Betty. When I told Tabby where I was going, she said, "Maybe after the funeral we can both visit," then asked when it was and why it was taking so long.

To the first question I told her I'd find out when after I'd talked with Miss Betty. To the second question, I explained that they not only had to do an autopsy to determine if there was anything medically wrong, or there was something in his system that might have contributed to his losing control of the plane. There was also the extra work the funeral home had to do to prepare the body for burial.

"You mean like a prescription that made him black out?" she asked. Apparently, she'd already forgotten about the equipment failure being the official cause of the accident.

"Yeah, something like that," I said.

When I left, Basil was nowhere to be found.

This time I drove by the lane down to the Renner Trailer. There was no activity. I took a left on Triple Bridge, two miles down to a right on Estercliff and the Weeks' home. I saw Patty Nixon coming down the driveway. I waited on the road for her to pull out and leave, but she stopped short of the road exit and waved me in. I obliged. I pulled off the to right and she rolled her window down — mine was already down.

Wondering if her mother had said anything to her about our telephone conversation, I asked, "Your mother home?" even though I saw her car in the driveway; testing the waters.

"Yeah. She's still a mess, but I'm sure she'll be happy to see a friendly face," which meant Miss Betty was mum about her mini rant at me. When I thought about it, I could understand why. "I'm going up to the store with a grocery list," Patty said. "Just trying to help with little things, at least until the funeral is over."

"Is that set?" I asked.

"Oh, didn't Bobby call and tell Aunt Tabby?" I told her Aunt Tabby had asked me about it just before I'd left to come over, and Patty said, "Oh, sorry. It's Thursday. There will be a brief memorial at the funeral home at 2:00 pm, then over to the Evergreen Cemetery for the grave side service there." Tears pooled in Patty's eyes.

"I'm really sorry about all this, Patty," the extent of the meaning she had no idea. "My folks would have been devastated if they were still with us."

"I know, Webb. I know. Thanks for being such a good friend." Then she rolled up her window, waved and pulled out of the driveway onto Estercliff.

Whether I was being a good friend or not was still open for interpretation and consideration.

Miss Betty opened the door, apparently expecting Patty had forgotten something and returned. When she saw it was me, she just stood there with her mouth hanging open.

"Miss Betty, we really need to talk," I said, trying to sound emphatic and at the same time solicitous. A trick from my interviewing suspects days in the Army.

I expected an angry reply. Instead, she looked embarrassed and, without a word, opened the screen door and let me inside. She left the inside door open. In case she changed her mind and decided to throw me out?

"Just talked to Patty in the driveway. Heading up to the store." Of course, Miss Betty would know that; just trying to make conversation; get things going.

Still no reply. I followed her into the living room where she sat down in one of the easy chairs. I took the end of the couch nearest to her so our talk would seem more intimate. More Army days tricks, although I hated to feel that way with an old family friend.

Finally, she said, "I'm still mad at you, Webb."

"And I'm here to tell you why you shouldn't be." I'd already decided that, even if there was something unscrupulous going on about Erskine's death, I would consider her an innocent victim. Why. Because that's how I wanted to feel. What I wanted to believe. If she wasn't, I'd deal with it.

Maybe I was chasing a fly without a swatter, but I had this feeling . . . .

She just stared at me, waiting.

"There are people, and don't ask me who, because I'm not going to say, but people who are concerned that Erskine's death was more than just an accident, a mistake, a simple malfunction of equipment."

"My God, who would think that?" jumping up and standing there, looking down at me.

"Betty, just sit down and hear me out."

Surprisingly, she did.

"First of all, I want you to know I'm sorry about getting in the middle of your business about trying to reconnect with Caroline."

"Are you? Really?"

"Yes, Miss Betty, I am," I lied. Personally, I thought it was a crock of shit, nothing but a con game, but telling her that would get me nowhere. Before she could reply, I asked, "What do you know about Bogdana Nicolescu?"

She gasped, and tears began to pool in her eyes.

I suspected I wasn't going to get a reply, or at least not one that was productive, so I said, "Did you know she spent eight years of a ten year sentence for murder in a New York penitentiary?"

Miss Betty's mouth dropped open. Then, "But, but . . . how do you know this? And who asked you to find out?" sniffing, but trying again for information I wasn't ready to give her.

I wasn't clear from her reply, so I asked again, "Did you know that?"

"No," demure.

"These days, with computers, there are few secrets," I said, shrugging hoping that would satisfy her. "May I ask you a question?" hoping to get her mind going in another direction. Without waiting for a reply, I asked, "Was there anyone Erskine was having trouble with? Business associates, competitors, unhappy farmers."

Betty shook her head, meaning I at least got her thinking in the direction I wanted her to go. I felt like an ass, but better me doing it now than by someone who hardly knew her doing it later; that is, if there was a reason for someone else to question her. I wanted to blame Aubrey Meads for getting me into this mess, but it wasn't just him. Even her own son-in-law was concerned, and the reports on Bogdana Nicolescu were troubling. I needed to find out more about her.

Miss Betty interrupted my thoughts saying, "The only trouble Erskine ever had with anyone was that guy, Landon Livermore."

I frowned. "I don't believe I know him."

"That's because he's not from around here. He lives over in Chowan County, but he's not from there either. From Wake County, I think."

I waited, but when that was all she said, I asked, "What trouble did Erskine have with him?"

"Oh," waving a hand in the air, "he wanted to buy Erskine's business, including his plane. Erskine had considered it, but I talked him out of it. I mean what else would he do? He'd talked about doing some long-haul trucking, but I didn't want him doing that. He'd be away from home too much and I don't like being alone." Tears came. "Oh, what am I going to do, Webb?"

"You still have family and friends who love and care about you and will be here if you need them."

"But I'll still be alone at night," sniffing.

"Maybe Patty can stay with you for a bit." I wasn't sure what else to say.

Betty just looked at the floor. "You said he had trouble with this Livermore. What trouble?" pushing.

"Oh," again with the hand wave, "I guess Livermore thought he had Erskine convinced, and he wasn't too happy when Erskine backed away. Told Livermore he wanted to give it a few more years."

"Huh. I take it this Livermore is a crop duster."

"Oh, yes." Still tears, but trying to keep her composure. "He does Chowan, Bertie and Gates Counties. Guess he wants to be the crop duster kingpin of northeast North Carolina. Not satisfied with that and his farming. I guess he'll get his wish now." Then the tears began to flow and they didn't stop.

Holy crap!

What in hell have I gotten myself into?

Or was it all just a series of might-could-be suspicious events and facts. It was all very convoluted and confusing.

The only thing I knew for sure was, only a few days ago someone had taken two shots at me, and they weren't meant to miss.

Chapter 13

WHEN I PULLED back into Aunt Tabby's yard, Basil was sitting there on the front porch, waiting. On the short drive over I'd developed my next plan of attack. I had three options:

One, to spend my time following up on the girl in the jeep wrangler. However, besides the color and the make of the vehicle, and a youngish girl/woman with black hair and an accent of undetermined origin I had nothing. For now, I had to hope the sheriff's office might spot the vehicle and come up with something, even if only a license plate number. Or, if she was the one who sniped me, maybe she'd try again and I'd simply catch her in the act. Or she'd kill me and I wouldn't have to think about it.

That got me thinking again about the identity of the shooter. If it was the black-haired girl, who was she and why was she after me? I'd told Aubrey that, while there wasn't any angry ex-girlfriends in my life, I had made some other enemies. Since the shooting, the possibilities were constantly on my mind, itching at my deep consciousness. I just couldn't scratch them to the surface. I went over it one more time.

The serial killer from Hertford was dead, killed by a deputy sheriff and, as I said before, the nutcase who kidnapped my friend, Blythe Parsons, was locked up in the looney bin. The Colombian guy, Tito Carijona, who was involved in kidnappings over at Pelican Point, had been eaten by an alligator after he'd almost shot me.

Thinking of Carijona brought me back to the funny accent Margie had mentioned. She wasn't sure if it was Latino or not. Even though the incident with the Colombian was a few years back, somebody might have loved him enough to seek revenge. Carijona had worked at IPS on Bear Island, the quasi-military training camp providing personal protection both foreign and domestic. Maybe I'd call the CEO, Ben Rankin, and see what he thought. He'd once offered me a job there—which I'd declined. Even so, he might be helpful.

In the meantime, a second option was to concentrate on Bogdana Nicolescu. I had some general information to go on. However, the only one who really knew her around these parts was her live-in whatever he was, Perry Adams, and Miss Betty, whose relationship appeared to be nothing more than giving the self-proclaimed psychic money to support her con game. Seems as though without any help from the sheriff's office I'd have to go to Nicolescu's old haunts in New York to dig something up. Time and money I wasn't sure I wanted to spend. If all else failed, maybe I'd have to.

The third option was something I could accomplish more easily. I figured Bobby Nixon, who was well-connected in the county, could probably help me learn something about the Chowan County crop duster named Landon Livermore. Also, maybe Erskine had said something to his son-in-law about Livermore's interest in buying him out.

On the matter of Bogdana Nicolescu, even though Miss Betty didn't want me talking about her business with the con artist, under the circumstances I needed to talk to Bobby about it. If nothing else, maybe he could convince his mother-in-law to get some mental health counseling. Also, if he had the means, it might be a good idea for him to find out how much the Nicolescu woman drained out of Betty and Erskine's account for her "professional services." Most of the time, one bad deed led to another, and money was usually a catalyst for criminal acts.

Basil followed me inside, strutting, tail high, as if he owned the place and had just granted me access.

"That you, Webb?" from Aunt Tabby.

When I said it was, she asked if I was hungry. I told her I was, but needed to make a phone call first. When I asked if I could use the one in her bedroom, she sang out, "Oooh. Calling that lady friend of yours?"

I said, "Maybe." *Or maybe not.*

I caught Bobby on his way out of the office and asked if he could see me after lunch. That I'd drive down. He must have been in a hurry because he didn't ask me why. Said to come by the office at one-thirty if that would work. I said it would.

Lunch was a ham and tomato sandwich with plenty of mayo on fluffy white bread, which is what I called that brand I won't name, but rhymes with "Blunder." The ham was of the processed variety, not my standard fare, but guests shouldn't complain, so I didn't. At least the tomatoes were fresh from a local produce stand. One out of three ain't bad in baseball, but for food, not so much. Even so, it took three sandwiches to fill me up. I did tell Tabby that I'd be back for supper and she could have the evening off from kitchen duty as I planned on cooking one of the big mouth bass I'd caught, including the preparation of the sides of coleslaw and potato salad. I was surprised when she said that would be lovely.

When I left, Basil strutted out with me and followed me to the truck. I didn't have the heart to tell him no. It wouldn't have mattered anyway. I had left the windows down and he leaped up and through the passenger side onto the seat.

I drove up Tyler Swamp to Union Church, then headed to the Weeksville Junction Grocery. Two things: I needed gas and, if Margie was working, check with her about any further Wrangler sightings. The pumps on the driver's side were open. There was a small panel truck on the other side. Basil got up and looked out the window, then laid back down on the seat. The tank was near empty, so it took over nineteen of the full twenty gallons. I went inside to pick up some cat snacks and pay for the gas.

Margie was on duty. I gave her two twenties and asked her, "Seen any more of that Black Wrangler?"

She shook her head. "No. You?"

"Me neither." I didn't bother getting into my encounter on Tyler Swamp Road.

"This accent you said the girl had." Margie waited. "You said you weren't sure if it was Latino or not. Did the black-haired girl speak with, how should I put this, in an educated manner?"

Margie laughed. "You mean how some people just talk dumb or like they have marbles in their mouths and some speak English you can understand?" in her thick, Down East North Carolina twang.

I had to smile. "Yeah, something like that."

"Well . . . hey wait. I was watching the news last night and there was this guy, you know, the guy that runs Russia?" shrugging. "I think it was Russia. Patton, or something like that."

"Vladimir Putin?"

"Yeah, that's him. She sounded a little bit like him. Not her voice, but the way she pronounced things. Like maybe Roosha instead of Russia."

"So she might have been Russian?"

Margie shrugged. "Maybe."

Or Serbian, I thought. "Huh." *Maybe I had to start thinking further back.*

Margie handed me my change: $4.50, which included Basil's treats. I hadn't seen the price of gas this low in decades. Of course, in Europe they consider Americans spoiled, even when gas here was four bucks a gallon. Most of the continentals were paying double that.

"Is that helpful?" she asked.

"Yep. Sure is. Appreciate it, Margie." I wished her a good day and headed out the door.

I'd started between two parked cars, thinking about the black-haired girl in the Wrangler, when I caught a glint of something across the road.

Everything happened fast. My mind said, *Gun in second floor window!*

I hit the pavement.

I heard a crack, then the metallic thunk of the bullet hitting the car on my left.

"Son of a bitch!"

Then, the sound of a vehicle entering the parking lot caught my attention. All I could see was its wheels. Staying next to the car on my right, I crawled forward. It was another delivery truck. This one, beer. High enough for me to hide behind while I made it back to Trusty Rusty. This time, the shooter wasn't getting away. I got up in a crouching position and, when the cab of the truck passed in front of me, I jumped up and ran toward the trailer.

As soon as the end of the trailer passed me, keeping low, I ran behind it, crossed a ten foot open area and dove into the back of Trusty Rusty. I crawled up to the lock box and, on my knees, reached for the combination lock and worked the knob: three turns to the right to 17, two turns to the left to 31, one turn back to the right to 5. I pulled the lock open and dropped it on the truck bed.

I could see Basil looking at me through the back window and yelled at him to get down on the seat, as if he would know what I was saying. There was another crack, and a bullet twanged against the roof of the cab, just above and to the right of my head.

"Shit!"

I pushed up the lock box cover and, holding it up, reached inside and retrieved my new handgun.

It held a loaded clip. I didn't bother with the rifle. I didn't want to start a shootout right there next to the gas pumps. I wanted to get up close and personal. My next thought was, Shit! If the shooter starts aiming at the pumps, a well-placed shot could blow me Basil and the guy in the panel truck to smithereens.

The shooter was stationed at the second floor window of an old abandoned house across the road, just to the right of the grocery. The structure was overgrown with vines and other vegetation, some growing from the inside. The place wasn't fit for hogs. The window was on the side of the house facing the caution light, which didn't give the shooter the best angle toward the grocery and the pumps, but apparently good enough to get a bead on me. There was a second floor window above the front door, but the only thing I could figure was the floor had probably given away and there was no place for the shooter to set up. As far as I could remember, nobody had lived in the place for at least forty years, maybe longer. It was a miracle it was still standing.

I had a plan. In retrospect, it was a stupid plan. But I was bat-shit angry and had only one thought in mind.

End this now!

I dropped the top of the lock box, made sure the safety was on the Springfield XDS 45, jammed the weapon in my belt in back, rolled over the drivers side of the truck bed, duck-walked up to the door, opened it and, staying beneath the windshield, crawled into the seat and started the truck. I could see Basil cowering on the floorboard, up under the passenger side dash. Then, in the brief moment I took to move my head as close as I could to the post between the windshield and the door window so I could see where I was going, a bullet smashed through the windshield. Instinctively, I put my head down and closed my eyes.

"I'm going to get you, you son-of-a-bitch!" I growled. Then, peeking up just enough to see over the hood, I punched the accelerator and headed straight toward the house. I heard one more shot, but had already driven past the open line of fire.

It's a good thing no one was coming in either direction because either they would have hit me or I them. When I got across the road I jammed on the breaks, turned the steering wheel to the right, and slid sideways into a ten-foot wide strip of weeds. The house was built in the days when paved roads and in Weeksville were only a dream and the owner didn't give a shit about a front yard.

As soon as Trusty Rusty came to a complete stop, I pulled on the emergency break, turned off the ignition, opened the door and hit the ground running, pulling the .45 out of my belt as I went up onto the front porch.

The porch was inset on the left side of the house, leading about seven feet straight back to the front door. To the left of that was a window that had been boarded up. For some reason, the downstairs windows had all been boarded shut, but the second story side windows, which were in various stages of breakage, were not. Which was why the shooter was upstairs.

I stayed to the left of the front door, got low and put an ear against the wood. I could hear yelling from across the street, but I had to ignore it. Then, from inside, the sound of a crash and a shout

"*Govno!*"

Pronounced Guvnyo. It was Serbian for "Shit!"

A female voice!

The black-haired girl in the Jeep Wrangler. Had to be.

Weapon in hand, I stood back and took a run at the front door, slamming into it with my right shoulder. The door flew off of whatever was left of its hinges, and I went to floor with it.

Immediately, I did a three-sixty roll to my right and brought up the .45. There was no one in sight, but I could hear her crashing through the brush and trees out back. I jumped to my feet and ran to the non-existent back door, stopped, peeked around the edge to make sure she wasn't waiting there to take me out if I made myself a target.

She wasn't. I could see her running, or I should say sloshing, through the trees and underbrush. She had on black pants, a dark blue lightweight windbreaker with a hoodie and black tennis shoes. I knew where she was heading.

Behind the house and back yard, such as it was, the land was swampy from a small creek that ran off a waterway out to the Pasquotank River, three miles east. The swampy area was only about a hundred feet or so across, leading to a side road that cut the angle off between Weeksville Road and Peachtree. There was a two-story concrete building the telephone company used as a switching station. Next to it was a small, graveled, pull-in parking area. That had to be where she'd left the Wrangler.

I yelled at her to stop or I'd shoot. In retrospect, I wished I'd just shot, but I didn't have my official permit yet and I didn't want it to turn out that she became the victim and I was the one charged with attempted murder, or worse.

Justice, sometimes . . . .

Of course, she ignored me. As I neared the edge of the swamp I felt a sharp pain on the calf of my left leg, just above ankle. Nothing like bacteria-laden swamp detritus for a nice infection. I didn't have time to worry about that. I heard the door slam and the engine start. By the time I'd reached the road, she was about fifty yards away, burning rubber toward Peachtree, but not before I caught the Virginia license plate number. I emptied all five bullets in the clip into the back of the Jeep. There was nothing I could do but stand there, arms at my side, and watch her get away.

Be on the lookout for a slight-built girl with long black hair driving a black Jeep Wrangler with five holes in the back of it. I wondered if that was how I should tell it, weapons permit or not.

I put the .45 in my right rear pocket and jogged back to the grocery down the side street and the short hike up Weeksville Road. When I got to the abandoned house, there were a couple of young guys next to Trusty Rusty; another person, an older man, was coming off the front porch. They all turned and gawked at me.

I stopped and looked in the truck. There was no sign of Basil. "Anyone see a gray, tiger-striped cat?" When no one answered, I said, "About sixteen pounds, emerald eyes, perpetual smile on his face?"

"Was someone shooting at you?" the older man said. It was then I noticed a deer rifle in his hand.

Instead of answering, I asked, "Anyone got a cell phone to dial 911?"

"Already done it," one of the young guys said.

"I take it you're all right," the older man said.

"Well, she didn't get me, so I guess that makes me all right."

"She?"

I started to answer, when I found myself falling against the side of the truck.

"You sure you're okay, mister?" one of the young guys asked.

That was the last thing I remembered.

Chapter 14

I WOKE UP. It was dark. Odd smells. Someone snoring.

What the hell? Where the hell am I?

Did she double back and shoot me from behind?

The only place on my body that hurts is my lower left leg.

I drifted back off into netherland.

I heard voices and my eyes fluttered open.

Lights on. In a bed.

"Are you awake, Mr. Sawyer?" A female voice. "Dr. Robertson is here if you feel up to speaking with him."

"Robertson?" I mumbled. The inside of my mouth felt like it was full of the sands of Mogadishu. God awful place.

A man stepped into view. Blue, pin-striped buttoned-down shirt and khaki pants. "Good morning, Mr. Sawyer. I'm Dr. Robertson. Hear you lost the fight with a cottonmouth," smiling.

So that's what happened. Got me on the damn leg when I was running through the swamp. Me instead of the damned black-haired bitch. No justice. "Cottonmouth? That's exactly what the inside of my mouth feels like." I didn't think he'd get the Mogadishu reference.

"If he's making a joke, he must be feeling better," the woman said.

I peered at her name tag. I was still a little fuzzy, but it looked like Janice Echols, RN.

Robertson let her take the lead. "I'm Janice Echols, your nurse. This is Dr. Robertson. He administered to you yesterday afternoon when you were brought in."

In the meantime, Robertson had pulled up the blanket and had peeled up the gauze on my leg. I looked over to my left. The other bed was empty. Maybe I was dreaming when I heard someone snoring.

Robertson prodded around the bite wound area, nodded, and said, "You were lucky. He didn't get a clean strike. Only got one fang into you, not a full dose of venom, so I guess you were moving and not just standing there. Anyway, we cleaned it up and administered CroFab. Got the first vial into you within forty-five minutes after you were bit."

"Crowfab?"

"It's CroFab," spelling it for me. It's the commercial name for Crotalidae Polyvalent Immune Fab. A fancy name for pit viper anti venom. So far you've had six vials spaced over twelve hours, but that may be enough. Some good Samaritan didn't wait around for an ambulance. Brought you straight in."

"Who?" I asked, wondering if it was the older guy with the deer rifle.

"Don't know. They'll have his name in the ER At any rate, we'll just need to monitor you for the next several days to make sure there's no allergic reaction."

"Few days?"

Robertson laughed. "If your vitals look good by this afternoon, we can probably release you back into the wild." Then, "By the way, the man who brought you in said something about someone shooting at you and you chasing them through a swampy area."

"I think that's where he got me. The snake. I didn't realize it at the time," I mumbled. I wasn't interested in relating my would-be assassination attempt story. I was sure the police would be here soon enough about that. "Any chance I can get some food?" I asked.

Nurse Echols said, "I'll be sure something is sent in shortly."

After the doctor left, Nurse Echols leaned over and whispered to me, "All you personal effects are there in the night stand next to you," pointing. "All except one. They made us take the handgun and lock it up behind the nurse's desk."

I managed a smile and said, "Well, I guess I won't be able to shoot my way out of here, then."

I was struggling through dry toast, a bowl of oatmush and a glass of OJ with just a hint of orange in it when Sheriff Grimes and a man I didn't recognize came through the door.

I swallowed and asked, "Did you bring me something palatable to eat?" Grimes smiled. The other man didn't.

"How're you doing, Mr. Sawyer?" Grimes asked.

"I'm alive. Does that count?"

Grimes chuckled, I gave your Aunt a call. Let her know you'd been bit by a cottonmouth. She came up last evening but you were sedated. Said for you to call her when you could this morning. I didn't say anything about the shooting, just the snake bite."

"Thanks for that," I said. "She's had enough excitement this past week to last a lifetime. By the way, how'd I get here?"

"Eldon Edgerton. Know him?" I shook my head. "He was there when you came back to the truck and passed out."

The older man.

"Did a quick check and saw you had the bite on your leg. Didn't wait for my guys or an ambulance to show up. Just put you in his truck and brought you straight here."

"I'll look him up and thank him," I said. Then, "Oh . . . !"

"What?"

"Basil."

"Your cat?"

"Yeah. He was in the truck with me. Wasn't there when I got back to it."

"I'll check again with the people who were there," Grimes said.

"Appreciate that. If someone finds him, tell them to take him over to Tabby's. Although he's pretty resourceful. He may find his way over there himself." Then I asked, "What about the truck?"

"One of Eldon's son's drove it into the grocery parking lot, taped up the windshield with a plastic cover, locked it up, including the lock box in the truck bed and gave the keys to Mr. Beekins."

Mr. Beekins owned the grocery. "Guess I owe a lot of people thanks."

"You want me to call someone to get 'em to patch 'er up?"

"No. I'll deal with it," I said. "You have better things to do, like finding the shooter." Then, "Oh, I got the license plate for the shooter's vehicle. The black Jeep Wrangler."

"Yeah, we found it here in Elizabeth City. Left it over behind an abandoned warehouse by Knobb's Creek. Five bullet holes in the back of it. Shoulda aimed a little higher," smiling. "Anyway, the tread marks Henderson got matches the back tires, so it's the same vehicle. Virginia State Police have it as stolen in Alexandria, Virginia. Sent off prints to FBI to see if they have any matches."

"No sign of the girl?"

"Long gone. Makes me wonder if she's got an accomplice. You know, leaving the Jeep behind. Or maybe staying with someone in town. In the meantime, give Detective Jenkins here a statement on exactly what happened, including the background of events to date. Any description, thoughts on the shooter. When you being released?"

"One way or another, this afternoon. Got some largemouth bass I was supposed to cook last night that's still waiting to be eaten."

Grimes laughed. "Got any extra?" Before I could answer, he said, "Deputy Meads is off today. Said he was going to stop by."

"Good, because I need wheels out of here."

"Besides the humiliating wheelchair ride to the front door, you mean?"

"Oh, geeze. I forgot about that."

Grimes said, "Hang in there," and turned to leave, then turned back around and said, "Oh, here. Forgot to give you this, reaching in his back pocket and pulling out an partially crinkled envelope and handed it to me. "Your gun permits, including conceal and carry for the handgun. Which, by the way, I'll let the nurses station know to release to you when you leave. Be careful, Mr. Sawyer. Whoever she is, she's oh and two, but she may not miss the next time around. In the meantime, we'll do our best to find her, but we're getting the FBI in on it, too.

"Thanks, sheriff."

Grimes gave a half salute and left.

The whole time the sheriff and I were talking, the detective stood there with his arms folded across his chest, an annoyed look on his face. The minute Grimes was gone, Detective Jenkins pulled up the visitor's chair and sat down. The first thing he said to me was, "You know, it's a good thing you have friends around here, 'cause where I come from, you'd be getting an unlawful possession of a firearm charge thrown at you."

"Then I guess I'm glad I don't come from where you're from."

He gave me an unfriendly frown.

I spent the next hour and a half telling Jenkins everything that happened from the time I pulled into the gas station to when I woke up in the middle of the night and found myself in an unknown bed in a funny smelling place. Even though there was a report on file about the first shooting in Tabby's back yard, he wanted it all over again. I also told him about the events leading up to the encounter with the Wrangler on Tyler Swamp when Henderson was with me.

Jenkins also wanted to know if I had any idea who the black-haired suspect was and why she wanted to kill me. I spent another half hour telling him about what had happened in Bosnia and about Radovan Tadić, including the events that led up to my shooting him in the face while he sat in his jail cell.

"With all that in mind," I said, "I suggest you check with the FBI, or Homeland Security, or whoever is responsible these days to see if someone fitting the black-haired girl's description recently came into the country, presumably into D.C., since the Wrangler was stolen there. Maybe she's from Serbia, but maybe not. Name could be Tadić, but maybe not."

When I was done, he said, "And you're not breaking rocks at Leavenworth, why?" When I didn't answer, he said, "More friends in high places, I presume," in a disgusted tone.

I shrugged. I didn't like Jenkins and I didn't care if he knew it. "Does this mean I'll be put on the back burner while you deal with your other important cases, like the case of the ex-wife's stolen dining room table?"

"Don't be a fucking smartass, Sawyer. I'll do my job no matter—"

Jenkins was interrupted by a nurse, a different one from earlier, who came in to check my vitals. He got up and said, "I may need to talk to you again. Stick around."

"You mean here?" with a straight face.

He grimaced and left me to my fate with the nurse, who asked how the food was.

"How do you think?"

She laughed.

As soon as she was done, I picked up the phone and called Aunt Tabby. She answered, all out of breath. When I asked if she was doing all right, she gasped and went into a flutter of words so disjointed and discombobulated I could hardly understand what she was saying, although I did catch the words "hospital" and "Bobby." I presumed he'd called to find out why I hadn't shown up for our appointment.

Finally, I asked, "Has Basil shown up?"

"Basil? He's not with you?"

"They didn't have a free bed for him here," I joked. She didn't get it, so I mentioned that he'd apparently jumped out of the truck and had gone missing, and she went off on another long ramble about what we should do about it.

When she was done with that, I finally got out of her that she was just leaving to come up to the hospital to see me, at which I suggested that I was going to be released soon (one way or another, I was going to be out of there as soon as Aubrey showed up) and that Aubrey Meads was going to give me a ride back home.

"But there are a couple of things you can do for me," I said, then went on to ask her to go up to the grocery and ask them to keep a lookout for Basil, but first to call City Auto Glass and ask if they could come out and do an on-site install on Trusty Rusty's windshield.

"What happened to your windshield?" Tabby asked.

"Got broken," I said. I figured she was going to find out sooner than later about the shooting, but I'd let the Weeksville Gossip Vine take care of it for now. Later, I'd give her my version of what I thought she needed to know.

Next, I called Bobby Nixon. Fortunately, his office number was one of those easy-to-remember jobs with lots of threes and zeros. It turned out he wasn't in, but a female voice clicked me over to his voice mail and I left a brief message about what happened—the snake bite part—and said I'd reschedule with him as soon as possible. After I hung up, it hit me that today was Wednesday and Erskine's funeral was tomorrow and I'd see Bobby there. I wondered if the dog killer and the psychic would show up.

As it turned out, Aubrey didn't show up until just before 2:00 pm and I had to suffer through another meal from down under—I couldn't believe it was a ham sandwich on "Blunder" Bread. Will wonders never cease. With it was a small salad in a plastic bowl, wrapped in cellophane, and a cup of cherry Jello.

Just after Aubrey walked in and we'd exchanged some pleasantries, yet another nurse, different than the first two, came breezing in to take my vitals and change the dressing on the bite wound.

When she was done, I said, "If Dr. Robertson is around, tell him that I plan on checking out in the next half hour, so if he wants to give me the CroFab seal of approval he'd better shake a stethoscope."

The nurse just smiled and said, "You know you can't be released without his approval."

To which I answered, "Huh! I didn't realize this was the prison ward. Better find him chop-chop or I'll have to send my regards via postcard."

To which, Nurse Whateverhernamewas gave me a horrified look and rushed out of the room.

Aubrey stood there chuckling and shaking his head. "You know, Webb. You may be the most colorful person Weeksville has ever grown."

"Or maybe just a weed."

I had already dressed when Dr. Robertson came blowing into the room.

"Mr. Sawyer. I see you're anxious to get out of here. How are you doing this afternoon?" he asked.

"Feel fine," I replied. "Anything I need to be aware of. After effects from the bite or the medication?"

Robertson laughed. "You know, when Miss Hutchinson, she's the nurse, tracked me down all in a panic about you're going to check yourself out, it didn't surprise me. My colleague, Dr. Korkovsky, who practices down at the beach, told me about the time you were admitted to Dare County Regional after being knocked on the head and you pulled the same stunt on them. I told her, 'I guess I'd better get up there, because there was no doubt about it, he'll do it.'"

Then the doctor noticed Aubrey standing there. "Aren't you a Deputy Sheriff for Sheriff Grimes?" When Aubrey said he was, Robertson said, "Huh! This time, he's even got a police escort for his escape." Then, back to me, "Well," looking at the medical chart, "I guess we're both busy people. Let me check you out. Take a peek at the leg."

Once he was finished with that, he said, "Okay, Mr. Sawyer. Like I said, not much venom got into your bloodstream, so I think you're good to go," then spent some time advising of any possible side effects to look out for, such as hives or rash or any other allergic reaction, which if it was a problem I most likely would have experienced it by now.

Robertson gave me his business card. "Call my office for a follow-up appointment for Friday. In the meantime, if anything doesn't seem right call my emergency number or come straight here to the emergency room. I'll let the nurse's desk know you're checking out. Oh, and by the way, do me a favor and humor the volunteer. She'll be in shortly with the wheelchair. She's sweet and young and I know you don't want to make her cry," smiling.

I took a deep breath and sighed. "Alrighty then."

On the way out we stopped by the nurse's station and they gave me some papers to sign and a small cloth bag. Nobody said anything, but we all knew what was inside. Well, maybe not the volunteer. I also found out that I didn't have to bother with the accounting office. When they brought me into the emergency room, someone there knew who I was, got my insurance card out of my wallet and I was good to go.

I'd told Aubrey I'd give him a full update on the way back to Weeksville.

Chapter 15

I HATE WAKES and funerals.

After my parents died, I'd vowed that the next funeral I'd go to was my own. A stupid vow. There would be more I'd either feel obligated to attend or feel guilty if I didn't. Erskine's was somewhere in between those two self-indictments.

I drove Tabby's car, a late model Buick four-door sedan of the type a lot of the people over sixty who live out in the country, particularly women, drive. The men pretty much stuck to their pickups. I guess I wouldn't be any different.

When Aubrey had brought me back from the hospital, Trusty Rusty was still in the grocery store parking lot. City Glass hadn't been out yet, but when I'd retrieved the keys from Mr. Beekins he'd said Clyde Henderson had come around 9:30 that morning and dug a bullet out of the back of the driver's side of my seat.

"Between the bullets and the snake bite, you're lucky you're still here, Mr. Sawyer," Beekins had said. I'd agreed with him.

Beekins also told me that Henderson vacuumed up the broken glass best he could but said I should go over it again to be sure. Beekins wanted to talk about the shooting event but I'd told him I'd get together with him sometime and tell him all about it, which was unlikely. I'd then thanked him for holding the keys for me, then had gone outside and peeled enough of the windshield cover off so I could see where I was going. I'd driven home, with Aubrey following behind to be sure I got there in one piece. Before he left, I'd given Aubrey some information which, as a favor, he'd agreed to track down.

While I wasn't all that thrilled to go into town and stand around the funeral home to mingle, then follow the procession back to the Weeksville United Methodist Church, where Erskine was to be buried, Tabby wanted to go and she wanted me to drive. I didn't have a suit, but did have a pair of dress pants and a clean, plain blue, buttoned-down shirt, which would have to be good enough. However, when I'd first arrived at Tabby's, besides my tennis shoes, the only other footwear I'd brought was a pair of Frog Togs, neither of which Tabby thought was funeral appropriate. Not to be thwarted, Tabby brought out several pairs of Uncle John's dress shoes and I finally found a pair that I could squeeze my feet into and walk around with only a modest level of discomfort. Why she'd kept them I didn't ask. Even so, I brought along my tennis shoes for a quick change when the funeral service was over.

At the funeral home, Bobby saw me and came over. Tabby was off mingling. She'd heard the Weeksville Junction Grocery customers and staff accounting of the events, including everything from the shootout at OK Corral version to a story about the guy who lived next door who went after a fox who was trying to steal his chickens and, instead, ended up shooting out her nephew's truck window and put a bullet in the right rear fender of Kenny Shaw's 2003 Chevy Impala. Tabby liked the shooting-the-fox story. The shootout story was just too unbelievable.

"People make up the stupidest stuff," she'd said. Then got serious with, "You sure are unlucky, Webb. But I still don't understand how you got bit by a snake."

I'd told her I didn't either.

Bobby sidled up to me and whispered, "We still on for after the burial service?"

He'd called after I'd gotten back to Tabby's and was all over me about getting bit by a cottonmouth. "That's some bad doo-doo," he'd said, then went on to say, "When I called Tabby after you didn't show, she told me about it." He'd wanted to know the details. All I'd said was that it had been a snake-bit day and I'd tell him about it in person. We'd agreed to talk at Betty's house after the funeral. Do a little walk-around the yard. He still hadn't asked what I wanted to talk about, which was fine by me. Our conversation wasn't for cocked ears.

Next to the funeral itself, there is nothing worse than driving in a line of vehicles behind a cop and a hearse. I waited to be sure I was the last car in the conga line. Last in, first out.

Neither the dog killer nor the physic were in attendance. I didn't expect them to be. Too bad. I had worked out a scenario to sidle up to the woman who held conversations with the dead. Just in case.

When the funeral was over and people started wandering toward their vehicles, I hustled Tabby to the car and tastefully hightailed it out of the churchyard and bee-lined it for Miss Betty's. When I turned into the driveway, I did a Uey and parked in the grass next to the entrance so I wouldn't have to beg car movers when I decided to leave. I didn't waste any time changing into my tennis shoes.

We waited in the car until Bobby Nixon and several other mourners showed up. The two guys across the street were there again, this time power washing their house. I waved to them when we got out and walked the long driveway up to Betty's. Tabby had made a fish casserole with the leftover bass I'd finally got to cook. She was worried that no one would like it. I told her, if that happened, not to leave for home without it.

I lasted about twenty minutes inside before the sniffling and boo-hooing got the best of me. I wandered outside and sat on one of the patio chairs. Eventually, Bobby found me and we decided not to take any chances for interruption and walked up the field road out toward Erskine's hanger shed.

We were about a hundred yards up the lane before Bobby asked, "So what did you want to see me about? Any other ideas on . . . you know?"

"A couple of things, Bobby. First, let me say again how sad I am for Erskine's loss. Unexpected events like that are always a shock to friends and family, and I know you and he were close." Then I told him about my talk with Perry Adams, and about Miss Betty's dealings with the psychic, Bogdana Nicolescu."

Bobby's initial reaction was relief that his mother-in-law wasn't having an affair, but when I mentioned the fact that maybe the Nicolescu woman was taking Miss Betty for a financial ride, his anxiety returned.

"Jesus, Webb. When Patty said something about tension between her and Erskine, I thought . . . well, you know what I thought. But maybe it was money.

How much do you think this Bog-whatever-her-name-is scammed her for?"

"If she actually did, I don't have a clue, Bobby. Is there anyway you can find out?"

Bobby Nixon stopped walking and looked me and frowned. "I can try, Webb. But Miss Betty is the executrix of Erskine's estate. Maybe I can convince her to have Patty deal with the paperwork, and that way, Patty will give it to me because numbers and such aren't her forte."

"Worth a shot," I said.

The thought that popped into my mind was, if Erskine found out about what Betty was doing and wouldn't let her continue giving them money, Perry and Bogdana, realizing their cash would cease, made sure Erskine was out of the picture. Was there enough money involved for them to actually commit murder? How much is enough, I didn't know. Depended on the level of desperation or psychopathy. Maybe Bobby could find out how much, if any, money was drained out of their accounts to Nicolescu's benefit.

Once that matter was settled, I asked him what he could tell me about Landon Livermore.

"Landon Livermore? You mean the farmer and crop duster?"

"Yeah, him. Lives and has his business in Chowan County, right?"

"His main business is in Chowan, but he does business in Bertie, Gates and Perquimans, too. In fact, he's one of my best clients," frowning. "Why do you want to know about him?"

I told him what Miss Betty said about Livermore wanting to buy out Erskine's crop-dusting business. "She said he wasn't too happy about being turned down."

"Huh. Well, to tell you the truth, it was Erskine who came to me and asked if I'd approach Livermore about it."

That surprised me. "That so?"

"Sure. Erskine was toying with the idea of giving the aerial stuff up and doing some long-haul trucking for a while. Said it was the easiest way to see the country and make some money at the same time." Then he asked me, "What does Landon have to do with anything?"

I wasn't sure how to answer but, before I could come up with something plausible without alarming him, he asked, "You don't think . . . ?" Then, "No way. Betty must be confused. Like I said, it was Erskine who came to me to check it out. I talked to Landon about it and he said he'd think on it. He did consider it for a couple of months, then told me it was tempting, but right then he was spread pretty thin and didn't think he could handle it."

"Hmm," wondering why Miss Betty said it was Livermore who'd come to Erskine. Maybe that's what Erskine told her so she wouldn't know it was his idea.

"I wonder how she got the impression that Livermore was angry about it?" I asked.

Bobby shrugged. "Landon did tell me that his son, Ralphie . . . his name is Ralph, but they call him Ralphie, had pushed his father to make the deal and wasn't too happy about it when Landon decided to pass on it. But I don't see how Betty would know about that."

"Hmm. This Ralphie kid — "

"Well, he'd not a kid anymore," Bobby interrupted. "His like thirty-two. Landon's in his mid fifties."

"So, what's Ralphie's story?" probing in a new direction.

Bobby shrugged. "Had some trouble a ways back before the family moved to Chowan from Wake County. Don't know for sure why, but I heard Ralphie spent some time in jail for an assault of some kind. Landon's never said anything about it and I didn't want to ask. Anyway, I guess his son got his act together because he's part of the various businesses now."

Curious, I asked, "What are the various businesses?"

"Well, the crop dusting. They spray in Gates, Chowan and the western part of Perquimans. Erskine did the part east of the Perquimans River.

Then, they have extensive acreage in clary sage. That was Landon's father's business until he died. That's when Landon moved over here and took it over."

I knew about clary sage. It was a good crop because of the steady prices. The prices for the other crops of the region were all over the place. Clary sage is planted in August, grows about a foot tall, then goes dormant over the winter until it begins growing again. It's a sea of either pink or white until it's harvested in June. It produces something called sclareolide, which is then exported to Europe and used in fragrances, then the products are sold back to the U. S. for use in perfumes and colognes, laundry detergents, dish soaps and the like.

"A beautiful crop when it's in full bloom," I said.

"Yeah," Bobby said. "People driving through are always asking what it is. Anyway, Landon also owns an extraction facility over in Bertie County, where they process not only his crop, but the crops from the other farmers in Chowan, and also in Bertie and Martin Counties."

"So, it's just him and his reformed son who run the businesses?"

"Actually, he has two sons and a daughter. Joey, Ralphie and Corine. Corine and Ralphie do the crop dusting. Well most of the time. Landon flies when one of them can't. He and his wife Tammy deal with the sage crops, and Joey, the other son, runs the extraction plant in Millstown."

"Huh. I can see why he was reluctant to take on another crop dusting area without a third, full-time pilot."

"Yeah. I guess Ralphie tried to convince him that he and Corine could handle it, but his dad said no."

"Is this Ralphie a hothead?"

Bobby shrugged. "Don't know. Only met him once and he seemed okay, but who knows."

We'd started walking again, heading out toward the hangar when, from behind, we heard Patty's voice calling for Bobby.

"Guess we'd best head back," he said.

On the way, I asked him one more favor. "Can you get hold of Erskine's logs that show when the last time he went out before the accident?"

"I can," Bobby said, "but I don't have to. Three days earlier he'd flown over to Camden County to spray some fields over there. I know because I was here the night before and he'd told me. I remember because he'd said there was a lot more Coast Guard traffic these days and he'd have to check with the station for the schedules."

Bobby never did mention the snake bite event again, which was fine by me.

Before Tabby and I returned to her place, I went by the Weeksville Junction Grocery to see if anyone had seen Basil. No one had. I spent an hour or more driving around the area, stopping along the side of the road, getting out of the car and calling for him without success. Even Tabby did her part and yoo-hoo'd for him. It had been over thirty hours since he'd gone missing and I was now very concerned.

Aubrey had given me his number, and when we got back to Tabby's, I called and talked to his wife, KiKi, and asked her to have Aubrey call me when he got home. Not only did I want to have him alert the other two deputies who patrolled the area to be on the lookout for Basil, but I had two other new requests for him.

He was the one who'd got me into this business with Erskine and I was running out of resources, so he had to do his part.

Chapter 16

AUNT TABBY WAS humiliated that the fish casserole wasn't a big hit. In fact, only one serving had been taken. I didn't tell her it was I who scooped it. Most people left their offerings at Miss Betty's. Fortunately, Tabby followed my advice and absconded with hers.

"Well I've never . . . ," she complained.

I just laughed and said, "More for us, Aunt Tabby."

"I guess," she groaned, "but it's still an insult. And you know what else was an insult?" I pursed my lips and shook my head. "When I gave my sorrys to Miss Betty, she just gave a weak little smile and nodded her head, like it was an effort to acknowledge my presence."

I took a deep breath. "You know, Aunt Tabby, this has been an ordeal for her. I don't think she was all that responsive to anyone."

"Well, I guess," Tabby said. "But it was my yard Mr. Erskine crashed into."

I put a hand on Tabby's shoulder. "You and Miss Betty can probably talk about it in due course. After things have settled down a bit."

Tabby frowned, then asked, "Later, would you like some sweet corn and sliced tomatoes with this?" meaning the casserole.

I told her that would be fine.

While I brewed a pot of snickerdoodle, Tabby told me all about several conversations she'd overheard at Miss Betty's house. Tabby liked to keep up with what was going on in the community so she could pass it on as if she was the front line of the local happenings.

I was out on the front porch, having a manly mug of coffee and sorting things out when Tabby came to the door and said Aubrey Meads was on the phone. I got up and brought my coffee with me. I wished Tabby had a mobile device so I could talk privately without using the device in her bedroom.

When I got on the line, Aubrey asked if it was alright if he swung by to give me some information; that he couldn't stay long as he was still on duty. I told him sure. That I'd be out in the shed, figuring it was more conducive for privacy. Tabby is a little cock-eared about people's conversations.

I went out to the shed and retrieved a Handivac from my lock box, taking Henderson's advice, making sure there were no leftover shards of glass left in the crevices of the seats or floorboards. I told Trusty Rusty that I felt bad for his recent trauma and would make it up to him as soon as possible with a wash and maybe even a wax—I hoped I wasn't over-promising with the wax.

It wasn't long before Aubrey pulled his cruiser into the yard. He drove it all the way back to the shed, got out and came up to see what I was doing. When I turned off the vac, Aubrey said, "I thought City Auto Glass was coming out this afternoon."

"Supposed to," I said, pulling myself out of Trusty Rusty. "Whatcha got?"

"I made some notes." handing me three sheets of paper. "One is for Bogdana Nicolescu and Perry Adams. The other two are on Landon Livermore and his family members. Mainly vehicle and property info on Perry. Nothing in Nicolescu's name. Lots of stuff on the Livermore family but nothing out of the ordinary, except for the son Ralph's prior criminal record. Any questions, give me a call later. I'll be home after six, but give me an hour or so to settle in with the family for dinner."

"Thanks, Aubrey." Then, "If you hear anything about tracing that Wrangler, let me know. Detective Jenkins wasn't all that friendly, but I guess he'll do his job. Doubt he'll be quick to share anything with me, though."

Aubrey laughed. "Grimes will know. He'll probably keep you informed, but if I have any contact with him, I'll drop a casual query. Gotta run."

"Onward!"

I got myself a Grolsch from the fridge and went out to the front porch.

The page with Nicolescu's name on it was devoid of information: no driver's license, no car registered in her name, no property in her name, no library card, not a registered voter . . . nothing at all in North Carolina. Did she still really exist? Well Perry Adams and Miss Betty seemed to think so, so I suppose she did. I had to find a way to talk to her.

Below the Nicolescu non-information was Perry Adams' name. He owned the property on Fairfield Road, he had a driver's license and a vehicle (Aubrey gave me the license and tag numbers, including a description of the truck; a 2013 blue Dodge Ram pickup). Next to the property info, Aubrey made a note, saying that he could get me a print of an aerial view if I wanted it (was he encouraging me to sneak in there to see what was up?).

Adams was a registered Independent, had a library card, belonged to the local art guild (he was a found-objects metal sculptor) and since his set-tos with the local hunters and hunt clubs, had been active in lobbying local and state officials about restrictions on hunting dogs running loose and the homeowners right to shoot them to protect their property.

My question to this, of course, was if he didn't like the hunting practices, why in hell did he want to live around here? However, when I mulled it over, I figured that was the last thing on his mind when he bought the property and moved in. What I couldn't figure was, since he was obviously obsessed with privacy, why he'd become involved in an ongoing confrontation with the local hunters which not only brought undue attention to him, but had landed him in jail.

None of it made sense.

When I first encountered him on the speaker at the chain barrier in his driveway, Adams was clearly agitated and confrontational. I suppose that was understandable, since he didn't exactly enjoy a cordial relationship with others in the community. However, when I spoke with him at the Y, while I could tell he was annoyed, he didn't appear overly agitated. On the contrary, he'd taken the time to speak with me, which he did in a generally non-confrontational manner.

Perry Adams was definitely a conundrum.

I was still contemplating Bogdana Nicolescu.

I turned my attention to the information pages on the Livermores, which Aubrey had compiled both from official records and from his uncle on his mother's side. The uncle was a county ag official in Chowan County and knew the family quite well.

The Livermores were an interesting bunch.

I offer Aubrey's notes as a narrative, adding information that I know from being the son of a farming family. Why? Because it makes it easier for me to conjure up a picture of the Livermores and their story.

Landon Livermore, age 53, the father, graduated from State in 1984, came back to Chowan County to work for the family farm, located outside of Linden Crossroads. His father, Davis Livermore, had been the largest individual owner of farm acreage in Chowan County. He worked 1892 acres, growing soybeans in the summer, harvesting in late fall, then winter wheat from late fall to the harvest in late spring.

As Bobby Nixon had told me, when Davis Livermore passed, Landon and his wife took over the business. Soon, Landon's daughter, Corine, age 30, recently divorced, joined him on the farm. Like her father, she had a pilot's license and, soon, Landon bought an Ayres S3R-T34 crop duster for her to spray their own acreage. Soon, other farmers in the area who knew the family were contracting

Corine to spray their fields. It wasn't long before a man named Cordell Deets of Gates County, who had been spraying the farms in Chowan County, had lost so much business that he sold out to the Livermores, including all of his accounts in Gates County.

With another plane, a Thrush 550P from Deets, and no one to fly it but Landon, enter Ralphie, age 27, Landon's youngest son, recently out of the poky for busting his now ex wife, Samantha, in the chops. Ralphie also had a pilot's license and began flying the Thrush for their ever-expanding crop dusting business. It wasn't long before they had pushed into western Perquimans County, taking some accounts away from Erskine Weeks in the southern part of the county west of the Perquimans River; they'd already had Deets' accounts in the northern section of the county.

Joseph Maynard "Joey." Age 33, oldest child of Landon and Tammy LeAnne (nee Zindowski) was the only one not in the family business. That was when Landon decided to change over from soybeans and winter wheat to a crop with more stability in pricing and less competition for markets, clary sage. Once he'd done that, he purchased the only clary sage extraction facility in the area, which was located across the Chowan River at Milltown in Bertie County, then put Joey in charge of that operation. Joey, single, moved over from Wake to live on the family farm and commute to Milltown.

Landon and Tammy's youngest, Ralph Dalton "Ralphie" Livermore, dropped out of State in his Sophomore year, married Samantha Ann Powers on March 31, 2008, she pregnant with their daughter Melissa Elizabeth; divorced on November 13, 2010. On July 4, 2009, Ralphie was charged with domestic violence and spent 90 days in Jail. After the divorce, he lost custody to the child and moved east to work with his father as a crop duster.

The following is a list of vehicles owned by the Livermores:

2014 Dodge Ram, Silver, NC Lic AGT 4141 (Landon)

2012 Toyota Corolla, Silver, NC Lic DDW 1390 (Tammy)

2015 Ford F-350, Red, NC Lic XTC 9163 (Joey)

2010 Mini Cooper Convertible, Yellow, Lic DDW 5511 (Corine)

2015 Ford F-150, Black, NC Lic XMI 1883 (Ralphie)

I'd just finished going through Aubrey's notes when City Auto Glass pulled into the yard. I waved them back to the shed.

"Heard you got your window shot out," the short, beefy middle-aged guy with a flushed face said. He had a sidekick who looked like it could have been his son, but Beefy didn't introduce himself or the kid, so who knew.

"Something like that." Then, "Appreciate it if you would run a vacuum, too, jut in case the police didn't get it all." I didn't say I'd just done a run-through myself, figuring who knew where all the little shards ended up. "I'll be on the front porch when you're done." I double checked the lock on the lock box to be sure it was secure as I didn't know these guys from Tweedledee and Tweedledum.

I headed back to the porch to go over Aubrey's notes one more time and come up with my next plan of action. I felt as if I was back in a war zone with too many things going on at once and trying to triage the threats and problems.

I was still working on the Grolsch, sorting out information when the young guy from City Auto Glass came up with a paper for me to sign, saying they'd bill the insurance company.

"That was quick," I said.

"Got'er down to a science," the kid said.

Before I signed anything, I walked back to be sure Trusty Rusty was all back in one piece. Beefy was already in the City Auto Glass truck, radio on too loud with country music filling the air. T. R. was fine and I signed the paper.

The kid said thanks, jumped into their truck and off they went. I meant to ask if they had, in fact, vacuumed again, but what the hell. Either they had or they hadn't.

Back on the porch, Grolsch almost gone—I was a swigger, not a guzzler—I decided that there were two things I needed to do. One was to find a way to talk to the psychic. Sneaking up on the house in the morning when the dog killer was at the Y and hoping Bogdana would open the door (or hell, even answer it) was an option, but not a very good one. I quickly dismissed that idea, relegating it to Plan B, since I did have a Plan A.

Plan A, was to head back up to the YMCA in the morning and hope I could convince Perry Adams to let me talk with her. I'd work on an approach for that. If that didn't work, maybe I'd have to go back to plan B because I had no Plan C.

Even if Adams did allow me into his home to speak to the psychic, I figured I wouldn't get any hard information. The best I could hope for was to assess her demeanor; make an investigator's best guess as to whether she and/or Perry had any culpability regarding Erskine. I'd already decided they were probably guilty of flim-flamming Miss Betty.

Next, I needed to go over to the Livermore farm and get a feel for what they were up to, if anything, regarding Erskine. I hoped I could accomplish both those things tomorrow, because the weekend was coming up and Nan was coming home Saturday. I wanted to be done with all of this business about Erskine. At this point I just wanted to satisfy myself and Aubrey—maybe even Bobby—that in all likelihood, Erskine had the bad fortune to have suffered a fatal crash due to a mechanical malfunction.

Of course, the main problem I had was that someone unknown, for some unknown reason, was trying to kill me. But now that was in the hands of law enforcement, including the F.B.I. and, most likely, homeland security, all of whom at this point had more resources than I to track down the shooter.

I finished the Grolsch and got up to head back inside, when I noticed a pickup with a dog crate in the bed coming down the road from the direction of Union Church. When he slowed as it approached Tabby's, and the driver's side window came down, I was about to hit the deck when a finger presented itself. Then the driver sped off.

I watched it disappear behind the tree line.

It was Jeb Renner.

He'd washed the truck since I'd last seen it.

Chapter 17

THE FINGER FROM Jeb Renner I could handle, as long as that was all he was shooting.

As soon as I stepped back inside, the phone rang. Tabby hollered from the hall bathroom, asking me to get it. It was Dr. Robertson's office.

Once the female voice on the other end of the line knew she had me, she said, "You didn't call this morning for an appointment. Dr. Robertson needs to do a follow-up on your snake bite."

I laughed. "Tell him that the CroFab was so-fab, I'm good to go-fab."

There was a long pause on the line. Then, "We can squeeze you in at 1:30 today."

"How about this. I'll be there at 9:00 am tomorrow, but if I'm not out of there by 10:00 am I'll have to see you next month sometime . . . maybe."

Another long pause. Then, "Hold on a minute."
I held on for three minutes.
Then, "Dr. Robertson can see you at 9:30 am."

"I'll be there, but one way or another, I'm leaving at ten."

"Ah..."

"Look," I said. "I'm sorry to bust your chops, but I stopped jumping through hoops when I left the Army. See you at 9:30 tomorrow morning and not a second later."

By then, Tabby had wandered out into the kitchen, asking, "Who was that?"

I told her, then asked if there were any of Uncle John's rubber boots still around, figuring she'd kept most everything else so...."

"I think so, why?"

"Because I'm going to look for Basil and I don't want to get snake-bit again," I was also going to check out the abandoned house and the route the shooter took to escape, but I didn't tell her that.

"Oh!"

The boots were snug but, like the shoes, manageable. I turned right at the grocery, went past the abandoned house and then left on the cut off between Weeksville and Peachtree Roads to the cinder block telephone building. I pulled into the gravel parking area where the shooter had parked her Wrangler.

I got out of Trusty Rusty and walked back around onto Weeksville Road. My plan was to knock on the doors of dwellings as I worked my way around, back up to the grocery, then through the abandoned house, then out back through the swamp to the truck. There were a few homes on the cut-through and on a side street that wound its way behind, then across the narrow side creek back out to Weeksville Road. I'd go by those places, working my way around in a big circle. Basil was sociable and friendly. Surely, someone had seen him, maybe even fed him.

There were two homes on the same side of the road close to the grocery. I went to them first. The ones further down, between the cut-off road and the larger creek that led out to the river I'd get on the final loop around back to the truck.

The first house, no one answered the door. I wished I'd had some flyers or something to leave behind, but I didn't. My best hope was the Weeksville Grapevine was in full swing. The second house, the one next to the grocery, a sixtyish woman with a road map of wrinkles for a face and unruly gray hair, wearing a pink-flowered dress that looked as if it were two sizes too big, opened the door with a big toothless smile.

She looked me up and down and said, "Well, Mister, whatever yer sellin', I'm buyin'," then cackled like the hens she had running loose in the side yard between her place and the store.

I laughed, then gave her my spiel about my missing sixteen pound, male, tiger-striped cat with emerald eyes named Basil. She hadn't seen him, but wanted to invite me in to talk about it. When I told her maybe another time, that I needed to continue my search, she said, "Say, didn't you just drive by here in that old beat-up lookin' blue pickup?"

When I said that was me, she said, "Huh! Ain't you the one who caused all that ruckus the other day, guns a blazin' and all?"

When I told her I was involved, but was the shootee, not the shooter—I think my quip went by her—she said, "Some of them wetbacks that hangs around next door started a rumor it was me shootin' at some fox tryin' to git my chickens."

Her reference to "wetbacks" soured my joviality, and I said, "Well, ma'am, if you see my cat, he don't take kindly to people shooting at him. He's from Mexico, you know, and he just might shoot back."

She stood there with a stupid look on her face as I walked away across her front yard, heading for the grocery.

I thought I might as well check there again, even though I was sure they would have called me if they'd seen Basil. Wouldn't hurt to remind them to pass the word to their customers.

Margie wasn't there, but Mr. Beekins was working the register. Before I could say anything, he asked if I'd found my cat yet, which let me know nobody there had seen him. I asked if he'd been sure to tell his customers to be on the lookout. He said he would. He started to ask me about the events of yesterday when two other people got in line behind me and I said, "Catch up with you later on that, sir."

I walked across the street to the abandoned house. Someone had picked up the front door from where I'd shouldered it in to the floor and had leaned it against the opening. It was a futile effort. The first good northeasterly wind would blow it back down. Except for the fact that it would hasten the demise of the structure, it really didn't matter.

I walked back and forth from one side of the house to the other, calling for Basil. I'd call, wait and listen. Call, wait and listen.

Nothing.

I edged the door aside and went inside. I stood there for a moment, taking in what was before me. When I'd broken in after the shooter, I hadn't time to see just how bad it was inside what was probably once a nice comfortable home at the crossroads of local activity.

To my right a small jungle of vines and brambles grew through a broken floor. A gum tree, or was it two that had grown together, reached for the roof past the non-existent second floor. I turned and looked up. No floor directly above me either, which was why the shooter didn't use the window above the front door.

I repeated my routine, calling, waiting and listening for any sign of Basil, but there was none.

At the back of the house a staircase, still intact, just barely, let up to a section of floor about six or seven feet wide, tenaciously hanging on for dear life. I went over and eased my way up the stairs. The rotted wood, broken through in places, creaked and groaned all the way up. I wondered if the any of the cops made their way up there. Or did they just send Henderson up, figuring better him than them if everything gave way?

Apparently, that's what happened, because I found chalk circles where spent casings were marked, photographed and taken away in evidence bags. I eased my way around the window area, hoping to find something Henderson might have overlooked, but there was nothing.

I eased my way back down the stairs. Apparently, the shooter fell during her hasty retreat from upstairs, and I spent the next ten minutes checking the stairs and the area beneath them.

Nothing.

I went through the open back door, or, at least where the door used to be. I saw no sign of it.

What could be billed as the back yard was partially cleared. Aunt Tabby had mentioned that a few years ago someone made an attempt to use the space behind the house to set up a saw mill. Apparently, that's when a partial clearing took place. The log cutting operation didn't last very long and now the vegetation was slowly reclaiming the empty space.

Once again, my calls for Basil went unanswered.

I did what the police call walking the grid, back and forth between the back of the house and where the swamp began, covering an area about ten feet wide.

Nothing.

I looked around and found myself a sturdy-looking stick, about five feet long, then went over to the edge of the swamp. I stood there for several minutes, visualizing the path the shooter took. I thought about going back around to the truck and getting the rifle, but I was here and I had on Uncle John's boots, so . . . .

I called again for Basil, listened, heard nothing, then stepped into the swamp, my eyes scanning the mucky water, tree branches and shrubbery around me. To my right, a snapping turtle, sunning itself, slid off a log and into the water.

I moved slowly, stopping periodically to study my surroundings. I was about two-thirds of the way across when I sloshed through a narrow passage between two trees. I had no recollection of the girl or me going through there,

It was then that two things caught my eye; something to my right, dangling from a branch; something on my left, in the water, coming toward me. I turned my attention to the water. A goddamned snake. I couldn't tell if it was a mocassin or a simple water snake. Either way, it was coming into my space.

I placed the stick into the water and used it to guide the snake out of my path. Fortunately for me, it complied and swam past. I watched it until it disappeared into the brush, then turned my attention to the item in the tree.

I guess Henderson hadn't bothered to track the shooter through the swamp, because what I held in my hand was a medal attached to a royal blue ribbed cloth necklace.

This was the gold version of the medal, awarded to officers by the Serbian Army after the Second Balkan War of 1913. One side of the medal had the Serbian national, heraldic eagle. The other side, the Serbian Cyrillic text that read ЗА РЕВНОСНУ СЛУЖбУ, pronounced *Za Revnosnu Sluzbu*. In English, that reads "For Zealous Service."

I recognized it right away; knew where I'd seen it before.

It had been around the neck of Radovan Tadić when I shot him. Based on his age and when the time frame the medal had been awarded, I presumed it was his grandfather's, or maybe a great uncle; maybe he'd just stolen it.

More than likely, it was from someone in his family, which made me think the shooter was either his daughter or his niece; someone in the family who was out to avenge his death.

I still have nightmares about Bosnia and about the part that Radovan Tadić played. There are some events in your life that never seem to go away. I stuck the medal in my right front pocket.

I knew what I had to do; as soon as I returned to Tabby's.

I continued making my way through the swamp. I figured nothing short of a body would have forced Henderson in here. After what had happened to me, I couldn't blame him.

Once I was back on dry land, I spent a short amount of time scanning the parking area next to the telephone switching station. Even though I figured Henderson and the deputies went over the area, sometimes things were missed.

I found nothing else.

I should have brought my sneakers to change into, was my thought as I trudged up the road and began knocking on doors. On the cut-through road, only one of the four houses answered the door. It was a middle-aged man in sandals, shorts and a black t-shirt that announced in yellow, "I'm not lazy, I'm physically conservative."

When I gave him my spiel about Basil, the man said, "Don't like cats. Never have, never will."

I thought about a smart comeback, but wasn't in the mood for it. By the time I'd turned to go, he'd shut the door.

I worked my way back around to the wide creek end of Weeksville Road and started back up, crisscrossing back and forth to catch the houses on both sides of the street. I caught someone home at about four of the eight houses, but no one had seen Basil. One woman who had cats said she fed them outside and maybe he'd come by and helped himself to the food; that she'd make a special effort to keep an eye out for him.

While I was happy to find the lead on my would-be assassin, I was sad that I couldn't come up with any leads on Basil. I guessed that the shooting and the bullets creasing the roof of the cab and crashing through the windshield freaked him out, although once before, when the Colombian and his team of three others came to my home in Blue Heron Marsh to kill me, he'd been through an incident with gunfire. Where would that rascal have gone? I felt as if I'd lost my best friend.

By the time I was back at Tabby's, I was ready for something stronger than Grolsch. I always kept a bottle of Jack Daniels Black Label enclosed in bubble wrap in the truck's lock box—for emergencies.

I declared an emergency.

Once was inside, Tabby first asked about Basil — she was as disappointed as I was — then asked if I was ready for supper. I was hungry, but my adrenalin was pumping and I needed something to settle me down. I poured myself a blackjack on ice and hit it with a few splashes of water. I'd already taken a healthy swallow when I thought, *I hope if there's any Crofab still in my body they don't start an argument.*

I dug my miniature, low tech address book out of my wallet and looked up the last number I had for General Brad Tillman, asked Tabby if I could use the phone in her room, and set out on my mission to get some answers.

Chapter 18

IT TOOK ME almost an hour to track down a number where I could leave a message for General Brad Tillman. I was surprised he was still on active duty, expecting that he might have retired by now and I'd have to find a computer and look him up on line. The last time I heard from him was a card he'd sent me after I was released from the U. S. Army psychiatric facility at Fort Bragg. He'd wished me good luck in civilian life; said to call him if I ever needed anything.

Well, I needed something now.

I'd already decided that I was not going to give the Serbian medal to Detective Jenkins, the FBI, Homeland Security or anyone else. That baby was going to be framed and hung in a place of honor in my house. Which also meant, if I was able to come up with the name of the shooter, I would also have to come up with a plausible story to give Jenkins about how I got the information.

***

"I just don't understand why no one at Betty Weeks' liked this casserole, Webb. It's simply delicious. Don't you think?" Tabby's voice rising in pitch.

I told her it was absolutely delicious. She smiled, got up and came around the kitchen table and kissed me on the forehead.

About halfway into the meal she asked me about Preston. Preston Everret Sawyer is my son. He's now twenty-two and living in New Zealand. He is my only offspring with my ex wife, Claire.

Not to be unkind, but Claire was a trailer park girl in Fayetteville who I met at a bar and fell in lust. Since then, I have a rule: don't date women you meet in bars. It's a hundred to one it will actually work out. That's not based on a scientific study. It's just my personal assessment. At any rate, she cheated on me while I was stationed in Europe (various assignments on my part, various men on hers) and we divorced. Long story short, since she was in the States and I was in Europe, she was awarded custody of Preston. She soon moved to California, where she hooked up with a doctor of the medical variety. I hadn't seen Preston since, until . . .

. . . one day he showed up on my dock, saying he didn't like California and wanted to live with me. He also wanted to go to college and study music. I helped him get admitted to Elizabeth City State University.

It wasn't long before he became embroiled in a murder case that turned into a kidnapping and, if I hadn't tracked him down, probably his demise. Apparently, none of that mattered. He told me he wanted to move to a place that was civilized and not prone to acts of violence, his words, and, for whatever reason, convinced himself that New Zealand was that place. Maybe it is. I've never been there.

"He recently graduated from the New Zealand School of Music in Wellington," I told Tabby. "I don't hear from him very often."

"That's a shame, Webb. A shame."

Aunt Tabby and Uncle John never had children and she had a simplistic view of parent/child relationships. Honestly, I can't claim to be an expert on that, either.

"He's doing fine, Tabby, and more importantly, he's doing something he loves."

"I guess," was her reply.

We had just finished supper and were clearing the table when the doorbell rang. I told Tabby that I'd finish up if she answered the door. "But look through the peephole and see who it is, first," I cautioned.

It was Sarah Aycock.

"Oooh, Sarah, I didn't have a chance to talk to you after the funeral," I heard Tabby say. Tabby invited Sarah inside, saying, "We just finished supper. Would you like some coffee and pie? I made a nice peach pie."

"Oh, my, yes," I heard Sarah say. "That would be lovely."

Aunt Tabby had Sarah take a seat in the living room, then came into the kitchen. "Oh, Webb, I'm sorry to abandon you when we're cleaning up, but I have a guest . . ." as if I wasn't aware, ". . . so don't you worry about all this mess. I'll take care of it later."

I told her she should just get coffee and pie for herself and Miss Sarah and I would take care of cleaning up the kitchen and putting the dishes into the dishwasher—at home I did everything by hand, so a dishwasher was a luxury for me. Even so, I'm glad I didn't have one. Just one more thing to dump gray water in the marsh, if it didn't break first.

More stuff, more repair bills.

As soon as they were settled with their coffee and pie, their conversation turned to the funeral and the after-service event at Miss Betty's. With my mind on what I was going to say to General Tillman, my attention was not on Tabby and Sarah's *tete-a-tete*. The trouble was, their so called private conversation wasn't private at all, as both of them spoke in loud, animated tones.

Even so, I did my best to block it out. I had my own problems to solve, playing out different what-ifs and what-nexts while I rinsed and put down the dishes and cookware. At home, I tended to clean up as I prepared and cooked, and I would never have this much to deal with, even if Nan was over for a meal . . . or two. I think men are better in the kitchen than women.

When I was finished, I made myself a cup of snickerdoodle and went out back. I stood on the back porch. Tabby called it a porch, but it was really a small deck with no railings. The only thing on it was a round, wood-top table with two metal chairs that had been spray painted a light gray-green. I sat down in the one facing across the soy bean field toward the tree line.

I studied the trees for a few moments, looking for movement or the glint of light off a scope. I wondered where the Serbian girl was now. What next move she was planning.

And I knew she was still out there.

Coming after me

For vengeance.

Two cups of coffee later, and the sun going down, Aunt Tabby came out onto the back deck and sat down across from me.

"Whew! That woman wears me out with her talking."

I smiled.

Tabby leaned over and said in a low voice, as if someone might be standing around the corner at the side of the house, listening, "You know what Sarah Aycock told me?"

"I can't begin to guess," I said.

"Well, she said she heard Linda Slayton tell Martha Temple that Jolene Evenston said that Erskine and Richard Trueblood had a falling out. You know Richard Trueblood, don't you?"

I said I did.

"He died of a heart condition last year, you know."

"I'd heard." In fact, Tabby had told me on a previous visit.

"Well, anyway, Jolene said . . . I mean Linda said Jolene said that Richard was unhappy with Erskine about something he did and wouldn't speak to him any longer. And they'd been friends since grade school days. I don't know why I've never heard about this before," Tabby added.

That sorta of peaked my interest. "Dad always liked Richard, even though a lot of people in the community didn't. I think he and Erskine were Richard's only true friends."

"Right. That Richard could be a pip," pulling a face.

I chuckled. "He just didn't take any guff or funny dealing off of anyone, that's all. I always liked him."

"Well anyway, that wasn't a very nice thing to talk about right after Erskine was put in the ground. And with Miss Harriet in the same room."

Miss Harriet was Richard's widow. She was a kind lady, always willing to give a helping hand to anyone who needed it, sometimes much to the chagrin of Richard, who looked with jaundiced eye on anyone who didn't pull their own weight.

"No hint of the problem?" I asked.

"Oh, no," Tabby said. "But you know Linda and Jolene. They're the two biggest gossips in Weeksville. I think they make stuff up just to have something to talk about."

I had to laugh about that. But only inside.

"Besides, Erskine was a very nice man and wouldn't do anything unkind to anyone," Tabby huffed.

I agreed. On the other hand, if he had, and someone was angry enough about it, they might have . . . .

I'd hoped for a call back from Tillman and stayed up until midnight, reading some of Uncle J's old fishing magazines that Tabby still had lying around. Finally, I gave it up about fifteen minutes into the next day and went to bed.

I was lying there on top of the covers in my shorts and t-shirt (I usually slept naked at home but didn't think it was a good idea here), unable to sleep, when I heard the phone ring. I swung my feet off the bed and grabbed for my pants. The clock on the night stand said it was 1:37 am.

By the time I'd reached my bedroom door, there had been three rings. When I opened the door I could hear Tabby's sleep voice saying, "Yes, but it's the middle of the night and—"

I hadn't wanted to invite questions and hadn't said anything to Tabby about expecting a call, certainly not from who. I knocked on her door. "Aunt Tabby, that may be for me."

I heard her say, "Hold on," and shortly her door opened.

"I'm sorry, Aunt Tabby. I didn't expect this call until tomorrow," even though it was already tomorrow.

"Oh, it's okay," she said, rubbing her eyes. "I hope I can get back to sleep."

"Maybe read for a while," I suggested. "I'll take the call in the kitchen," then headed down the hall.

When I picked up I said, "Is that you, General?" He said it was. Then, "You can hang up now, Tabby." After a couple of silent beats I heard a soft click. "That's my Aunt Tabby," I said. "She had some trouble and I'm staying at her place in Weeksville for a few days."

Accepting that without questions, he said, "Been a long time, Sarge."

I had worked for General Tillman at NATO Headquarters in Brussels when he was still a colonel. When he was promoted and transferred to another command, I ended up in Sarajevo, the capital of Bosnia, on a mission to hunt down a man named Radovan Tadić, the leader of a Serbian death squad. They should have called them destroying squads, because they not only killed people, but they raped, tortured and maimed not only individuals and families, but whole communities. The press preferred catch phrases like genocide and ethnic cleansing.

When we finally caught him and put him in a military holding cell for ultimate transportation to The Hague to be tried for war crimes, I took justice into my own hands.

During my investigations I had interviewed a family by the name of Musa, and had fallen in love with a twenty-year old girl named Daliya. I had just returned from a trip to Mostar when I learned what had happened. Apparently, someone had reported my visits to the family and Tadić and his thugs showed up at the Musa home, gang raped Daliya in front of her father and brother, then made her watch as they executed them. That night, she'd committed suicide by stabbing herself in the heart.

I'd talked my way past the guards, saying I was there to interrogate Tadić. When I saw him there in his cell, smoking a cigarette and laughing with one of the guards, I lost it. I had checked my M16 at the front desk, but I'd always carried a non-military 350 Magnum under my pant leg in a holster strapped to my calf.

Here's the thing. Once, when I was in The Hague on military business with Colonel Tillman, he'd said to me, "The leaders of these Serbian death squads should be caught and shot. Bringing them here to The Hague is nothing but a spectacle and a show. They'll just convict them and send them to prison for thirty years because here in Europe they don't believe in the death penalty. If it was up to me, I'd forget the trial bullshit. I'd just line them up and shoot the bastards."

I followed his line of thinking.

I pulled out the .350, aimed it through the bars at that son-of-a-bitch, saying, "This is for Daliya Musa and her family," and emptied the clip into him. When I was done, there wasn't much remaining of his face.

There was a long wait and a short trial. When the courts martial came, the deal had been struck. Colonel, then General Tillman interceded, called in some chips with his higher-ups, and saved my ass from spending the rest of my life at hard labor at Fort Leavenworth, Kansas. Instead, I spent a year in the psych ward at Fort Bragg here in North Carolina.

I owed Brad Tillman big time. Now here I was asking for a favor.

I didn't bother him about my problems with Jeb Renner or the death of Erskine weeks. Neither one had anything to do with the sniper. I gave the general the whole story about the shooter.

When I was done, he said, "Jesus, Webb. Some things just won't go away," which was exactly what I had thought. Then, "This medal. I can make some calls and check on his personal effects. Who they were released to . . . if they were released. I'm sure there's a list."

"I'd appreciate that, sir. And not to be pushy or unappreciative, but time is of the essence here. She's on the loose and I'm sure once she thinks things have settled down here, she'll come after me again."

"Do you think she knows that you live in Nags Head?" he asked. Apparently, he'd either kept up or quickly found out about my life after the Army.

"Don't know. But I can't take the chance of going back there and her coming here and taking it out on my aunt. You know, an-eye-for-an-eye thing."

"Yeah, I do know, Sarge. These people are a little nuts the way they think."

While I wasn't ready to condemn all of the Serbians for some of their citizens' criminal actions, I knew what he meant. "Thanks, sir. Anything you can do will be helpful."

"So you want me to tell you and not anyone else?" he asked.

I knew what he was asking. "Just me, sir. It's my problem and I'll handle it."

"I understand," he said. "But tread carefully, Sarge. Be sure you can call it self-defense and get away with it, because I won't be able to help you this time around."

"For once, the authorities here are behind me on this one," I said.

Tillman chuckled. "Back at you as soon as possible." And then he hung up.

I pulled the Serbian Zealous Service medal out of my pocket and looked at it.

Zealous!

Now there's a appropriate term if I ever heard one.

Chapter 19

IT WAS ANOTHER night of sleeping in fits and starts. There were so many things going on in my mind, as soon as I shut one thought down and relegated it to some storage box in my cerebral cortex, something else took its place.

A nightmare about Basil in the swamp, being attacked by snakes, woke me up. The clock on the night stand said 7:02 am. I dragged myself out of bed and took a long hot shower.

I had a plan.

A hearty breakfast, compliments of Aunt Tabby, and two mugs of coffee later, at forty-two minutes after seven I hit the road.

I headed down Tyler Swamp to Triple Bridge. When I went past Jeb Renner's, I slowed down and glanced down the driveway, but there was nothing to see but the north end of their mobile home. I turned right on Triple Bridge and took it to the end where it T'd at Little River Road. To head back toward town I'd turn right. Instead I turned left, heading toward Harriet Trueblood's. It had been well over a decade since I'd last seen her.

I hoped she was home.

She was.

After I knocked, I could hear her coming before she opened the door. Harriet stood there, using a walker to brace and keep her steady. The last time I saw her she was in her late fifties. Now she looked as if she'd aged thirty years instead of only a dozen.

Miss Harriet threw a hand to her mouth, then said, "Oh, my word! Webb Sawyer. Is that really you?" She still had a voice with a fiftyish lilt to it.

She was the second person who'd asked me that. This time I resisted a smart-ass remark. Instead, I gave her the biggest smile I could muster. "Yes, ma'am, Miss Harriet. It is. And I hope I'm not bothering you too early, but I have a lot of appointments ahead of me today and this might be the only chance I have to see you."

Harriet smiled back and said, "I just made me up a pot of coffee and it's always better to share it with someone."

For once, I decided this was no time to let my coffee prejudice rear it's bitter head. I'd drink it, no matter what it tasted like. Well, maybe some of it. "That'd be fine Miss Harriet."

"Why don't you just call me Harry, Webb. That's what Richard used to call me. In private, of course. I used to call him Dicky Boy," she giggled. Then, shaking a finger at me, "But don't you go tellin' anyone else this, you hear? It's just between us chickens." She giggled again.

Contrary to Richard, Harriet Trueblood always had a more effervescent nature. They were like yin and yang. Even so, it worked for them for over sixty years. So who was I to question it? I hoped she was still giggling when I asked about Richard and Erskine.

"Got some blueberry muffins I made up from scratch yesterday," she said. "Made a batch of 'em thinking my daughter Pauline was a comin' over, but she got called into work and couldn't make it. So's I got me plenty to share." She pronounced her words more like a mountain woman than a low-country lady.

I figured I could drink almost anything if I had homemade blueberry muffins to go with it. "I'd love that, Miss Harriet—"

She wagged another finger. "Harry. We agreed."

"I think you should save that for your memories," I said, chuckling. She just laughed in her girlish way.

They'd lived in their house for at least thirty years. Richard had built it for them after they'd lived in the family farmhouse for the first twenty years of their marriage. Once Richard's parents had died, he'd no longer felt an obligation to live there. At least that's what my dad had told me.

This house, while more modern, had been built without air conditioning. Within two months after Richard's death, Miss Harriet had installed central air. While I always liked Richard, he was tight with a buck and very old-fashioned in his thinking. Sometimes that was a good thing. Other times, not so much.

She wanted me to sit in Richard's old easy chair — and I do mean "old" easy chair. A year after his passing, the odor of his inexpensive stogies still permeated the fabric.

"Why don't you let me help you, Miss Harriet," looking at the walker.

Harriet laughed. "Okay, Webb. I'll leave you off the hook. You can still call me Miss Harriet." Then, "No, you sit yourself right down there," pointing at Richard's chair.

"You see this here space-age walker? Got wheels and a tray in front for me to carry things around. What more could an old lady ask for?"

She nodded toward Richard's chair, then turned and propelled her walker-on-wheels toward the kitchen.

I was happy that Miss Harriet had already turned on the air conditioning. Even with it running, the smell of Richard's Nicaraguan Maduros, his favorites, if I remembered correctly, lingered. I always hated the smell of cigars. My dad had been a pipe man. His tobacco was Prince Albert. I can still picture the red, 14-ounce can with yellow lettering and a picture of Prince Albert inside a white oval. I never took up smoking. If you've ever seen a picture of a person's lungs after they'd been smoking for ten years, you'd know why.

I was considering my approach when she interrupted my thoughts with "Well, here we are. Coffee and muffins. Dicky Bo—ah," shaking her head. "Richard," a faint smile crossing her face, "always loved his blueberry muffins."

I took one of the two cups of coffee she'd poured, along with a muffin.

"There's cream and sugar," she said.

I thanked her and said I took mine black. "Muffin is delicious," I said. "I can see why they were Richard's favorite."

Harriet smiled as she gingerly lowered herself into her own easy chair. "That was terrible what happened to Erskine," she said. "And right in your Aunt Tabby's yard, too." Using two hands, she took the other cup of coffee off the tray. I thought her hands might be shaky, but they weren't. "That woulda plum scairt me to death."

"She was pretty shook up about it all," I said. Then, I leaped in with, "Dad and Erskine and

Richard were all pretty good friends. Now they're all gone," looking at the floor, shaking my head. Until that moment, I hadn't thought of it that way. The three of them. Time and unexpected events cull the herd.

"Yes. They were all friends," Harriet said.

I looked up. "May I ask you something personal, Miss Harriet?"

"Sure," she said, shrugging.

"It's about Richard and Erskine," looking her in the eyes, trying to assess her reaction. I felt uneasy about playing her, but something told me this was an important piece of information. With all the guilt I'd been feeling lately, you'd think I was Catholic.

"But he didn't . . . I didn't . . . ."

I decided to go for broke. "I just thought it was a shame they'd had a falling out, and now they're both gone. Shame to end a lifelong friendship over, you know, whatever it was." I looked at her. She was making involuntary cheek movements. "Was it really that bad? Whatever Erskine had done that made Richard disavow him as a friend?"

Harriet took a deep breath. "I told Richard he shouldn't judge Erskine. Friends don't judge friends. It's the Christian way to be. Friends are supposed to be there to support and counsel each other in times of crises," she continued. "I talked to Richard, but he wouldn't listen. Then I asked the preacher to say that in one of his sermons. I didn't say why, but he did what I asked. It didn't make no difference."

"At least you tried," I said.

"Richard," she said, "was just so doggoned strict. You know how he was." When I didn't say anything, she said, "Well, maybe you didn't, but your father did."

I did know, but I didn't say so.

"Your father would have tried, too, if he was still alive. Richard was stubborn sometimes"

Most of the time, as I remembered him.

She then digressed. "You know, sometimes Jenson used to go around and smooth things over for Richard when he'd get into it with others. Once Richard . . ."

Harriet then told me the story of how Richard had bought a lawn tractor from a guy out on Peachtree Road (if she remembered right, it was Elwood Turner) and how the first time Richard used the mower he discovered there was a hairline crack in the bottom of the gas tank and gas was leaking out. Angry, Richard replaced the offending tank, then took the one with the crack in it, and a bill for the new one over to Turner.

When Richard found Turner working out in the yard, he threw the faulty tank at the man's feet, called him a cheatin' so-and-so (Harriet couldn't bring herself to say the actual words), handed him the bill and told him he expected a check in the mail within the next few days.

"Of course, Richard never got a check," Harriet said, shaking her head, but half chuckling, too. "So he put up a sign in our yard, letting everyone know that Elwood Turner was a crook and not to ever buy nothin' from him. Well, Webb, Mr. Turner came by one day and ripped the sign off our lawn and told Richard he was gonna use it as evidence and sue him for slander.

"That's when your dad got involved and went over and calmed that Turner fella down. Afterwards, Jenson came by here with cash money for Richard. Claimed Turner had given it to him to pay Richard." Then Harriet did chuckle. "You know, I always suspected it was your father's money, not Turner's."

I wasn't sure if this was going anywhere or if it was just an old lady's reminiscence, but I nodded and said, "I wouldn't doubt it if it was. He liked to keep things in the community running calm." He wasn't a troublemaker like me.

Then I tried, "That's what I meant when I said those three stuck together and stuck up for each other. And that's why I was bothered when I heard there was a problem between Richard and Erskine. I won't ever believe Erskine cheated Richard over anything. He just wasn't that kind of person."

"It wasn't Richard he cheated," Harriet blurted out.

Now I was on to something.

I frowned. "You mean Erskine had some misunderstanding with someone else, then told Richard about it and Richard took the other person's side? That doesn't sound like Richard."

Harriet was shaking her head. "No. It wasn't that at all. But I will only tell you if you promise not to tell anyone else that I told you."

I had to tread carefully. I knew if circumstances arose, I might have to tell someone else. Maybe more than someone else. But if I promised and didn't say Harriet told me, while it wouldn't comply with the spirit of the promise, I could live with that. Now I was thinking like an attorney.

I took a chance, saying, "You know, Miss Harriet, if you are uncomfortable talking about this, you don't have to." Somehow, however, I knew she felt she had to. Besides, Colonel Tillman once told me, one of the reasons I was a good investigator was that people liked to tell me things. That I had a sympathetic face. Maybe that was true. Although I've looked in the mirror trying to see what he was talking about and thought, I *wouldn't tell this son-of-a-bitch anything.*

"No, Webb. Like you said, the three of them are gone. It's only Betty and me left now."

I found mentioning Betty Weeks both curious and interesting. She didn't mention Tabby because, even though my aunt was part of our family, she had never been particularly close to either Harriet or Betty.

When she didn't continue, I prompted with, "It had to be something bad to have affected their friendship that way."

"It was," she replied, nodding. There was another long pause and I thought I'd lost her. Finally, she blurted out, "Erskine was having an affair with another woman. Some long-hauler who lived up in Chapanoke. You know where that is?"

"The northern part of Perquimans County," I said, trying to respond and process the information all at the same time. "Did Miss Betty know about this?" pushing for more.

A look of sadness on her face, Miss Harriet said, "I don't know, Webb. I hope not." Then, shaking her head, "And Erskine and Richard were so close all their lives." Now tears ran down her wrinkled cheeks.

"I'm really sorry to hear all of this, Miss Harriet. Then changed the subject to, "I hear you had a fall," gesturing toward the walker. How's that coming along?"

I think she was happy to move on to something else and began a long oration on what happened and how, and all about the hospital and doctors and so on. Older women love to talk about their ailments. While she talked I had two more muffins and, to be polite, a few sips of coffee to wash them down.

I don't carry a watch, but there was a wall clock at the end of the room and I realized it was getting close to the time when I had to leave. Finally, I said, "I'm going to have to run. I have an appointment in town I can't miss."

"Oh, that's too bad. Can you come back and tell me what you've been doin' over the past few years?"

I said I would do my best, although I didn't know if that was true. I liked her and she was an old friend of the family, but a dead family friend. A person trying to kill me and a missing cat currently occupied my time and energy.

I had to move on.

"The muffins were delicious," I said. She wanted me to take some with me. I told her I'd take one, that she'd best keep the rest in case her daughter came by later.

When I left, I kissed her on the left cheek and, once again, told her I would do my best to come back soon.

More guilt.

As I drove away, I realized I'd never actually promised Miss Harriet anything regarding Erskine.

In my mind, If I needed to share information, I was off the hook.

Sometimes I wanted to kick myself in the ass.

Chapter 20

I WAS DUE at Dr. Robertson's office in thirty-five minutes, which meant I had between ten to fifteen minutes to spare. By the time I reached Weeksville Junction, I had less than ten minutes to spare. I spent that time calling for Basil, mainly in the area around the abandoned house and the swampy woods behind it.

Someone had to have taken him in and was feeding him. I thought maybe it was time to make flyers and either drop them off or post them with every home and business within the Weeksville Junction area. If I didn't find him by Sunday, I would get someone to help me produce the flyer. There was a big chain office supply store in town with a copy center that I could probably use. I wished Nan was around to help me with the Basil problem.

I walked through the doors at Dr. Robertson's at exactly 9:29 am, and that was by their clock. I went up to the window, which in this case didn't have a sliding glass. I always wondered what a person was supposed to do if there was a glass door and it was closed, and the person behind there didn't look up. Should a person stand and wait for them to wake up and realize someone was staring into their cage? Knock on the glass, even though it said not to? Or maybe press a nose against the window and make faces; or dance like a monkey, as if they were the spectators and the person waiting was the one in the cage?

Brain working overtime.

I was saved from those choices when, after a ten-second beat, the girl looked up from the file she was studying and acknowledged my presence.

"Webb Sawyer for my nine-thirty with Dr. Robertson," I said.

The girl had dark chocolate skin with a round face and large oval coal black eyes. The eyes had lashes that had to be fake — an inch long and turned up at the ends. Really? She clicked information into her computer, then looked back at me, saying, "Please have a seat, Mr. Sawyer. Dr. Robertson will be with you shortly."

I smiled. "Well, if shortly means by ten minutes to ten, allowing ten minutes for his time, that will work. But please remind him that at 10:00 am sharp

I'll be heading out the door for an appointment for which I don't intend to be late." I smiled again.

She looked at me with a dumbfound look on her face.

"Not kidding," I said, then turned and walked across the room and sat down.

I saw her pick up the phone and say something into it.

Eight minutes later, by the time on their wall clock, an unattractive woman with a pleasant voice and demeanor opened a door and called for me. Frankly, I'll take pleasantry over looks every day of the week. Speaking of looks, when I jumped the line I got a variety from curious to annoyed from those already there when I'd arrived.

I got the usual step-on-the-scale routine and was quickly led into a room. I wasn't there a minute when another woman came in, this one older and craggy-faced but, again, pleasant. She didn't waste any time with chit-chat and took my temp and blood pressure.

Before she was done, Robertson breezed in with a "Howdy, Mr. Sawyer," glancing at the numbers from the nurse or medical assistant, or whatever she was, then said, "I heard you weren't in any mood to hang around, so I hurried you in."

"The rest of the sheep in the pen were not too happy," I said.

Robertson gave me a knowing snicker.

After a closer look at the results from the temp-taking and blood pressure, he nodded, and asked, "You feeling okay since your left the hospital?" I told him I was. "No dizziness, cramps, numbness, shortness of breath or anything else unusual?" I shook my head. "Gonna take a blood sample and let you go," he said, nodding to the woman. "Will let you know if anything that needs attention turns up."

"CroFabulous," I said.

The woman gave me a funny look. Robertson laughed, saying, "Gotta get back to the cranky ewe I left next door."

"Just tell her you had a demanding celebrity to take care of," I said,

Robertson, smiled, nodded, said, "Take care, Mr. Sawyer. "Call if you need anything," then breezed back out.

"Are you really a celebrity?" the woman asked after she'd taken a blood sample.

"In my own mind," I said.

It was a few minutes after ten when I strolled into the YMCA. The girl behind the counter recognized me from before and said, "He's probably in the locker room. Down the end of this hall," pointing. "Then turn right and go to the end of that one. Last door on the right."

"Gotcha," I said, and headed that way.

I was about half way down when I saw him emerge from the hall further down, then go to the right. When he went to the left and disappeared from view, I picked up the pace. At the end of the hallway I turned left and stopped. Straight ahead was a door to the outside marked EXIT. To the right were two doors, both open. To the left was a closed door without a sign. I took a quick peek into the two open doors. They were activity rooms, both empty.

I decided the closed door must be a stairwell, leading up to the workout area. I opened it. I was correct. Straight ahead, stairs led to a mid-floor landing, then switch-backed to the left. I started up when something to the left caught my eye. There was a set mirrors high on the wall that enabled a view of the space that led back under the stairwell.

Someone was back there.

It was the dog killer. He was looking right at me via the mirror. As I turned and retreated down the stairs, he came out of his hiding place.

"You again," he growled. "What do you want this time?"

"Guess you saw me through the mirrors at the end of the hall," laughing, trying to keep it light.

Perry Adams just glared at me.

"Actually, I need a favor," hoping to bait him with a sanguine request. Another technique I used in the Army.

Before he could answer, the door opened and I moved out of the way to let a woman by. She headed up the stairs.

As soon as she was gone, I said, "There's a couple of empty rooms across the hall. Maybe we should use one of them so we won't be in anyone's way."

Ignoring me, Adams asked, "What kind of favor?"

I opened the door and nodded across the hall. "One I don't want anyone else to hear." When he didn't move I said, "It's something only you can assist me with. I really would appreciate your help," I added, sounding as sincere as I could.

Without answering, he brushed past me and stepped out into the hall, gave a quick look at both open doors, then headed toward the one farthest away from the stairwell.

I followed.

Adams went inside, then stood by the door until I came in, closing the door behind us. We both moved toward the center of the room, where he stopped and asked again, "What kind of favor?"

"I'm concerned about our mutual friend."

He frowned.

"I'm talking about Miss Betty. Betty Weeks."

"I thought we already got that settled," he said, suspicion creeping over his reddening face.

"This is about something else. I'm worried about her. About her mental health. The business with her wanting to connect with her deceased daughter, and now her husband killed in a tragic accident." I wanted him to hone in on the word accident. "She's becoming withdrawn. Won't talk to her family or her friends," I lied, trying the spread the honey on as think as I could. "As I told you before, she and my parents were long-time friends from way back when the all went to grade school together."

"Big deal. Maybe you should just butt out," he sneered.

Ignoring that, I said, "I'm trying to be helpful."

"So, what's that have to do with me?"

"Not so much you, Mr. Adams. I was hoping your friend, Miss Nicolescu, could be helpful. Maybe if I could talk with her about Miss Betty. Maybe enlist her help in counseling my friend about her problems. Since, obviously, Miss Betty trusts her."

"Oh, so before it was all about some investigation into Mr. Weeks' death, and now it's all about Mrs. Weeks' mental state. Why should we help you with anything?"

"I can't give you an argument why you should, Mr. Adams. I can only ask, for Miss Betty's sake, for your help. I hope you and your friend will consider it."

Adams made a noise that sounded like a pig rutting around in a pile of slop.

"So, first you show up in my driveway unannounced and uninvited, lying to me about why you were there. Then you came here and interrupted my workout, claiming that I'd better speak to you because there was an investigation in the circumstances of Erskine Weeks' death, as if I might have something to do with it. And, by the way, I called the sheriff and he was a jackass about it. He told me to mind my own damn business and stay out of trouble..."

That surprised me. I wondered why the sheriff didn't say anything about it when he saw me in the hospital. I guess I had more "street cred" as they call it, than the dog killer, who had spread resentment like a fart joke at a funeral.

"... and now you're pestering me again to do you a favor? Jerk-off," making his way toward the door.

I thought I'd give Adams one last shot and said, "Well, we don't have to be friends, but I thought because we have a mutual enemy maybe we could at least help each other out." I was grasping at straws, but what the hell... you never know.

Adams stopped and turned around. "What the hell are you talking about?"

"Jeb Renner," I said.

"Jeb Renner? What does that son-of-a-bitch have to do with anything?" When I started to answer, Adams said, "What exactly is your game, Sawyer?"

"There's no game," I replied, innocence written all over my face. "It's just that Renner shoved a rifle in my face and threatened to shoot me. And I understand he put three 22-250 .45 grain slugs into your house."

Adams chuffed. "You seem to know a lot about my business, which is something that disturbs me, because one thing I value more than anything is my privacy, and you've been encroaching on it. Am I going to have to get a restraining order?"

I knew I'd lost him, so I decided to indulge my inner Mr. Hyde. "You know, Mr. Adams, if you enjoyed your privacy so much, maybe you shouldn't've shot those hunting dogs just because they had the misfortune to wander on to your property. Kind of a dumb-ass thing to do for a man who values his privacy, don't you think?"

Adams face screwed up and his eyes bore into me like a corkscrew into a wine cork. "Fuck you, Sawyer. You come anywhere near me or my property again, I'll finish the job that asshole Renner started."

He wheeled and stormed out of the room, slamming the door behind him.

"Hmm!" After my original conversation with Adams I'd relegated him and Bogdana to my mental pending file about having anything to do with Erskine's accident. Then after what Miss Harriet told me about Erskine's indiscretion, I'd almost locked the file drawer on them. I figured, now that Erskine was gone, if Betty wanted to waste her money on a phony psychic, that was her business.

However, once again, there were darker thoughts scrambling to get out of the cabinet. Was Betty caught in the middle of unfortunate events? Assuming she knew about Erskine's indiscretion, was it crazy for me to think she was having an affair with Perry Adams as a way of getting back at her husband? But if that was so, what about Bogdana? What was her part in it? Since I wasn't sure about her relationship with the dog killer, I wasn't sure how that idea played out. Unless they were having a *menage a trois*. The very idea of that made me cringe. Then again, how well do we really know what goes on behind closed doors with our friends and neighbors? Sometimes even our families.

The weird thing is, none of this would have crossed my mind until the unfortunate event in Aunt Tabby's front yard and, subsequently, Aubrey's and Bobby's suspicions about it.

In any event, Mr. Perry "The Dog Killer" Adams and Bogdana "The Psychic" Nicolescu were out of the file drawer and, once again, back on my radar.

Chapter 21

AS I HEADED out of Elizabeth City and Pasquotank County on my way to Chowan County and Linden Crossroads, once again I tried to process all the convoluted and confusing information I'd gathered about Erskine and Betty Weeks. There were just too many possible scenarios, one being that I was chasing my tail; that I was on a fool's mission. Not that I thought Aubrey Meads was a fool. Far from it. But maybe he had read too much into Betty's clandestine meetings at Perry Adams' house with Bogdana Nicolescu, assuming they were, in fact, clandestine. Either way, I was going around in circles.

The one good thing about it, it was keeping me busy while the F.B.I. and/or Homeland Security tried to find the girl who wanted to kill me. I assumed they were. Maybe in the scheme of things it wasn't a priority. And the nature of the problem left Detective Jenkins in the woods, so he'd be of no help. And I had no resources available to do anything about it. Hell I didn't even have the shooter's name. Yet. Maybe I'd hear from Tillman by this evening. I thought about finding a pay phone — if that was still possible these days. Call Aunt Tabby to see if he'd called, but the more I thought about it, the less appealing it became.

Once I passed Fairfield Road where Adams lived, my thoughts shifted to the long-hauler who was supposed to be Erskine's sideline. I didn't have her name, but Miss Harriet said she'd lived in Caratoke, which was nothing but a blink on a four-number state road, so how hard would it be to find a woman truck driver who lived there?

Rhetorical.

It was only a matter of minutes before I came to the turnoff for Route 1293. There was no actual route number sign, at least not where it intersected with Route 17 South. There was a sign that announced **CARATOKE** →, but that was it. I turned right onto a narrow two-lane country road. About two miles up I saw the route number sign.

I had been to Caratoke only once in my life. That was with my dad when I was about fourteen. The road had been only recently paved then. I'm not sure it's ever been repaved since.

Caratoke was farther up the road than I'd remembered. Of course, when you're a kid out with your dad, you don't really pay much attention to time and distance. Finally, I reached a sign that announced the town limits. There were a few shotgun style houses, outnumbered by single-wides, with a double-wide scattered here and there. The only commercial operation was the same little country store I remembered from way back when. If there had once been paint on it—I couldn't remember—it had long since peeled off and never been redone.

The sign above the covered front porch said **SAM'S GROCERY**. On the porch there was an elderly man in denim bib overalls with a pipe dangling from his mouth. He was asleep in a rocker. When I pulled in front, the man came alive, the pipe falling onto his lap. I wondered if he was the older version of the Sam who was here back when my dad and I came through.

When I popped out of the truck, the old man was brushing tobacco off his lap. Once I'd gone up the two steps to the porch he said, "The heat and humidity puts me to sleep every time."

I laughed. "Good thing the pipe had gone out or you'd be havin' some heat where you didn't want it."

When he grinned, the few teeth he had left were nicotine stained. "Now wouldn't that be somethin'," clearing his throat as he said it. "What can I gitcha?" hauling himself out of the chair.

"You Sam?" I asked, wondering . . .

"Yep. Still alive and kickin'. Well, alive, anyway," letting out something between a snort and a chuckle.

"Good for you," I said. "Got any cold root beer?"

"Oh yeah. I got me plenty a that," hobbling toward the screen door.

I followed him inside. "Tell you what. I'll buy two of 'em if you'll have one with me out on the front porch."

It hurt to watch him walk around the check out counter and over to an old time floor refrigerator and pull up the top. I followed him over and held the top up for him while he searched around inside. Between the bottles of Coca Cola an 7-Up—there was even some Nehi grape juice in there—he came up with two bottles of Stewarts root beer.

"Bet you never seen root beer like this," he said.

Actually I had, and I told him how when I was a kid Dad and I had come through on some business and the only thing I could remember was the Stewarts root beer. "And a younger version of you," I added.

"When was that? Nineteen hundred and froze to death?" chuckling. Then, "Say, I'm hungry. You want a sandwich? Made fresh this mornin' by my niece. Ham and tomato and lettuce with mayo and horseradish mustard. On me. The root beer, too."

I started to tell him it was all my treat, but he held up a hand and said, "Humor an old man. Besides, I need someone to chat with. You're the first one by in the last two hours. Maybe even three. I don't know."

I'd been so ramped up for the past several days that it was kinda nice to just sit there, munch on a homemade sandwich, sip on an old-fashioned root beer and shoot the breeze . . . and watch the traffic go by—averaging one vehicle every twenty minutes. That based on the fact I was there about an hour and waved to three passers by: a John Deere tractor, a red pick-up, and a light blue, beat-up, early 1990s something or other.

The tractor was the first one by and Sam and I had a long discussion on the attributes of the various makes and models. I told him that when I was a kid most every one out our way favored John Deeres. Of course, the reason for that was probably because back then John Deere had the only dealership in the area and nobody wanted to drive fifty miles or more to buy something else.

"Even so, I remember a few old Ford tractors here and there," I said.

"Never drove one my whole life," Sam said. "Always been in the grocery business."

"Sandwich was good," I said. "I was hungrier than I thought. Root beer was great, too." Then,

"Speaking of driving, you know of a woman truck driver who lives in the area? I'm talking big rigs. Semis."

"Oh, you mean Cookie Goode. She spells Goode with an 'e' on the end. Yeah, she don't live too far from here. Just up the road apiece. Down a dirt road off to the right. You know her?"

"Actually, never met her, but she's the reason I came up here today. See, she and I recently lost a good friend and I wanted to talk to her about him."

"Oh, yeah. That friend of hers, Pete somethin'."

So Erskine went by Pete up here so no one would know his real name and start putting two and two together. Sam rubbed his whiskered chin and thought for a minute. I waited while he pondered.

"Come to think of it, Cookie never did tell me his last name. Just came in with him one mornin' on her way out for a run and said, 'Mr. Sam, this here's Pete. He thinks he might want to go into the long haul business and I invited him to make a run with me, see if he likes bein' on the road.' Seemed like a nice fella, too. When she went out Tuesday mornin' she told me he'd been killed in some kinda wreck, but didn't say what kind or how it happened. So you was friends with Pete, too?"

"Family friend," I said. "My dad and him grew up together."

"What happened?" Sam asked.

"Unfortunate accident," I said. "You know how those things just come out of nowhere and the next thing you know it's lights out," telling the truth without the details.

"Yeah, I know what you mean. One day, about eight years ago . . ." a hand going to his chin again, ". . . hmm, maybe closer to nine or ten. Anyway," waving a hand, "some kid come a flyin' down the wrong side of the road and hit this woman goin' over to Hertford to see her sister. Hit her head on, right out there in front of the store," pointing. "I'd just come out onto the porch and seen it all. BOOM!" smacking a fist in a hand. "And they were both dead. Just like your friend Pete. Kid was drunk, they said. Damn fool wants to kill himself, that's one thing, but takin' someone else along with him is just wrong."

Getting back to Cookie Goode, I asked, "So you said Miss Cookie went out Tuesday morning. She back yet?"

"Oh, no," Sam said, shaking his head. "She don't get back until Saturday mornin's. You see," turning his whole body toward me, "she comes in here at 8:00 am on the dot every Tuesday mornin' when I open. Fills up her coolers. One cooler is for drinks. She likes that Nehi grape soda." Then he went off on a tangent telling me how there was a bottler that specialized in vintage sodas, like the Nehi and the Stewarts, that he buys from because the people in the area like the good stuff. "Like they used to make it, you know?"

I told him I did indeed know and I agreed with them.

"Anyway, she stocks up on the sodas in one cooler and sandwiches in the other one. On Monday evenin's, my niece, Mandy—she's the one made them sandwiches we just ate—makes up a whole batch of Cookie's favorite kind so's she has them to take on her run with her. Cookie 'specially likes liverwurst with lettuce and mayo. Never cottoned to that stuff myself, but Cookie likes it. You like liverwurst?" he asked.

Actually, Mom used to pack a lot of it for my school lunch box, and I liked it back then, but I hadn't eaten any in decades. "Haven't had any lately," I said.

"Yeah, well like I said, I'm not much for it. Anyway, Cookie stocks up on the drinks and sandwiches and snacks and heads out Tuesday mornin' on her run. She goes up to Norfolk somewhere and loads up with some kind of finished goods. That's what she calls 'em. Finished goods. Then takes them down to Dallas, where she unloads, picks up somethin' there, then takes that to Kansas City, then gets somethin' else there and brings it back to Norfolk. Then she's back in here on Saturday mornin'. She comes by around 10:00 am and returns the empty bottles, buys herself a Nehi and a sandwich and heads over to her house. Does that every week. Same routine. Sounds mighty borin' to me," he added.

"Huh," I said. "So she won't be home until tomorrow morning?"

"That's right. You want me to tell her you came by?" Sam asked. "By the way, you never did say your name. Who do I say was askin' for her?"

I laughed and reached a paw over. "Sorry for being rude. Name's Webb Sawyer."

Sam held out a hand and shook mine. "Pleased to met you, Mr. Sawyer."

"Webb's fine," I said.

"Well, Webb, I'll tell Cookie you came on up to see her. But, say, you didn't mention where you came on up from."

"I live in Nags Head," I told him, afraid that if I said Weeksville it might spook Cookie Goode when he told her. Then, "Tell you what. You can go ahead and tell her when she comes by, but I'd like to leave a note on her door, anyway. Can you tell me which dirt road I turn off on to find her house?" I had no intention of leaving a note, but wanted to see where she lived. Get a sense of her.

"Sure," Sam said. "Second road on the right. More a lane than a road really. Only three houses up there. She's the last one on the right."

* * *

I found her place easy enough. It was at the end of the dirt lane, about two hundred yards from the other two homes, which were right next to each other (presumably, two related families). For some reason I expected a run down place with a couple of left over beaters in the yard, good for only scrap metal and cannibalized parts . . . maybe even an old washing machine and fridge, to boot. Instead, I pulled into a nicely kept yard with a well-maintained double-wide at the end of a freshly-graveled driveway. The one-acre lot had been cut into a stand of mostly pine trees, interspersed with oak and gums. There was a well-established Bradford pear in the middle of the front lawn and a nice-sized garden shed next to a weeping willow in back. A late model white Toyota Tacoma was parked on the right side of the house. To the right of that, I could see tire tracks where she parked her semi cab when she was home.

I didn't bother getting out of the car to walk around the property or try to look inside. No need for that, really.

On the way past Sam's Grocery I was ready to wave, but there was a pickup outside and he was no longer on the front porch.

I liked Sam the country grocer.

Back out on 17 South I soon crossed the bridge over the Perquimans River. Off to the right, over the cypress-scaped water toward the edge of the town of Hertford, was like looking at a real-life picture postcard. However, once you got past that, it was no more than a sleepy, time-ravaged southern village made famous by the Hall of Fame baseball great, Jim "Catfish" Hunter.

My all-too-recent experience there with the serial killer by the name of David Nigel Wilkerson, a man who was evil beyond comprehension, still haunted my mind.

The good news was, he was dead and I was alive.

In Chowan County, outside of Edenton, I exited North on Route 32, heading for Linden Crossroads. I didn't know where Landon Livermore's farm was, but since everyone in the county knew him, I was sure someone would.

However, I had one more stop to make before I intruded on the Livermore family. The ham sandwich at Sam's didn't cut it. I was still hungry.

I didn't remember any real restaurants along 32 and, once I was off 17, all I saw were fast food joints. I wasn't a big fan of the 1,000 calorie fare, and I didn't think a salad would carry me far. But, as Dad used to say, "If you're hungry enough, even Grandma's blood pudding tastes good."

I stopped and bought myself a double cheeseburger, forgoing the fries, and a large (may the

Gods of Food Additives forgive me) Mountain Dew, the Dew in order to keep me going. It was only noon and I was already beginning to flag.

About fifteen minutes later I arrived at the sign announcing Linden Crossroads. I say sign because there was no town. There was an abandoned building with a saddleback roof not long for this world (probably the original corner grocery), and catercorner across the road a barn that had already gone to the land of rural buildings graveyards.

Now the problem was, go straight, go left or go right. I guess this was why people had GPS and cell phones. On the other hand, it made my life more interesting to fly by the seat of my guesses. The stop signs were on the crossing road and I was stopped on Route 32, contemplating, when off to my right I saw an old Case International tractor coming down the road.

I pulled through the intersection and off on the shoulder, got out of Trusty Rusty and stood there, waiting for the driver to come up to the stop sign. When he did, I moved toward the machine, indicating I needed to talk to the guy.

The kid looked to be about fourteen. That didn't surprise me. I was driving my dad's equipment when I was twelve. The kid turned off his engine and asked if he could help me.

"Looking for the Livermore farm," I said. "The guy who plants the clary sage."

"Lotta people around here planting clary sage these days. My dad's been doing it for the last six years now." Then, "I'm going right by Livermore's house, if you want, you can follow me."

I wanted to laugh but I didn't. Following behind a tractor for who knows how many miles was for a person more patient than I. "Just point me in the right direction and I'll find it."

"Straight ahead," the kid said. "About three miles on the right."

I thanked him and walked back to my truck, did a uey, then turned west down the country crossroad. I'll give the kid this. He waited for me to get ahead of him so I wouldn't have to pass. I waved as I turned in front of him and he waved back. It was probably the highlight of his day.

Three miles later, almost to the tenth of a mile, there it was: two big signs, each engraved on matching stone gateways that announced **LIVERMORE FARMS**.

I turned in, thinking, *This should be interesting.*

Chapter 22

ACTUALLY, IT WAS more interesting than I imagined.

I drove up the quarter mile unpaved and un-graveled oak-lined driveway to a civil war era house that had been redone with a brick façade. It was a two-story structure with a metal hip roof and elaborate window hoods. The eaves had heavy, paired brackets and there was a full-width porch with turned balusters and posts with finely-detailed capitals.

The place reeked of money.

My thought was, this guy doesn't need to sabotage anyone's crop duster just to get the extra business. Maybe his supposedly hot-headed son might be so inclined but not Landon Livermore.

Along both sides of the driveway the fields had been recently disced in preparation for the next planting. There was white picket-board fencing around the house with an open entrance where it became a short, black-topped driveway that T'd into an oval in front of the house. It was wide enough for two vehicles. There was a 2014 silver Dodge Ram and a 2012 silver Toyota Corolla parked there, the same vehicles on the list Aubrey gave me for Mr. And Mrs. Livermore. I pulled past them and parked.

They had a fancy lion-head knocker which I used to announce my presence. For some reason I expected a maid or butler or some other house servant to greet me, but it was a well-coiffured middle aged woman who I soon found out was Mrs. Livermore, herself.

Tammy Livermore might have once been a comely girl, but those days were a couple of decades behind her. She was a small, thin woman, maybe pushing five-foot-five, with a long narrow face and sun-mottled skin. She sported a wide, narrow-lipped mouth and a long, thin pointed nose—unflattering features. Murky brown, close set eyes sat deep in their sockets. Her short hair had already turned gray, but kudos to her hairdresser, who had done a nice job drawing attention away from the face it surrounded.

The good news was, besides the hair, she had a pleasant voice and demeanor that, once I had announced myself as Webb Sawyer from Weeksville in Pasquotank County, and apologized for showing up to see Mr. Livermore without an appointment, greeted me with playful and welcoming words.

"Well, Mr. Webb Sawyer of Weeksville in Pasquotank County," she said, "please follow me," which I happily did.

She led me into a kitchen large enough for an informal table that seated six.

"Landon," she said. "This is Mr. Webb Sawyer of Weeksville in Pasquotank County."

At first I thought maybe she was being facetious, but I soon learned that was just how she talked.

"He's here to see you," she added.

Landon Livermore was a large man. Not in girth but in general build. He was surely six-foot-five with a frame north of 225 pounds. He had very little fat and a lot of solid muscle. His square-jawed face told of a man with conviction and purpose, and his piercing dark eyes offered a strange mixture of friendliness and resolve. He reminded me of my mentor and ass-saver, General Tillman; a leader of men. That said, Landon Livermore wasn't waiting around for his wife, Tammy, to wait on him. He was already setting plates and silverware on the table.

"Landon waits for no woman," Tammy said.

Her husband chuckled at her jest. It was easy to see they had a comfortable relationship.

"Mr. Sawyer," he said, putting down a plate and coming around the table, right hand extended. "Landon Livermore. I don't believe we've met."

I shook his hand. Suddenly, I was uncomfortable that I had thoughtlessly intruded upon their lunch hour. I guess it showed, because he smiled and said, "You've arrived just in time for one of Tammy's famous hearty lunches."

"He's been up and working in the fields since six this morning. He needs a hearty lunch," Tammy said. "There's plenty and your welcome to join us."

I noticed a pitcher of ice tea on the table. "Just some tea, thank you. I've already eaten."

Livermore motioned me to a chair and we both sat. "What can I do for you Mr. Sawyer?"

"Webb, please."

"Webb it is," he said.

"My friend, Betty Weeks' son-in-law told me about you," I said, probing.

"You mean Bobby Nixon?" Livermore asked.

Tammy Livermore procured a glass and filled it with tea. I took a sip. It was sweetened, but I didn't complain.

"Yep, Bobby."

"Very sad news about Erskine's accident. Is this about his spraying business?"

Here's the thing. When I left Caratoke, I had no idea what approach I would take with the Livermores. But by the time I'd turned north on Route 32,

I had the makings of a plan, which I decided on over the double-cheese and Dew. The key was, I was there not to accuse, or ask tricky questions. Landon Livermore was no fool. His status in the county and the way he had built the business after his father had died made that obvious. And now, meeting him solidified that idea. No, I was there to gather some facts and make an assessment about the family dynamic. I would have to find a way to meet the son. In any event, I would play the reluctant advance man on the crop dusting issue and, at the same time, sidle up to him on his crop of clary sage, which, in fact, I actually had some interest. And maybe I could even gain some information to help Miss Betty.

"It was very sad," I said, "and let me answer your question this way," ready to tell a healthy mixture of truths and lies. "My family and the Weeks have been friends since Erskine and my dad were in grade school. Obviously, Miss Betty, Erskine's widow, is in a state of both mourning and confusion. In addition, Erskine's clients are wondering what will happen to their contracts with him." I was sure that was true. "She wonders who will pick up the slack and spray their crops. I'm sure she's worried about the loss of income, too. Anyway, she asked me if I would look into it and give her some advice." That one, a fabrication.

"Hmm," nodding. Then, "Why you and not Bobby?"

"Good question. The same one I asked Miss Betty. She wouldn't say. Only said that she trusted my judgement because I knew the farming business. If there was more to it than that, I didn't ask. Of course, I'll share our talk with Bobby. I like and respect him. I may know the farmers, but he knows the financial and contract arrangements better than I do," showing my humble side. "And it is family business," I added.

I quickly segued to, "Also, I'm interested in knowing more about your sage crop. I figured while I was here it would be a good opportunity to discuss both matters."

"So you're a farmer again," he said, smiling.

I think he had my number, but was being kind. I decided to come clean on that point. "Not since I left home to join the Army," I said, "but I still own the rights to Dad's farm land and lease it out to other farmers in the area. I know them all quite well, which is why I thought I could be of assistance to Miss Betty," circling back to the crop dusting.

"Why me?" he asked. "Didn't Bobby tell you that before Erskine died he'd approached us about buying him out."

"Yeah, Bobby mentioned that. Something about Erskine wanting to switch over to some long haul trucking," seeing if I'd get a response to that.

I didn't.

"We considered it but decided we didn't want to bite off more than we could chew."

"Right. Bobby did tell me that. This is more about me getting good advice for Miss Betty. She's really in a quandary about what to do. I told her I didn't know you but knew of you." I shrugged, acting nonchalant. "I figured since you're a client of Bobby's and he seems to think highly of you, it would be worth a shot." I hoped Landon was buying my line of bullshit.

"What about Mr. Chapman over in Currituck. I'll bet he's chomping at the bit to get Erskine's clients and expand in Camden, Pasquotank and the eastern part of Perquimans."

"More tea," Tammy Livermore interrupted. She'd gotten up from her seat and stood there with the pitcher of ice tea in her hand. I obliged and told her thanks, I would. While her husband and I were talking, she'd served up her hearty lunch of leftover sliced ham, potatoes and carrots. Once again, she tried to tempt me, but I passed. While I probably could have indulged myself, I already felt guilty enough about lying to them while interrupting their lunch and drinking their tea.

"Oh, he's chomping all right," I said. "He even eased up to her at the funeral home and asked if he could give her a call in a week or so. He didn't say why, but Miss Betty knew why. Rather unseemly, I thought." If there was a Hell, I'd surely be heading there for that one.

"Hmm," biding for time while he finished a mouthful of ham. When he was finished, he asked, "Bobby know about that?"

I shook my head. "He was off somewhere else and I was standing nearby. Eddie Chapman didn't know I was there. If Miss Betty told Bobby later I don't know. I haven't talked to him since the funeral. In any case, I figured he might refuse to deal with Chapman because of it, and we both know that at some point he's going to have to."

"You're absolutely right on that one, Webb," Livermore said, jabbing his fork in the air. " Then, "Since we both know that's the reality of it, what makes you think I can be of help?"

"Ah, Mr. Livermore. As Shakespeare had Hamlet say, 'There's the rub.' The problem the farmers have with Chapman is that he charges higher prices, and they are afraid he won't honor the agreement they had with Erskine. Chapman has the upper hand, because they need the service. So here's my thought. Even though you don't want Erskine's contracts, if Chapman thinks you do, the farmers may get a more favorable deal. I know that's asking a lot, but it is Bobby's wife's family, and Bobby was very close with Erskine. And you and Bobby are friends and business associates . . . so . . . ," I shrugged.

"Hmm. Clever ploy, Webb."

I smiled. "It's a reach, but I understand that originally your son was interested . . . ," letting that thought linger; see where it went.

It went nowhere. Livermore was chuckling. "You know, I've actually read about you, Webb. Your tracking down that serial killer over in Perquimans and some other things . . ."

Thankfully, he didn't bring up the Army business.

". . . And here I thought you were just a man of action. I didn't realize you were a conspirator and back room negotiator, too."

I returned the laugh. "Actually, no one has ever accused me of that before. I'm usually pretty straight forward and blunt," trying to put on my nonchalant, innocent act.

"Man of action, huh?" Tammy put in. "My kinda man," turning to her husband and wiggling her eyebrows.

"Two of us at the same table," Landon said grinning. "You're a lucky girl." Then, "Speaking of Ralphie, I guess he and Corine are running late today." Then to me, "They're usually home for lunch. In case Bobby didn't tell you, Corine is our daughter. She runs the crop dusting business with her brother."

I nodded. "Bobby mentioned her."

"They should be here shortly, Landon," Tammy said. "Since Mr. Sawyer is interested in the sage, why don't you take him out into the field with you." Then to me, "We don't start planting until next month, but we're discing now. Landon knows everything there is to know about clary sage."

"Right," I said. "I saw the disced front fields as I drove up. Very impressive entrance by the way. And you've done a nice job with the house, too."

"Papa Livermore did most of that," Tammy said. Then, "You sure you don't want anything to eat, Mr. Sawyer, man of action?"

"Thanks, but I'm good."

She was an interesting woman. It made me think of something my dad once told me after things went south with Claire. He'd said, "Next time marry an ugly woman. She'll be so grateful she'll never leave you." I don't know whether it would be a good thing or not, but if she had a personality like Tammy Livermore, it might be a worthy idea.

"Great," Livermore said, pushing back his chair and standing up. Let's go over to the barn complex, then we'll go out to the back fields. We'll talk about Mrs. Weeks' problem and I'll tell you all about clary sage, one of the greatest crops nobody ever heard of."

"One of the prettiest, too," I said.

"That it is, Webb."

We went down a hall and out onto a porch on the north side of the house, then out the screen door, down two steps and across the lawn to a wide double gate. The gate was open and we walked on to a field road that followed the other side of the fence out to a complex of barns.

There were tire tracks in the yard. I guess Livermore saw me looking and said, "Yeah, I have to do something about that. Maybe put some blacktop from the driveway to the gate. Ralphie and Corine drive their vehicles out there and park them next to the hangar."

We talked as we walked. "I take it your dad wasn't in the crop dusting business."

"Nope. Wasn't in the sage business either, but after he passed and I took over, I decided having one steady, productive, stable-priced crop a year made more sense. Labor intensive only twice a year, August, maybe the first part of September, depending on the weather, when we plant, and June when we harvest. In between, it's monitoring and light maintenance. Tammy and I like to travel, so it suits our lifestyle much better than trying to deal with two to three crops a year."

"Makes sense to me," I said. "Is it the soil or the mind set why the farmers over my way don't plant clary sage?"

"Maybe some of both," he said. "Soil and moisture content is critical for a fast start. It grows best on medium textured, well-drained soil."

"If I was still in the business, I'd have an ag guy come out and test the soil on the family lands and see if they're compatible. If my dad was still alive, he'd probably consider it, but the farmers over my way are pretty set in their ways."

"Well, someone has to grow feed corn and beans," he laughed.

"I understand you have another son who runs an extraction plant in Millstown."

"Right. Joey. Lives here and commutes for now, but just bought some property in the Millstown area. Is going to build his own place. I should say, their own place. He just got engaged to a girl from over in Windsor."

"Good for him," I said. "Hope she's a good catch."

Landon snorted. "Much better than Ralphie did. That wife he got rid of was a real piece of work."

Was he just being protective and supportive of his youngest son, or was there more to the story than the criminal report?

Landon Livermore stopped, cocked and ear and listened. "Ralphie and Corine. I can hear the engines. You?"

I had good ears but I couldn't hear them.

"Just that I have my ear tuned to them. If you were here all the time you would, too."

It wasn't long before I heard the drone of their engines, although I couldn't tell there were two planes. Landon pointed to the northwest. I shaded my eyes and soon I saw them low on the horizon, one behind the other.

"I'm just glad Ralphie never had any kids with that woman. That would have been a double disaster." Then, "They'll be landing soon. Come on," nodding his head. "Lets get out to the hangar and meet them."

We stood in one of the double bays of the hangar, watching them come in. Ralphie's Thrush landed first. It was a fine looking craft: white with wide red stripes under the engine that swept up to just above the wings. The wing tips were also red. Behind him was Corine's Ayers, which looked a lot like Erskine's plane with its yellow body, except the Ayers had a silver cowl on the front.

They popped their canopies and crawled out of their respective aircrafts. Corine was tall and solid with a confident stride and looked like her father, where Ralphie was short, maybe five-eight, with a slight frame and sharp features like the mother.

Corine had taken the second spot on the landing, showing deference to her little brother. Was she doing her family part to prop him up after what he'd been through with his legal problems? Maybe. I couldn't say. However, now that they were on the ground, she charged ahead of Ralphie.

As she strode past, she said, "Howdy fella's. I'm hungry. Catch up with you on the way back out." Then she jumped in her yellow Mini-Cooper convertible and tore down the field road, leaving both tread marks and Ralphie behind.

This was exactly what I was hoping. Maybe I could clarify my imaginings about Ralphie Livermore, the supposed hothead. The guy who was not happy with his father's decision to pass on buying out Erskine's business. Suddenly, my mind was in overdrive, trying to decide how to play it, when his father saved me the trouble.

"So, Ralphie, this is Webb Sawyer. He's a personal friend of Betty Weeks, the wife of Erskine." When Ralphie frowned, his father said, "The crop duster over in Pasquotank who just had the fatal accident."

Recognition. "Oh, yeah. Man. That was a real bummer."

"We all agree on that, Ralphie," I said.

"So, Mr. Sawyer here is hoping to find a way to both protect Mrs. Weeks' interests and at the same time make sure the farmers Weeks served don't get a raw deal with Eddie Chapman."

Ralphie snorted in disgust. "That Eddie Chapman is a crook."

Ralphie's father laughed. "Well, I don't know if he's a crook, but he does charge high prices and the farmers pay it."

"He's a crook," Ralphie said. Then, to me, "That's why I thought we should try and buy out Mr. Weeks' contracts. 'Cause if he was going to sell, at least it would keep that Chapman guy from more of his overchargin' ways."

All of a sudden I had a newfound appreciation for Ralphie Livermore. I didn't think he was all that bright, but I didn't get the sense he was a killer.

Chapter 23

"MR. SAWYER HAS an idea about how we can help the farmers who did business with Erskine Weeks get a fair deal with Chapman."

"Deal with Chapman?"

"He may charge higher fees than we do or Mr. Weeks did, but from what I hear he's reliable and does a good job."

"But—"

Livermore held up a hand. "But what Mr. Sawyer suggests . . ."

I could tell that Ralphie's father was doing his best to be patient with his son.

". . . is that we let Mr. Chapman think we have changed our mind—"

Livermore broke off and looked at me. "We have to assume he might have got wind that we'd been approached and turned Weeks down. For all we know, Weeks might have approached Chapman, too, although I doubt it."

Then back to his son, "—So Chapman will think we changed our minds and are going to offer Mr. Weeks' clients a ten-percent discount for the first two years to entice them to sign with us. I think both Mr. Sawyer and I agree, Chapman wants these accounts and he'll be forced to make a favorable deal for them."

"Why are we getting involved?" Ralph asked, looking at me.

"Because Bobby Nixon is our friend and the Weeks are his family. Mr. Sawyer here is also a friend of the family and is trying to help Mr. Weeks' widow."

Ralphie thought about it for a while. Finally, he said, "So, how does Chapman know about what we want to do?"

"Not what we want to do, son. What we want him to think we want to do."

Livermore was exercising a lot more patience than I. Then again, Ralphie was his son, not mine — thank goodness.

Ralphie pondered that for a moment, then said, "Yeah, right. I get it."

Livermore looked at me and sighed. Then, to Ralphie, "Your friend, Buddy, who lives over in Point Harbor. He knows Chapman, right?"

"Yeah. Goes to the same church, I think."

Landon Livermore looked at me and smiled. "Now we're getting somewhere." Then, back to

Ralphie, "So here's what I want you to do, son. You get in touch with your friend Buddy—"

"Now?"

"After work will be fine. He works during the day doesn't he?"

"Yeah. Works at some tire place."

"So tonight you give him a call. Just to shoot the bull, you know."

Ralphie nodded.

"Then work it into the conversation. Tell him, 'Hey, guess what? Dad's getting in touch with Mr. Weeks' accounts and if they sign with us, we'll make a deal for a ten-percent less over the next two years,'" repeating what he'd told Ralphie before. Making sure it had sunk in.

"Yeah, Dad. Make Chapman think we want to get the dead guy's contracts so he'll give them a fair deal, since he's going to get them anyway. I get it."

"Good man, Ralphie," Livermore said, patting his son on the shoulder. "You better get down to the house and get some lunch before your sister eats it all."

Ralphie nodded and started to walk away when his dad called after him. "Let me know when you've talked to Buddy."

Ralphie looked back over his shoulder, saying, "I will, Dad," then broke into a jog down the field lane.

Livermore watched his son for a moment, then turned and said, "Let's go to the tractor barn." Then, as if making up for his son's dense behavior, said, "I'll tell you one thing, the boy is a hell of a crop dusting pilot."

And that was it for my experience with Ralphie Livermore.

Behind the hangar there were two equipment barns. One had two John Deere tractors, if not new, both of recent vintage, and another one parked outside, which was a little older model by maybe six or seven years. The other barn held two forage harvesters which, unless he was leasing out to other non-sage farmers, wouldn't be used until next season.

Livermore took some time telling me about the newer model tractors and the improvements since the days I helped my dad farm. We also looked at the harvesters, me telling him that the last one I remember my dad using was an old Case.

"When everyone else was buying Deeres, Dad didn't mind traveling fifty miles for a deal on a Case," I told Livermore. "He was always going against the conventional thinking."

"Like me with the sage," Livermore said. "Even though I wasn't the first to grow it around here, I was the first to expand the acreage for it and grow it full time. Now have over six-thousand acres in it.

That's why I bought the extraction plant in Bertie County. Figured I might as well process it, too, and if I was gonna do that I might as well process everyone else's."

Then he went into the details of growing clary sage.

"I plant about three pounds of seed an acre, using sorghum plates and a row-crop planter." He showed me the plates and how to adjust them for sage seeds. "Plant 'em about a fourth to three-eighths inches. You don't want to go under a half inch or there'll be delays on their coming up." Then he went into the pH ranges, which depended on the recommendations after soil tests. "I have mine tested before each season because, as you know, conditions can and will change."

I asked him about the fertilizer and he told me pre-planting fertilizer was not recommended. "Fertilize in the fall and spring," he said. Then we discussed the nitrogen levels that were best. It surprised me how quickly after all these years the nuances and details of farming came back to me.

Then we talked about herbicides and crop oil adjuvants and the current recommendations for what to use, when and how much, and the optimal time for spraying. "As you know, we harvest in June but, like soybeans and feed corn, the actual timing depends on moisture content."

I knew, for instance, that the price paid for soybeans depended on the moisture content: the higher the percentage of moisture, the lower the payment and vice-versa. Most farmers harvested at one-percent, unless there was a ton of rain coming in and they had to get the crop out earlier. The only other option was to spend money to store it in drying oasts. Some farmers invested in their own dryers, amortizing the major cost over their life span.

Farming is a lot like shooting craps.

"Since you're here, and since I've done you a favor, maybe you'd like to do me one and maybe even have some fun at the same time."

"Sure," I said.

"You think you could operate one of these Deeres?"

"No problem."

"You remember how to hook up a discer?"

"Yep."

"Want to disc one of the west fields? You do the north one, I'll do the south?"

"Sounds like a play date to me," I said, trying to keep a straight face.

It took us two and a half hours to turn the earth.

Afterwards, we shared a bourbon—he was an Ancient Age man and, oddly enough, I really liked it. Livermore called Bobby Nixon's cell and told him about what we were doing. Then I got on the phone and set a time at the coffee shop in Edenton to talk about a coordinated plan.

Bobby had invited me for dinner, but I didn't really want to include Patty in our discussions. All I could envision was more input and questions on a plan that was already in motion. If Bobby wanted to give her the details later, that was fine with me.

Finally, at least something positive was shaking loose.

I asked Livermore if I could use his phone to call Aunt Tabby. When Tabby picked up, the first thing she said was, "Some friend of yours from the Army named General Tillman called for you."

That was good news—I hoped. "Did he leave a message or say when I could call him back?"

"He said to tell you the name is Dragica Zorić. I wrote it down, right here. Then she spelled it for me. "Your general friend told me the 'c' in her last name has a little mark over it. He also said she's the niece, whatever that means," fishing for an answer.

I didn't giver her one.

I took a deep breath. "That's great, Tabby."

But when I started to tell her I was visiting a friend and would be late, so not to worry about dinner, she interrupted with, "Your friend, the general. Is he the one who, you know, helped you before?"

"Yes, he is," I said.

"Who is this Dragica person?" she asked.

"Just someone I wanted him to check up on. You know, from back in the Army days." Before she could ask more questions, I told her I had to run, and got off the phone. After I hung up, I wondered if I should just come clean with her, at least about the shooter.

Nah!

Besides, there'd be long conversations and too many questions.

I met up with Bobby at the Edenton Express Coffee House where, to my delight, they actually had a one pound bag of whole bean snickerdoodle for sale. If I bought the bag, they agreed to grind it for me, then take out enough to brew me a cup. I said it was a deal if they could make it two cups and put them in two of their large paper cups, which they did.

Sometimes you get the elevator and sometimes you get the shaft. Today the elevator was in operation.

While the barista was doing her thing for me, I sat down with Bobby, who right away said, "That's some deal you made with Landon. I don't know why I didn't think of that."

"Maybe because you're not as devious as I am," I said.

"What made you think of it?" Bobby asked.

I shrugged, "Just want to help Miss Betty. I know she's in a daze about everything." Then I passed on the lie about Eddie Chapman approaching her at the funeral home. I asked Bobby if he knew Chapman.

"Just heard the name but don't know him," Bobby said.

All the better, I thought. "Well, my thought now was to get in touch with Erskine's clients, at least the major ones, and set them up for how to deal with Chapman. I'll need a client list from you ASAP, because I plan on being out of Aunt Tammy's and back to Nag's Head by Sunday evening," although I figured I could get a head start without it.

Bobby frowned. "But what if Chapman doesn't go for it?"

I laughed. "From what Ralphie said, I think Chapman is a greedy little bastard who'll love the idea of trying to screw the Livermores out of a deal. Truth is, I don't give a damn about him. I just want the farmers, particularly those in Weeksville, to get a fair deal. In any event. It will be good for Miss Betty."

"Yeah, you're right," Bobby said.

"I'll leave it up to you about handling any contractual arrangements between her and Chapman. And I suggest you move quickly on it, because Chapman may just think he can take the poor widow lady for a ride and get the accounts from her on the cheap."

While Bobby sat there pondering, bobbing his head around, the barista brought over our coffee and my bag of ground snickerdoodle.

Bobby thanked me for the brew, then said, "Yeah, I guess you're right. I'll have to get on the paperwork for the Air Tractor, anyway." Then, "I tried to talk to Betty about it twice, but she doesn't seem interested. I guess I'm going to have to get Patty to talk to her. I know she's in shock about all this, but she just can't sit there in denial without at least letting me handle things for her."

Bobby, the practical one.

I told Bobby that as soon as I got home this evening, I would start calling the farmers I knew had dealt with Erskine and would call Bobby at home tomorrow, let him know of my progress, and get the names of the other accounts. There was no need to hang around, so I told Bobby I had an appointment and had to get going.

On the way out I thanked the barista for her kindness.

Actually, the only appointment I had was taking myself to the Office Barn in town to have them help me prepare a simple missing cat flyer, make a hundred copies, then, on the way to Tabby's, start spreading them around. I wished I had a picture of

Basil, but I'd just have to be sure the description on the flyer was self-explanatory.

In less than an hour, I was back in Elizabeth City, sitting in front of a desk across from a woman named Lila, who said she was a Copy Barn Specialist. I didn't know what that meant, but if she could help me I didn't care. Everyone has to have a fancy title for what they do.

After I told her what I wanted on the flyer, she came up with the idea to look online to see if we could find a photo of a Basil look-alike.

We actually found one that was 95% there. She copied and pasted it into the flyer, printed out a master, then made a hundred copies for me. Within less than forty minutes I had paid for them and was on my way back to Weeksville. I'd included a $500 reward as an enticement. I figured if someone had taken him in and was feeding him, they'd surely give him up for that. And I'd be happy to pay it.

I spent the next hour and a half knocking on doors and leaving flyers with those who answered, and sticking them in the door jambs for those who didn't. Margie at the Weeksville Junction store let me post one in the front window. When she asked about the girl in the Wrangler, I said she'd disappeared.

"Weird," was Margie's reply.

Margie also taped a flyer on the check out counter.

Thank you Margie!

There was no one at the nearby church, but I knew where the pastor's house was on Little River Road, so on the way back to Aunt Tabby's I drove by. I was lucky enough to catch the pastor's wife, who took a dozen or so of the flyers. She also agreed to have her husband make an announcement at church the coming Sunday and hand out a flyer to anyone who requested one.

There wasn't anything else I could do, so I headed back to Tabby's. It would be a sad day if I had to go back to Nags Head and Blue Heron Marsh without my four-legged friend.

Damn that Dragica Zorić!

Food had been relegated to the back burner, but Tabby had a matronly obsession with feeding her favorite, and only, nephew, so she was only too happy to drag out leftovers and feed me. And I was only too happy to oblige. However, since she had me cornered at the kitchen table, I had to fend of a rigorous cross-examination about General Tillman and Dragica Zorić

After the meal, Tabby said she was going outside to cut some fresh flowers, and I said I'd clean up. I used the time alone in the kitchen to call Detective Jenkins. I soon found out he was gone from the office, but when I told them who I was and that I had an important lead on the person who'd shot at me (twice, I emphasized) I was provided with his cell number.

As it turned out, it was an annoying call, with Jenkins annoying me more than was necessary.

It went like this:

Jenkins: What is it, Sawyer?

Me: I have the name of the person I believe was the shooter.

Jenkins: How did you get it?

Me: A confidential informant.

Jenkins: Don't be a smartass, Sawyer.

Me: Do you want the name or not? If not, give me the name and number of either the person who took over the case at the F.B.I. or Homeland Security.

Jenkins: So you're not going to tell me who told you?

Me: It was a person of high rank in the military. I'm not at liberty to give you his name.

Jenkins: You think the F.B.I. or Homeland Security is going to let you get away with that?

Me: That will be between me and them.

Jenkins: You're a real asshole, Sawyer. What's the fucking name?

Me: Dragica Zorić (I spelled it for him).

Jenkins: You have her address and phone number, too?

Me: If I had that, I'd go take care of her, myself.

Jenkins: Jesus! I need to find another place to work. One where a bunch of bubbas don't rule the roost.

Chapter 24

SATURDAY MORNING, BEFORE I left for Chapanoke, I finished making some calls to Erskine's Weeksville clients, all of whom were wondering what was going to happen to their spraying schedules. They were happy to hear from me—or anybody. One of them said he'd called and left a message for Eddie Chapman, which I thought was being disloyal to Betty Weeks, but I didn't say so.

I presented the idea to them as if it was Bobby Nixon's idea and told them he was in negotiations with Landon Livermore about a deal that would lower their spraying costs. Even the one who'd called Chapman was willing for Bobby to get in touch with him, which I said would be sometime next week. I'd be long gone by then.

I figured I didn't have to say anything about what to do if Chapman called them directly, figuring if Ralphie somehow screwed up his part, the

Currituck crop duster would still get the message via the farmers. On the other hand, if Ralphie had done his part, it would only reinforce what he'd put out there.

Win-win.

With two mugs of coffee flowing through my system, a little after 9:30 I was on my way back to Chapanoke.

Forty minutes later I pulled up in front of Sam's Grocery. He was right where he was the first time I saw him, except this time he was reading the newspaper. Sam looked up and waved.

When I came up on the porch, he said, "Thought you might be a comin' along soon. Why don't yah go inside and get us a couple of Stewarts."

"Miss Goode come back yet?" I asked.

"Oh, yeah. She was runnin' a little late, but she's in. Don't suppose she's goin' nowhere just yet, so's might as well humor an old man and sit a spell."

"I'll do that," I said, then went inside. I fished around inside the cooler and came up with two cold Stewarts, popped the tops on the built in opener, laid a couple of bucks on the counter and brought them back outside.

I handed one to Sam. He took it, then rattled the paper, saying, "Only get the paper for the weather and the baseball scores. The rest of it's bunk. I wanta know what's going on, I talk to my customers. Anyway, I like them Atlanta Braves. You a baseball fan?"

"Used to be when I was a kid. Haven't had much time for baseball since then."

We clinked bottles. "Here's to the Braves," he said.

"Here's to the best root beer in town," I said. Sam chuckled and we took a couple of healthy swigs.

"I told Cookie you came by to see her. Said you were gonna to leave a message on her door."

I just nodded.

Sam rambled on about the Braves' prospects, grousing about how they were only in fourth place and how things didn't look good for them for this season. After that we chatted about the weather. Finally, I extracted myself, saying I'd stop by on the way back from Cookie's.

A few minutes later I pulled into Cookie Goode's driveway. Next to her Toyota Tacoma was a big rig. When I got out of the car, I could hear the ticking of the engine cooling down after a few thousand miles on the road.

I got out of Trusty Rusty and was looking over at the rig when the front door to her double-wide opened up. A wiry woman with the frame of a person in her forties came out onto the stoop. The body may have said forties, but the tired, worn face placed her a decade later. She did have a nice head of short blonde curly hair, most likely dyed as there was no hint of gray.

She didn't say anything until she got closer. She had bright hazel eyes but, at the moment, they didn't present a pleasant look.

"Are you the Mr. Sawyer who found out where I lived from Mr. Sam?"

Confrontational.

"I am," I said.

"And who claimed he was going to leave a note on my door and didn't."

I shrugged. "I decided it wasn't necessary."

"Sam said you knew Pete."

"You mean Erskine, don't you?"

I got a stony face.

"What do you want?" she asked. It wasn't all that friendly.

"Well, Erskine and Betty are long-time family friends." I decided to lay it out. See what her reaction would be. "His crop-duster crashed in my aunt's front yard. I got there right after it happened."

Tears pooled in her eyes.

"Look, Miss Goode. I didn't blow your cover with Mr. Sam. And I don't want to upset you, but there are some people who are concerned that there might be more to Erskine's accident than what was reported by the NTSB." When she didn't say anything, I continued with, "I was hoping you might give me some insight about Erskine's . . . ah, relationships."

Cookie Goode snorted. "You mean his relationship with me, don't you?"

"I mean his relationships with anyone who might have wanted to . . . uh . . . do something to sabotage his plane."

"What? No! That's crazy." Then, she screwed up her face and said, "It was my fault Erskine died," her eyes rolling up toward the sky.

When she put her hands together, as if in prayer, I thought, *Oh, brother*. I kinda knew what was coming, and I wasn't looking forward to it.

She didn't disappoint. Or, maybe I should say, she was right on point.

"God punished us both for our sins." Then the flood gates open.

Oh, geeze. I had to find a way to get past this and extract some information. "Why don't we talk about this inside. I promise you I'm harmless."

All of a sudden she was back to being acerbic. "I'll kick your ass if you aren't," she said, then, sniffing, turned and strode with purpose back to the house.

I took that as an invitation, following behind, thinking, she's a strange one, evoking God one moment and threatening to whip my ass the next. I wondered what Erskine saw in her. Was it sex?

Maybe that was it. Not getting any at home and was with Cookie Goode. Whatever it was, I'd have to sift through the God business if I wanted to get anything out of her.

Once inside, tears still spilling, she told me to have a seat, asked me what I took in my coffee, didn't listen when I said I was fine, thank you, and disappeared around the faux stone fireplace into what I presumed was the kitchen. I sat on a wooden futon, the cushion covered by a red sheet with a white flower pattern. There was a mix and match of throw pillows, which I arranged for comfort.

The rest of the furniture, like the throw pillows, was eclectic. There were a few prints, poorly framed, hanging on the wall, including a head portrait of Jesus and another one on him on the cross. Everything else was the usual stuff: landscapes from here and there around the country, none that I could pinpoint as local. Maybe things she'd collected on her long haul travels.

Soon she was back with two nondescript mugs of coffee. Nothing fancy. Dollar Store fare.

"You didn't say, so I didn't put anything in it. Erskine liked his black, so I guessed you did, too."

I didn't bother telling her it didn't matter, that I would hate it anyway. I decided to humor her with a few sips, then set it down on a plastic coaster on the wood coffee table. She sat herself down into one of the two chairs across from me.

"You know, the only reason I told Sam, or anyone else who asked, his name was Pete so's to protect his . . . you know . . . ."

Before I could say anything, she changed her tone again and confronted me with, "Who thinks someone messed with his plane? That's what you're saying, isn't it?"

"Someone in the sheriff's department," I said. "I'd rather not mention his name."

"Then why aren't *they* out here talking to me?"

"Because they don't know about you," I said, calmly.

That one left her without a reply. But only for a half a minute. I could see the wheels turning.

She scrunched her wet eyes. "How do you know about me?"

I made a nondescript hand motion and said, "You know how small town and close-knit communities are. There's always somebody who knows something. I just knew you were a woman who did long haul trucking and lived in Caratoke. Can't be too many of those."

"God makes us pay—" she began before I interrupted her.

"Look, Miss Goode. If someone did cause Erskine's death, the only one who needs to make a payment to God is whoever it was." She started to interrupt me, but I held up a hand. "Maybe the suspicions are just that, and it was just an accident.

In that case, you can deal with God any way you see fit. I'm just trying to gather information to make a determination one way or another."

She shifted uncomfortably in her chair. "No matter . . . , "then she started in on the 'God works in mysterious ways' routine and I cut her off again.

"Why don't you just let me ask you some questions, then I'll leave you to your personal conference with the Man above."

She leaned forward and glared at me. "Don't treat my faith lightly," she growled. Then, just as quickly as she'd turned sour, her face took on a concerned look. "Surely, you don't think I did anything, do you?"

I didn't know if she did or not. So I lied to get what I wanted. "No I don't."

Relieved, she sat back in her chair and said, "So, what do you want to know?"

All of a sudden she left her self-incrimination behind and wanted to talk about Erskine. Probably a catharsis, A cleansing of the soul to the kindly Webb Sawyer in the confessional of her living room.

She was a strange woman.

She talked for over an hour.

She told me that she'd met Erskine after he'd seen an ad in the paper about a fellow trucker in Hertford who was getting out of the business and selling his rig.

"Emmet Delaney it was. By the time Erskine contacted him, he'd already sold his truck, a Freightliner, it was. I own a Peterbilt. A much better rig than any of the others. That's my opinion, anyway," Cookie said.

She went on to say that Erskine was just exploring the possibility of getting into the business and wanted to talk to someone who could tell him about getting a CDL, which is a commercial driver's license, and who could also give him some insight into the business.

There were plenty of truckers in the Weeksville area but apparently, early on, Erskine wanted to keep his wife out of the loop about what he was doing. At least about the fact that he was actively pursuing information on his thoughts about a late-life switch of careers. If that was true, it didn't say much about their relationship.

You think you know people, but you really don't.

"You know," she said. "The good, the bad and the ugly."

As she spoke, I just nodded or uh-huh'd her, not wanting to interrupt the flood gate of information.

Delaney had already packed up and was leaving for Florida the next day, she told me. So he referred Erskine to her. "He told him I was someone who knew the business. 'Inside, outside and upside down,'" Cookie said. She didn't even crack a smile when she repeated her truck driver friend's words.

"Emmet gave him my number, but when Erskine found out I lived here in Caratoke, he just drove out here. Like you, he stopped and Sam's store and found out where I lived. And like you, he came back on a Saturday morning."

"When was that?" I asked.

"When he first came over here?"

I nodded.

"It was almost two years ago." I could see her mind drifting back in time.

That would make sense if Richard Trueblood knew about it before he died.

When she didn't say anything else, I had to prompt with, "So you've been seeing each other for almost two years," a statement, not a question.

Once again, her eyes rolled to the heavens. Then she dropped her head, staring at her lap. Finally, she looked up and said, "At first it was just having some coffee and talking about the trucking business. There's more to it, you know, than just getting in a rig, hooking up a load and driving it someplace for delivery. A lot more."

She was back to her antagonistic tone.

Trying to ease her back down, I said, "I learned a long time ago that there's always more to any job than meets the eye: the rules and regulations, the politics, the inefficiencies and the slippery people you have to deal with. Dad had friends in long haul, so I know something about over-the-road trucking. Like cooking the books and end-running weighing stations. It's a rough business."

"I try to play it straight," she said, glaring at me, jaws clenched.

Try, being the key word, I thought. "I'm sure you do," I said. Then, "So did Erskine make any runs with you?"

She took a deep breath. "Only twice. During winter, when he wasn't flying."

"His wife approve?" I asked, knowing I was getting close to the information I wanted, but treading on dangerous ground.

Cookie snorted. "Hell, no! She was off visiting a sister in Atlanta both times. She probably would have killed him if she knew." When she saw the look on my face, she quickly toned it down and said, "I mean, I don't know what she would do," almost mumbling the words. Then, "I had a husband once. Caught him stepping out on me and that was the end of that."

I presumed she meant divorce. I was almost afraid to ask. Maybe Sam would know. If not, I could have Aubrey check for me.

Again, I wondered why in hell Erskine thought it was a good idea to get involved with this woman. One minute she's praying and feeling sorry for herself, the next minute she's all worked up and ready for a fight. Maybe she was just overtired, although I had a sense it was more than that.

"Miss Goode, I don't need to know the personal details of your relationship with Erskine. It's none of my business. But I would like to know one thing."

"What's that?" suspicious.

"You said his wife didn't know about you and Erskine. Are you sure about that?"

Suddenly, Cookie Goode stood up, and shouted, "The only reason she knew was because the damn fool told her!"

I was startled by her vehemence. "And he told her because he planned on leaving her?" I pushed, getting the sense I was close to an even more startling revelation. What that might be, I wasn't sure.

"I don't know what he was planning to do," she said, easing back down.

When I was in the Army, I once took a class on reading body language. How to tell if someone is lying. All I can say is, Cookie Goode's words said one thing, her eyes and body language another. Whatever it was he'd decided, she was lying. She knew.

"Besides," she said, plopping back into her seat, as if in resignation. "What difference does it make. He's dead. The Lord punishes sinners and we were both sinners." She'd returned to her penitent persona.

And here I thought the Lord was loving and forgiving. Maybe I was thinking of Buddha or Vishnu.

We sat there for several minutes, me watching her, she looking at her hands, which she'd folded and placed on her lap.

Without warning, she jumped up, went over to the front door, opened it, and said, "Thank you for coming, Mr. Sawyer, but I've been away for five days and have a lot of things to do."

Holy crap! While I wasn't happy about the sudden turn of events, it looked like I didn't have a choice. So, without a further word, I got up and left.

I was glad to be out of there.

If nothing else, I'd determined one thing. Cookie Goode must have been one hell of a piece of ass, because she was a fucking fruit loop.

I stopped at Sam's. He wasn't on the porch and there was a black, jacked-up pickup truck out front. I parked and waited until the customer came out—it was two early-twentyish kids wearing black, Grateful Dead t-shirts turned into wife-beaters. It looked liked they'd used their mother's pinking shears to do the job.

As they got into their pickup, I got out of mine. When they pulled out, they didn't even look my way.

Inside, Sam was still behind the counter.

"Well, back already," he said. "You talk to Cookie?"

"Sure did, Sam. She's an interesting woman." An understatement.

Sam chuckled.

I had one question for Sam, but didn't want to be obvious, so I said, "Thought I'd get a Stewarts to go," then walked over to the cooler and dug around inside until I found one.

I brought it over and set it on the counter, pondered for a minute, then went back to the cooler and got another one. "Another one for later," I said.

"Good thought," Sam said.

He rang them up, told me how much, and I paid him.

"Going back home?" he asked.

"Yep."

"Well, sure has been a pleasure havin' you come by. You come back real soon, yah hear? And hope you find your cat."

"Me, too, Sam. Been nice chatting with you." I headed for the door. Then, as if I'd forgotten something, I turned and said, "Felt bad about Cookie. We both lost a good friend. Heard she lost her husband, too," seeing where that led . . . if anywhere. I figured if she'd divorced the guy, Sam would know. And if not, he'd might know that, too.

"Oh, yeah. Danny Goode. That's where she got the name Goode. Although," making a face, "I hate to speak ill of the dead, but the man didn't live up to his name."

"That, so? Trouble with the law?"

"The law, drinkin', cattin' around, you name it. How Cookie got hooked up with him in the first place, I'll never know. But like she always says, 'the Lord has ways of dealin' with men like him.'"

"Huh," I grunted. "What happened?"

"She didn't tell you?"

I pursed my lips and shook my head.

"Danny drove like a fool. Always gettin' speedin' tickets and wreckin' cars. That was the death of him," Sam said.

"Car wreck, you mean?"

"Yeah. You know that sharp curve about a mile down the road from here headin' toward 17? Where it goes to the left?"

"Yep."

"You notice that oak tree dead ahead at the curve?"

"Yep. It's a big one. The oak, I mean. The curve is nasty, too. County roads can be like that."

Sam nodded. "Well, they say he musta been doin' eighty when come up on that curve. Brakes gave out. Hit that oak head on. BAM! Dead on impact."

"No kidding."

"That's what happened."

"Well I'll be darned."

Chapter 25

WHEN I CAME to the "L" curve in the road, I slowed down and eased around the corner past the mighty oak.

Brakes gave out, I thought. *Equipment failure. Familiar theme.*

I began running scenarios through my mind. If Cookie Goode sabotaged Erskine's plane, why would she do it? Because he'd decided not to leave Betty for her? Since Cookie already had almost two years invested in him and, as unstable as she appeared to be, could that have set her off? But how would she know how to sabotage a single-engine plane? The next problem was how would she be able to do it without anyone seeing her go out to his hangar? And wouldn't there have been signs of a break in?

I had another thought. I remembered those two guys across the street from the Weeks' house. Had noticed them on two different occasions, working on the two-story four-square, garage and barn. Maybe they saw something.

I decided that was my next stop.

First, I stopped at the Weeksville Junction Grocery to see if there were any reported sightings of Basil. There were none. I was finally resolved that I'd never see my four-legged buddy again, and that made me sadder than I could have imagined.

I left there in a sour mood.

I drove past Tyler Swamp Road and turned down Estercliff. I contemplated dropping in on Miss Betty, if she was there. Maybe I could get some clarity by talking one last time with her because, as it stood now, unless there was a witness to say Cookie Goode did something to Erskine's plane, and I thought there was a strong possibility she might have, I would just have to go back to Blue Heron Marsh and wait for Dragica Zorić to take another run at me. At least I would be on home turf.

Lastly, I'd have to have a sit-down with Aubrey and give him my thoughts and findings. Maybe tomorrow morning. I'd have to call and make an appointment. With tomorrow being Sunday I wasn't sure about his family schedule. I decided to sit down and do a hand-written report tonight.

Maybe Cookie did it. Maybe nobody did anything and it happened just as reported. Equipment failure and an accident. I wasn't naive. I knew law enforcement agencies didn't like to reopen investigations when there was already an agreed-upon conclusion. Either way, I'd know I'd done all I could. I'd leave with a clean conscience.

I needed a week of fishing.

The whole matter had been depressing.

I didn't see Betty's car in the driveway, but I did see the two guys still working at the property across the street. I pulled into their driveway.

Their names were Michael "Just call me Mike" Crawford and his step-son Bernard "Just call me Bernie" Pendergraft.

Once the intros were over, I told them I was a friend of their neighbor, the Weeks, and asked them how long they'd been living there. Want it or not, I got the whole story.

Bernie had done three tours with the Army in Iraq. Then, when that was done, he did another two in Afghanistan. They'd called him Mr. Miracle. He'd survived three IED events with only superficial injuries. At least those were the only ones they knew about. He'd watched three of his buddies die and another three who'd lost limbs.

He returned home with a full blown case of PTSD. His wife divorced him, got custody of his kids, moved to Washington State to live with her parents and made life impossible for him.

His step-father, Mike, had just retired as a Chief Master Sergeant in the Army. Widowed years ago, he took Bernard under his wing and decided it was time for a change . . . for both of them.

"I had a friend from here," Mike said. "Said I'd like to live here. These days, anything's better than the D.C. area. There, it's like living in a madhouse 24/7. It's congested, the people are rude and the traffic is horrific."

All this time, Bernie didn't have much to say. He was a bit antsy and I could tell he was ready to get back to work.

"Was born here in Weeksville," I said. "Now live in a stilt house at Blue Heron Marsh in Nags Head."

"Outer Banks, huh?" When I nodded, he said, "Nice down there, but used to be nicer. Even there is too busy for me."

"I'm lucky. I'm off to myself in a marshy eco-system while the world spins around me," thinking, *that's why I have to get back home as soon as possible.*

"Webb Sawyer, you say?" Mike asked.

"Yep."

"You're not one in the same as—"

"That's me," I interrupted.

"Huh!" Then to Bernie, he said, "This guy here should be given a medal for what he did." Then he related what he'd heard and read about my encounter with the Serbian death squad leader.

I stood by listening, mildly embarrassed. It wasn't that I was ashamed of what I'd done. I just wasn't all that happy to have conversations about it.

Finally, Bernie piped up and said, "Shot the fucker, huh?"

"Saved the people at The Hague the cost of a trial," I said.

Mike snorted. "Yeah. Where they'd spend a few years in a showcase trial, then find him guilty and give him a place to live and three squares a day for twenty years." Looking me in the eyes he said, "Thank you for your service, sir," then saluted me. So did his step-son.

Now I was really embarrassed, and it takes a lot for me to feel that way. Even so, I gave a half-assed salute back. I needed information, and if that's what it took to get it, that's what I'd do.

Changing the subject, I said, "So, looks like a lot of work still in front of you. Been working on it long?"

Mike laughed. "You're right about that. Place's been sitting empty for over a year. An estate situation. Anyway, we've been on it for a little over a month. Got the house habitable, but still a lot of work to make it comfortable. Since the weather's been good, trying to get the outside presentable. Will do the inside work when it gets too damn hot or when it rains."

"See you got a new roof on the place," I said.

"That's one of the first things we did, right Bernie?"

"That was a bugger," Bernie said.

I could tell he was wrapped tighter than a ball of yarn.

"So, you guys out here about every day?" I asked.

"Once we got some work done inside and the roof done, been outside every day for the past two weeks," Mike said.

"Wonder if could ask you a question," I said. "You heard about Mr. Weeks, I suppose. The crop duster."

"Oh, yeah. That was pretty bad. Heard he crashed in someone's front yard. Lucky he didn't hit the house."

"Yeah. That was my aunt's yard where he came down. She'd been watching him make his passes. It was a terrible thing for her to witness. I came on the scene right after it happened."

"Guess your aunt was lucky," Mike said.

"You never know when you're gonna get it," Bernie blurted out.

"Know what you mean, Bernie," I said, looking at him. As your dad probably knows, I spent time in both Somalia and Bosnia. Saw a lot of bad stuff."

Bernie just nodded.

"I've seen your truck over there," Mike said, "So I guess you know the family."

I gave him the short version about how my family and the Weeks' family had been friends since way back.

"You never know, do you?" Mike said, shaking his head," So what is it you want to know?"

"Well, Mike, I wonder if you and Bernie can remember back to the day of Mr. Weeks' accident. Do you?"

"Yeah, I do," Bernie said. "I remember seeing him go out there. He was walking, remember, Dad?"

"Yeah, he was. Walking."

Now that I had their mind on Erskine and his plane and hangar, I asked, "How about the day before. Do you have any recollection of that?"

Mike looked at me funny. "Is there something more going on than just Mr. Weeks having an accident?"

"Might be, Mike. And before you ask, the reason I'm asking around about it is, the NTSB, you know, the National Transportation Board, who did the investigation?"

Mike nodded.

"Well, they decided it was a connector joint that came loose and made him lose control. But there are others who wonder if that was the whole story."

"Ah. So you're the unofficial information gatherer to see if there might be anything to that."

"Not only unofficially but, by some, anyway, probably unwelcome." I gave him the eyebrow raise.

"I hear yah," Mike said. "Organizations. Don't matter if they're government or private. They get their mind set on they way they want things to be, and not how they might be or really are."

"I remember the day before," Bernie cut in.

He had an intense look on his face. I wondered what other memories were flashing in his mind. For a long time after Somalia and then Bosnia, I'd have bad stuff creeping into my thoughts, even when having an unrelated conversation.

"Remember, Dad. Weeks must not a been home that morning, 'cause a fuel truck pulled into their driveway. White with a red star. What's the name of that company?" frowning.

"Texaco, I think," Mike said.

"Makes sense," I said. "They do service aviation fuel." Then, switching to what I really wanted to know, "If I give you makes, models and colors of vehicles, can you tell me if you remember seeing any of them at the Weeks' house? Or even going up the field lane to Mr. Weeks' hangar, particularly the days before the accident."

"We'll do our best," Mike said.

I read off the list of Perry Adams' vehicle, all the Livermore's vehicles and last but not least, Cookie Goode's vehicle.

Mike's reply was the same for each one. "Don't remember seeing that one. You, Bernie?" Then Bernie said he hadn't seen any of them either.

I was disappointed.

"But what I was going to say about the fuel truck was, the driver pulled into field lane and stopped opposite the house and honked his horn," then went on to say that while he didn't know for sure, he figured that was the usual routine.

"Seems right, you know," Mike said. "So Mr. Weeks would know the guy was there to fill his tank... or tanks... however many he has."

"Yeah," Bernie said. "Anyway, Mrs. Weeks came out of the house and walked over to the fuel truck and talked to the driver. Like I said, Mr. Weeks wasn't home."

Bernie then related how she must have told him to go on out to the hangar, because he drove on up the lane. She'd gone back into the house and shortly came back out and got into her car, drove out of the driveway and around to the field lane.

"She drove up to the hangar and got out of the car, unlocked the place. Then went inside with him," Bernie said.

"That it?" I asked.

"Then I went inside the house to use the bathroom."

Mike was frowning.

"What?" I asked.

"There was something a little odd," he said.

From behind, I heard a vehicle slow down and I turned to see Miss Betty turning into her driveway. She looked over toward us, and I waved. She didn't wave back. I turned back and asked Mike, "What was odd?"

"Wonder why she didn't wave," he said.

I frowned. "What do you mean?"

"Oh, I meant just now. All of us waved at her and she didn't wave back. She always waves. That's one of the things I like about this area. Everyone waves at you."

"Yeah, and with all their fingers, too," Bernie chimed in.

I laughed. "The Weeksville wave, they call it." Then, "So what was odd about the day of the fuel delivery?"

"Oh, yeah. That. Well, when Bernie went inside, I went back to power washing the side of the garage. Wasn't too long before I saw the fuel truck coming back down the lane, but Mrs. Weeks wasn't coming along behind it."

"Her car was still parked out at the hangar?"

"Yeah, but I didn't think nothing of it. Figured she was probably straightening up the place. You know how women like to get into a man's space and help out whether he wants it or not."

"I know what you mean," I chuckled. I waited while Mike wrinkled his brows in thought.

Finally, he said, "You know. She was out there close to an hour before she came back down the lane. Only reason I know that was when I saw her turn onto the street and back around into her driveway, I looked at my watch, thinking, she probably cleaned up so good, Mr. Weeks would never find any of his stuff."

"Almost an hour, huh?"

Mike gave me a strange look. "Yeah. Almost an hour."

All three of us looked over toward the Weeks' house and watched as Betty Weeks disappeared through the side door.

Chapter 26

I TALKED WITH Mike and Bernie for a few minutes before I thanked them for their time, wished them luck with their restoration projects, got back into Trusty Rusty, backed out into the road and pulled down Betty Weeks' driveway.

She answered the door with, "Why were you talking to those two across the street? They're not from around here, you know?"

"Just being neighborly while I waited for you to return home."

"Hmmph! I suppose you want to know where I've been."

"Not really," I said. "Just wanted to talk to you about Erskine's crop dusting business."

"Oh, yeah, that. I heard you been talking to Bobby about it. I don't really understand why that's any of your concern."

"Now, Miss Betty," trying to ease down the tension. "You know all the farmers around here are friends of both our families. We've known them for ages and I just want to be sure they get a good deal from whoever buys Erskine's contracts. I talked to Bobby so's to make sure you don't get taken advantage of by whoever buys them out." Then, "May I come in so we can talk about it?"

Betty let out a big sigh, then said, "I suppose." "But I'm still angry at you for sticking' your nose into my business with Miss Danna."

I had a feeling she was going to be even more angry at me before our conversation was finished.

Once she had me seated in the living room, I was surprised when she asked if I wanted some coffee. I declined, saying I'd already had three cups and was coffeed out. I waited while she fixed herself a cup.

When she returned from the kitchen, she placed herself across from me on the couch, took a couple of dainty sips from her cup, then placed it on a coaster on the coffee table between us.

"Bobby told me the Livermores were reconsidering about taking over Erskine's accounts," she said.

For someone who'd full of angst and had just been through a funeral, she was pretty calm and collected.

"Did you talk to them, too?"

I wasn't sure if Bobby had told her that or if she was just fishing. To be on the safe side, I said, "I went over there to talk to Landon Livermore about his clary sage crop and we did have a brief conversation about the crop dusting business. I just passed his thoughts on to Bobby," not wanting to give away too much, too early. I wanted to find out what was going on in her mind.

"That he was interested and willing to give Erskine's clients a discount?"

"That's what he was hinting at," being as non-committal as I could.

"Did he say how much he was willing to pay me for the accounts?"

"No," I said. "That's for you and Bobby to work out with whoever wants to buy the accounts."

"Whoever? Is there someone else interested?"

"Not that I know of."

"Well. I suppose I should thank you for sticking your nose in, then."

"I'm sorry you see it that way," I said. Then, "There's something else I'd like to discuss with you."

She snorted. "More of my private business, I suppose?"

"Exactly that."

That took her off guard. First, her expression went blank. Then she sat back and looked at the ceiling. Then she leaned forward and glared across the coffee table at me. "I'm not saying anything else about Mr. Adams and Miss Nicolescu."

I ignored that and asked, "Do you remember an earlier conversation we had about the possibility that Erskine's wreck may have not been an accident? That someone may have tinkered with his plane?"

"That's ridiculous?" she said. "Who would do that?"

Here's the way it is, Miss Betty. As I told you before, I was asked to look into whether the preliminary report by the NTSB was accurate . . . or not," which was sorta true. "Their final report is being held up based on the report of my investigation." A lie.

"Who asked you to do this?" she asked.

As I've already told you, "I'm not at liberty to say. Someone may tell you later, but I can't."

"This is ridiculous," she said, but her look and body language said she wanted to know what I'd been doing.

Ignoring her again, I said, "So I want to get your opinion."

"My opinion?" snorting. Then she went back to, "I still don't understand why you're involved in this. You're not law enforcement and you're retirement from the Army, if it can be called that, was not under the best of circumstances."

If she was trying to annoy me, she wasn't. It just made me more suspicious of her. I learned long ago that people who have something to hide do their best to turn things back onto someone else. It would be interesting to see who she tried to turn it back on when I laid out my "so called" case.

For the third time, ignoring her, I said, "The first ones I looked at were your friends, Perry Adams and Bogdana Nicolescu."

"It figures," she interrupted. "And I've already said I wasn't going to discuss them."

I didn't care if she wanted to discuss them or not. I pressed on. "Everyone knows Perry Adams has a reputation for being a hot head. And I told you before that Miss Nicolescu has a criminal record."

Miss Betty's jaws clinched. "I asked her about that. She said it was self defense."

"That so."

"Anyway, what's any of that have to do with me?"

An interesting reply, I thought. "I didn't say it had anything to do with you." Then, "Maybe I'm wrong, but my first thought was that the two of them were scamming you for a lot of money and that Erskine knew about it and was putting pressure on you to stop seeing the woman. The psychic. Maybe they didn't want their gravy train to end."

"That's ridiculous," she said. That seemed to be her favorite word. I figured I'd hear it many more times if she let me keep talking.

"I told you why I was going there, and as soon as all this stupid mess is over, and you stop butting into my business, I'm going to try and get Miss Danna to take me back. We were getting so . . . so close . . . ." She let the thought drift.

"So you're saying you don't think either one of them had any reason to do harm to Erskine, even though he was on to them?" still pushing that idea.

"He wasn't on to anything."

"Okay. I'll note that you don't think they had any animosity toward Erskine."

But when I didn't say anything else, she leaned forward, waiting for more.

"Even though I was interested in his crops, I really went to talk to the Livermores because I wanted to get a feel for who they were and what they were all about because I'd heard that Erskine had contacted them about buying out his business."

"That's wrong. Erskine didn't contact them. He asked Bobby to contact them and they weren't interested. But now, all of a sudden, they are?" confrontational.

I guess she'd forgotten that she'd told me the Livermores had contacted Erskine and she'd talked her husband out of any deal with them.

"I'd heard that Landon Livermore's son had been unhappy that the deal wasn't going through." When she didn't respond, I said, "You know, since you said Erskine backed away."

Still nothing.

"And since the son wanted to expand his own crop dusting business."

She shrugged.

"Not only that, the kid does have the reputation as being a hothead. And, like Miss Nicolescu, he has a criminal record. His for assault. Maybe he had a reason to, let's say, make Erskine's clients available," throwing it out there for her to chew on.

I could see her wheels turning.

After a while, she said, "Maybe. Maybe your friends in law enforcement, whoever they are should check that out."

Once again, it was difficult to reconcile that over the past week Miss Betty had been so distraught she could hardly speak.

An act?

Now, both Erskine's death and her annoyance at me being a busybody in her personal life had taken a back seat to her sudden interest in what I'd been doing. What I might know.

I suspected her interest was more than simple curiosity. She had taken the bait and I was ready to reel her in.

I found it interesting that she was willing to protect the dog killer and the psychic, but ready to throw the Livermore kid under the bus. She was getting with the program.

"I'll make a note of that," I said. Then, "Then I ran across a piece of information which I'm embarrassed to have to discuss with you."

Her eyes went big. "What?" She knew what was coming but was doing her best to act surprised.

I decided to hit her with it, head on.

"Cookie Goode."

Betty's mouth fell open.

"You bastard," she said.

"So you do know about her."

Standing up, she shouted, "You get out of here right now! Right now!" Standing up and becoming irate was an unbecoming habit.

"Sit down Miss Betty. I've got something to say and I'm going to say it." I'd already decided to play it in reverse regarding Cookie Goode, like any good detective would do. Like Detective Jenkins would do if this ever got to his desk. While I didn't like Jenkins, I didn't question his competence.

She didn't budge, standing there glaring. She started toward the hallway that led to the side door, then came back, put her hands on her hips, and glared some more.

I just glared back. I'd already made up my mind that this whole relationship with the Weeks' family, at least this segment of it, was over. It was too bad, because I knew Aunt Tabby would be collateral damage. Maybe even Bobby and Patty, although I wasn't sure about Bobby. However, if that was the way it came down, so be it. I felt I owed it to Erskine to push for answers, even if there were none forthcoming. Even if there were no answers to give.

There was more prolonged glaring before she finally made some sound that was somewhere between a pig snorting and a bear chuffing. Eventually, she threw herself back down on the couch.

I've seen a lot of people squirm under interrogation, although I wouldn't use that word for our conversation. Betty Weeks wasn't the first one I'd ever seen who one minute could appear calm, the next minute go into a tirade.

"How . . . who told you . . . ?"

I waited her out.

"That bitch tried to take my husband away from me!" she screeched, startling me when she slapped the coffee table with the palm of her right hand, the liquid from her cup sloshing onto the highly polished wood surface.

I remember from my days in Brussels when I would do soft interrogations of terrorist suspects. How when I reached the critical point of the "interview," then dropped the bombshell piece of information on them, how their reaction was either indignance or a sudden display of anger.

Betty Weeks had left her indignance behind. There was real anger.

"I actually talked to Cookie," I said, not wanting to lose my momentum after Betty's outburst. "She gave me the impression that Erskine was going to leave you for a life of over-the-road trucking," adding fuel to the fire.

Once again, jumping to her feet and pointing at me, "That's it. She did it," now shaking the finger at me. "And you know how I know?"

I pursed my lips and shook my head.

"'Cause I checked out that 18-wheelin' tramp, that's how! You know what she did?"

Another head shake. Miss Betty was nothing like the kind, smiling, cake-baking lady I remembered when I was growing up. Somewhere along the line Betty Weeks had gone to some dark place and was stuck there. I didn't know how this was all going to play out, but I felt a twinge of empathy for her. If I hadn't known her all those years, I probably wouldn't give a damn. Just another looney tunes to deal with.

The person I really felt sorry for was Erskine. He'd ended up with one unstable person and then hooked up with another. A two-fer in the worst possible way. At least his part in it was over. Sometimes I wondered if the whole world had gone insane.

"She done went and killed her husband. You know how she did that?"

I decided to play dumb about Danny Goode's mishap. "No, I don't."

She snorted. "Some investigator you are. I hope whoever put you up to nosing around does a better job at pinning poor Erskine's death on her. It was that Detective Jenkins, wasn't it? I know Sheriff Grimes would never think anything bad about me."

"I thought we were talking about Ms. Goode. What makes you think anyone thinks bad of you?" trying to see where she'd go with that.

"Well, I know you do, Mister Sawyer," emphasizing the "Mister." She began to hyperventilate. "It's that Goode woman who everybody needs to look at. Everyone knows she tampered with her husband's brakes and made him have that car crash."

"Huh. If that's true, why is she still around?"

"Because," sitting back down, "nobody could prove it. Just like nobody can—" She stopped herself.

"Like nobody can prove what?" I asked, finishing her unspoken words.

"Prove nothin'," she growled. "Now get out of here and tell that Detective Jenkins to start looking at what Cookie Goode did to poor Erskine." For the third time, standing up, again pointing toward the side door.

For the moment, I kept myself planted in my seat. "So, let me ask you this, Miss Betty. How do you think Ms. Goode sneaked out to the hangar without anyone seeing her? And once she was there, how would she know about getting into the plane and finding the connector joint? How to loosen it to just the right tension? You follow me?"

Miss Betty just glared at me.

Now, for dramatic effect, I stood up. "I'll tell you how I think it happened. I think the morning before the accident, the Texaco delivery truck came up the field lane and honked for someone to come up and open up the hangar so's he could fill the tanks. I think someone came out of the house and followed him up there. Then, after the delivery was signed for and the driver left, the person stayed out at the hangar for as long as it took to sabotage the plane. Like maybe almost an hour. Of course it had to be someone who knew exactly what to do and how to do it. I suppose I could have someone check to see who signed for the fuel that day."

The arm with the finger pointing at the hallway to the door swung back around to me. "It was those two nosey parkers who told you that, wasn't it. Well I'll tell *you* something, Mr. Snoopy. It was me who went out there and it was me who signed for the fuel, and I was only out there a few minutes after, straightening up some things. So, what you think doesn't prove anything."

"But I'll tell you what will, Miss Betty."

The arm and the finger dropped to her side, but the eyes still bore into me like a drill.

Now was the time for the biggest lie of all. It was a calculated gamble. "You see, Miss Betty, the NTSB was asked to look for any fingerprints on the connector joint that didn't belong to Erskine. They were also asked to do swabs against the inside of the hull or anything else in there for traces of DNA. You know, where someone might have brushed up against it. So if the person didn't wear gloves, or even if they did, but accidently brushed up against something, they'll find out who it was."

I saw her look down at her hands.

"The results should be back by the first of next week I said."

Then I brushed past her and departed.

Chapter 27

BETWEEN COOKIE GOODE and Betty Weeks, I felt like I'd been on the end of a yo-yo string.

Tabby was so happy to see me, she hugged me and didn't want to let go, saying, "Oh, Webb. I was worried about you. I know you've been out there looking for that person who tried to shoot you." Then, "Did you find her yet?"

I gave a restrained laugh. "Not yet, Aunt Tabby, but the FBI has her on the run."

Tabby pulled back, looked at me and shook her head. "What's the matter with girls these days. Don't we have enough men who are criminals?"

You don't know the half of it, Aunt Tabby, I thought. *There are even kids these days that are as hard core as the adults.*

"Looks like your lawn needs mowing again," changing the subject. "But I'd like to make a call first." After the day I'd had, I thought about downing a Jack Daniels, but decided to use the mow to get my thoughts together for the report I would write.

"Oh, sure, Webb. Do you want me out of the way when you make it?" giving me a little half grin.

I little-grinned back. "No. Just want to touch base with Aubrey Meads."

"Oh, is he looking for the girl, too?"

"He's keeping his eyes peeled," was all I said.

"Oh, speaking of phone calls. Nan called after you left this morning. She wondered if you were going to pick her up at the airport this afternoon. I told her she'd better not count on it, because I didn't know where you'd gone or how long you'd be. We had a long discussion about your phone habits. I told her she should make you get a cell phone. Everyone has one these days."

"You don't," I said.

"Well that's different. I don't need one like you do."

I snorted.

Tabby headed to her bedroom to fold laundry and I went into the kitchen and punched in Aubrey's number from memory. I was surprised when he picked up.

"Surprised to catch you Aubrey," I said.

"Actually, was just getting ready to leave. Have an evening shift tonight."

"Well, wont keep you, but wanted to know if I could see you sometime tomorrow morning. I know it's Sunday and family and church and all that, but I'm heading back to the Outer Banks as soon as I'm finished with our business. I want to give you an in-person recap on my findings. In fact, I'm going to do a written report this evening, after dinner."

Aubrey laughed.

"What?"

"Aunt Tabby have an old Olivetti typewriter in the closet?"

"Actually, was going to use the even older method of pen and paper."

"Write plainly," he said. Then, "You have something worthwhile?"

"I think your eyes will be popping," I said. "But not sure if anyone can do anything with it."

"Hmm. Now you have me interested. Come over around 10:00 am. I'll send Kiki off to church with the kids, so we'll have the place to ourselves."

"Thanks, Aubrey."

"Gotta run," he said, then hung up.

I went to the back of the house, told Tabby I was gonna give the lawn a mow and headed out to the equipment shed. It was about an hour and a quarter job if I ran fast, but I wanted to mosey and think, so I figured an hour and a half or so.

About halfway through the mow I noticed Tabby on the back deck waving at me with one hand, with the thumb to her ear and the pinky finger to her lips, signing a phone call with the other. I drove the mower over to the deck and shut it off.

"It's Nan," she said.

I don't know if Tabby noticed the big smile on my face but it was sure as hell there. Finally, someone I really wanted to talk with.

Tabby left me alone in the kitchen.

"Good to hear your voice," I said.

"And I haven't even said anything yet," she said. Then, "What's this Aunt Tabby tells me about you getting threatened by the father of the kid who was messing with her." Before I could take a breath and answer, she said, "And then somebody shooting at you. Twice. And you getting bit by a moccasin and being taken to the hospital. And then finding out it was some girl from back in your Bosnia days. She says she thinks she's a terrorist. Is she the one who's been shooting at you? And, by the way, what happened to Basil? She said he went missing."

I knew by the time I finished with Nan, and got done with the lawn, I would need a triple shot of the JD.

I spent the next half hour giving her the rundown on all that had happened since I last spoke with her, at least in regards to Renner, Zorić, my snake bite episode, and Basil. I didn't get into the business with Erskine and Betty and the rest of them. That I could do at my leisure on the front deck of my house in the marsh . . . or better yet, in bed after getting hot and sweaty.

I did my best to convince her that, except for Basil, That I had everything under control and all was well in Weeksville.

"Uh-huh," she grunted.

I didn't tell her I was going to be home the next day, hopefully early afternoon, because I felt I needed some decompression time. I guess I was being selfish, but that was how it was going to be. When she asked, I told her to come over the first day she was free from catching up at work. I could tell from the tone of her voice she was a little put off, but she didn't say anything.

When we were done with the call, I went back outside and finished the lawn.

When I returned inside, Tabby immediately began to backpedal, saying, "I'm sorry. I didn't know Nan didn't know about your being shot at, and that Basil was missing."

I waved a hand. "Don't worry about it, Aunt Tabby. I've just been too busy to call her." Then I told her I planned to meet with Aubrey Meads in the morning, then head back home.

"You mean you're not going to church with me or staying for lunch?"

"I doubt you'll be back from church when I'm finished with Aubrey," I said.

"Oh." She seemed disappointed. Then, "You are coming back here first, aren't you?"

I'd thought about packing up and leaving straight from Aubrey's, but I suspected Tabby was considering skipping church and fixing me lunch before went—it was her way. So I said, "Sure, I'll come back before I leave."

She took a deep breath and smiled.

I fixed a double Jack Daniels—I figured a triple would cloud my mind and affect my report writing—and took it out onto the front porch. I declined Tabby's offer to take the day's paper with me. I just wanted to think.

I thought about what would happen should the unlikely event occur that Betty Weeks was brought to trial for the premeditated murder of her husband. Did I think she sabotaged his plane and caused his death? Yes, I did. Could any of it be proven?

Probably not.

I could hear the defense lawyer now, saying, "Isn't it true, Detective Jenkins, that Erskine Weeks had an illicit relationship with a woman named Cookie Goode of Caratoke in Perquimans County? Isn't it true, Detective Jenkins, that just before his accident, Erskine Weeks had broken it off with Miss Goode? Isn't it true, Detective Jenkins, that Erskine Weeks told this to his wife, Betty (a statement that surely Betty Weeks would have told the detective so as to move the suspicion from her to Cookie Goode)? Isn't it true, Detective Jenkins, that a few years earlier, Cookie Goode's late husband, Danny Goode, died under suspicious circumstances (the defense attorney's characterization, not based on any known fact or investigative report or supposition) when his brakes unexpectedly gave out and his car crashed into a tree, killing him?"

And it would go on and on like that, throwing any hint of motive and suspicion away from Betty toward Cookie.

Alternative theory.

Reasonable doubt.

No. I knew they'd never even be able to bring charges against Betty Weeks. She'd never see the inside of a courtroom on this matter. Hell, the truth was, there would never even be an investigation.

Erskine Weeks died when Yellow Bird did a one-point landing in Aunt Tabby's front yard. An accident? I didn't think so. Not any more. If I had to lay odds that it was murder, I'd give it 99 to 1 that it was and that Betty was responsible, 99 to 1 that Cookie Goode wasn't, and zero that the dog killer or the psychic, any of the Livermores or anyone else had anything to do with it.

I would just write my report just like Sergeant Joe Friday used to say on the old TV show *Dragnet*. "Just the facts, ma'am. Just the facts."

Chapter 28

I ARRIVED AT Aubrey's a few minutes after ten, Sunday morning. A low system had blown in over night and had turned things bleak and dreary. It was overcast and raining. It suited my mood.

Aubrey greeted me with a sullen look, which I attributed to the weather. I was wrong.

After I followed him into the living room, before we sat down, he turned and said, "I've got something for you from Terryberry."

"As in Deputy William Terryberry?"

Aubrey nodded, then said, "But before I hand it to you, I'll tell you what it is. If you don't want it, I'll just write 'Unable to find to make service.'"

"Sounds ominous," I said.

"You know I don't use swear words, Webb, so I'm just going to quote what Bill said."

"Okay."

"He said, 'I felt like finding that squirmy little rat-fucking bastard and sticking it up his ass.' Again, his words, not mine."

I laughed. "That's one way to get around personal rules."

Aubrey's face became flushed.

"Renner?" I guessed.

"Yeah. That . . . that fool had the nerve to file a civil suit against you for destruction of property and assault on a minor."

I threw my hands in the air. "I plead guilty as charged, your honor," I said, hamming it up. Already I was in a better mood.

"I don't find it all that funny," Aubrey said, frowning.

"Ah, Aubrey, relax. Hand it over and consider me served. It will just be another chance for that squirmy little rat-fucking bastard to show off what a damned jackass he is. And in public, no less."

Aubrey shrugged. "Suit yourself. He went over to their hand-me-down credenza, picked up some papers and brought them back to me. "You sure?" he tried again. "Because, as far as I'm concerned, by the time I got a chance to go over to Miss Tabby's you were long gone."

I held out a hand. "Lay it on me and let's get to the important stuff."

"Renner. I'd like to . . . ," letting the words trail off.

"Do I have to sign it?" I asked.

"No," but you do have the right to file an answer within thirty days and/or make a counter-claim."

I looked at the paper. The court date was set for the third Monday in September at 9:00 am. "I'll mark my calendar for a grand return to Elizabeth City."

Aubrey shook his head. Then, "I do have a more pleasant surprise for you."

"I'm all googly-eared," I said.

Aubrey laughed. "How'd they put up with you in the Army?"

"Things were going pretty well until I shot that guy in the face."

Aubrey grinned.

"What's the more pleasant surprise?" I asked.

"Oh, yeah. Hold on a sec." holding a finger in the air. Aubrey turned and went around into the kitchen. He was back in a flash with a small brown bag in his hand. "I know how particular you are about your coffee. So when I was in town the other day, I went by the Java Hut and asked the owner, Maria Salem, if she could grind me up a pound of your favorite and . . . here it is." He raised the bag up for me to see. It had the words "Webb's Favorite" written across the front in black marker.

"And," he said, "I hope you don't mind, but I already took some of it and brewed up a pot. I wanted to see what was so special about it, so I already had a cup. It's pretty darned good. I'm guessing you want a cup."

I nodded and thanked him, then giving him a hard time, said, "After a week of high-stepping through the dog poop of people's lives, that's the least you could do."

"Yeah, I agree," Aubrey said. "Sometimes you think you know people and you don't. Was it all worth it?"

My thoughts, exactly. "I'll let you decide. Meantime, you got anything bigger than a cup?"

Aubrey was back soon with a very manly mug in one hand and a plate of corn muffins in the other. "KiKi made them early this morning before she took the kids to church." He laid them on the coffee table, then hustled back into the kitchen. He returned with a jar of seedless raspberry jam in one hand and an opened tub of butter with a butter knife stuck in it in the other, saying, "I won't tell KiKi this is how I served it if you won't."

I made the zipped-lips sign.

We sat down on the couch and I handed him the envelope with my hand-written report inside. "Why don't you give it a quick read, then we can talk about it," I suggested.

"Sure," Aubrey said, then began reading.

I cut one of the corn muffins in half, fixed it up with butter and jam, then enjoyed it along with my manly mug while I watched him read.

When Aubrey was finished, he looked up and said, "Holy catfish! This isn't good, is it, Webb?"

"You sicced me on it, Aubrey. So now I'm dumping it back in your lap." Then, since I'd stuck to the mundane facts in the report, I spent time giving my personal thoughts about each of the main characters and supporting cast, answering any questions he had along the way. I also gave him my mental gyrations on what a court proceeding regarding Miss Betty might sound like.

When I was done with that, Aubrey said, "Unless we can find concrete evidence, I agree with you." Then, "So you really think she did it? Sabotaged Erskine's plane?"

"Ninety-nine to one," I said.

"What clinched it for you, or was it just a gut feeling?"

"The way she looked at her hands when I gave her the spiel about the finger prints," I said.

"My God," Aubrey said.

"Well, you were the one who put me on to her in the first place," I reminded him.

"Yeah, but I thought it might have something to do with Perry Adams. You know, if she had something going with him . . . I don't know what I thought, Webb. What a mess. A tragedy, really."

Then, "I can't believe how you found out that business with Erskine, either. Very strange."

"Strange?"

"You know, it turning out that I thought she was stepping out with Adams and it was Erskine who was doing the cheating."

"Nothing is ever as it appears," I said.

Shaking his head, Aubrey said, "I just don't believe that, Webb. Take KiKi and me. We're exactly as we appear to be."

It's that way now, I thought, but I would never say so. Aubrey was a good guy and KiKi seemed like a sweet girl and they had two nice kids. But who knew what unknown and unforseen events were lurking: something that could sneak up and create havoc with their lives.

Maybe, after this past week, I'd become more cynical than I already was about personal and intimate relationships.

"So, any idea what you're going to do about Miss Betty?" I asked.

A pained look crossed Aubrey's face. "I'm going to have to think on it, Webb. Maybe even pray on it. I mean, I know I'm going to have to show it to Jenkins, but . . . ."

"Maybe you can use it to convince him to talk to the NTSB. Ask them to take another look at that connector joint, or anything else inside of what was left of the fuselage. See what they can find."

"Yeah, I suppose you're right. I have to work again tonight, but have the next two days off. Maybe I'll take it up with Jenkins tomorrow."

We sat there for a few minutes without saying anything, Aubrey drumming his fingers on his leg. I fixed myself another corn muffin.

Eventually, Aubrey let out a big sigh and asked, "You hear anything from Jenkins or the FBI or Homeland about the shooter?"

I pulled the medal out of my pocket, showed it to him, then told him how I'd found it at the crime scene; how I'd recognized what it was; how I'd tracked down and talked to my old Army boss, General Brad Tillman. How he did some research and came up with Dragica Zorić's name.

"You know, of course, technically that's tampering with evidence," Aubrey said.

"And if your guys hadn't missed it and I hadn't found it, the shooter's name would probably never be known. I passed her name along to Jenkins who, I presume, passed in on to the FBI, Homeland Security and whoever else they're working with."

"He didn't ask how and where you got the name?"

"He asked," I scoffed . "I told him it was from a confidential informant and I wasn't at liberty to divulge the person's name."

Aubrey laughed. "If Jenkins didn't like you before, he probably hates you now."

"That's nothing new," I said. "Anyway, I hope that doesn't affect him taking any action. The report I gave you being from me, I mean."

"I could go over his head to the sheriff," Aubrey said.

"You know, of course, Grimes is a friend of the family. You might have to threaten to go to the FBI."

Aubrey shook his head. "What a mess." Then, "So, you didn't say if you'd heard anything from them. Jenkins, the FBI, anyone?"

"Nope. I figure Zorić either went underground or is in the process of reorganizing, replanning and maybe even reinventing herself to take another run at me."

"That's comforting," Aubrey said.

"I'll be ready for her." Then I told him about the time the Colombian guy brought three of his men with him to assassinate me in my own home at Blue Heron Marsh.

"Jesus, Webb!" Then Aubrey caught himself and said, "Sorry. It's just that . . . Holy catfish!"

I made a sound something akin to a laugh and said, "You better stop hanging around me, Aubrey. I seem to bring out the worst in you. I don't want to corrupt you." I told him how Randy Fearing's wife thinks that's what I did to him. "She thinks I lead what she calls a dangerous and Bohemian life style."

He laughed. "That's a term I haven't heard in a while. Like they say, 'To each his own.' I guess I prefer the quiet family life of a deputy sheriff in a rural county."

"I'm sure you have your share of crazies here, Aubrey."

Aubrey shook his head, "More and more lately. As the population grows, so do the crimes."

"Not to mention the Jeb Renners and the Perry Adams of the world."

"And now Miss Betty," again shaking his head. Then, "I guess you're going to keep the medal as a souvenir?"

"What medal?"

"Right. What medal?"

Chapter 29

WHEN I PULLED into Aunt Tabby's yard, besides hers, there was a vehicle I recognized.

I guess she wasn't satisfied with my answer about when I'd see her next.

It had turned into a nasty morning. On the way back from Aubrey's, the rain had picked up from light and intermittent to heavy and steady. I parked Trusty Rusty behind Nan's three-week old, fancy-schmancy, pyrite mica-colored Toyota Tacoma with its sand beige interior, got out and high-tailed it between the rain drops to Tabby's front porch.

The front door was unlocked and I turned the handle and stepped inside . . .

And Froze.

Ahead and to the right, Nan was sitting on an easy chair, her right profile toward me. Sitting in the matching chair across from her was Aunt Tabby, eyes wide open, staring at me, a look of terror on her face. And behind her, holding a gun in her right hand to the back of Tabby's head, was Dragica Zorić. She had her left hand on Tabby's shoulder, as if they were old friends. The couch with the coffee table in front of it, and in front of me, was between me and the Serbian girl.

Cleverly staged positioning.

Zorić had changed her hair from long and black to short and blonde, but it was her. How had she gotten inside? Assuming Aunt Tabby stayed home from church, was Zorić already there when Nan showed up? Or had she surprised or tricked them both?

"Finally we meet face to face, Mr. Webb Sawyer," pronouncing it Weeb.

Nan never once looked over at me, keeping her eyes on the Serbian girl. I knew what was going through Nan's mind, but she was too far away to do anything, which was why Zorić placed her there.

"It's me you want Dragica," I said. "You can let them go, then we'll deal with each other together."

"Ah," smiling, ignoring my request. "So you know my name. It would be interesting to know how you found out."

My executioner was actually quite attractive. She had a well proportioned face with a perfect nose, nice full lips and well coiffured hair and fingernails. Her dark eyes under full eyebrows held a steady gaze. She was attempting to put on an air of ease and friendliness, but the eyes gave away a deadly intensity and purpose.

She was here to kill me, and that was that.

"I'll tell you how if you let these two ladies go."

Zorić let out a deep-throated laugh. It was forced and more menacing than amused. "So they can call your police? I think not. Besides, I have plans for them . . . and then you."

I didn't like the way that sounded.

"Ah, so you understand what I'm going to do?"

I had to keep her talking, hoping an opportunity would become available for either me or Nan. I sure as hell wasn't going to stand there and watch her shoot Aunt Tabby, then Nan, before she turned her gun on me.

I looked at the weapon in her hand. It was a Sig Sauer P229, the same kind used by Homeland Security, Customs and many other Federal agencies. I knew it fired a .40 or a .357 caliber bullet, depending on the barrel, and I couldn't tell which kind she had. The weapon had a little bit of a recoil but, for someone familiar with it, at close range it didn't really matter. Either caliber would kill you without question. I did know the clips carried at least ten rounds and some as many as twelve to thirteen. Once she started shooting, there would be no reloading necessary.

"Are you angry because you missed the first two times, Dragica? You have me in front of you now.

No need to involve anyone else. Lock them in a closet if you don't want to let them go. They don't have to be a witness to our business. Our business is between us. It has nothing to do with them."

"Oh, Mr. Webb Sawyer, but it does. I wish I had thought of it earlier . . ."

Zorić was doing her best to seem composed and play the role of the sweet, understanding girl. It was like watching a high school girl cast in the leading role of an amateur production of *American Psycho*, only this was real and she was a Serbian nutcase bent on not only my demise, but of those who I loved and cared for.

This was one scary-ass bitch.

Poor Tabby's face was frozen in absolute terror and she trembled like a dog going into a vet's office.

". . . but now with us all together—"

I knew there would be no reasoning with this person. I'd shot her uncle to death while he sat in his cell, and she was bent on repaying the compliment. I'd killed a member of her family and now she was ready for what the Serbians called *osveta*—revenge.

"I think it's time for your Aunt Tabby to stand up." Zorić pronounced her name Tobby. When Tabby didn't move, Zorić gave her a tap on the back of her head with the muzzle of her gun and Tabby yelped.

"I said, stand up."

Time had run out. I had to do something that could very well make Tabby a casualty of the Serbian's vendetta. But if I did nothing, she would surely die.

Tabby stood up.

From behind Zorić, in the hall, I saw movement. A low shadow hugging the far wall

"Turn around and face me," Zorić ordered.

I knew exactly what the Serbian girl had in mind. While I watched helplessly, she would shoot Tabby in the face, maybe two or three times. She had plenty of ammo in the clip. Then she'd do the same to Nan. Then, finally, me.

I wasn't going to let that happen.

"I have something of yours," I said, reaching into my right front pocket.

She swung her Sig towards me. I didn't think she'd shoot unless she saw a weapon. It would ruin the scenario she'd so vividly planned out. Unfortunately, both my handgun and rifle were in the truck, in the lock box behind the cab.

"This," I said, holding up the Serbian Service Medal she'd left behind in the swamp.

"So that's how you found out who I am."

"You want it? I'll trade," buying a few moments, knowing she wouldn't.

I saw Nan's eyes dark quickly toward me, then back toward the Serbian.

Zorić snorted. "I'll get it when I'm done with you and your loved ones."

Just as she started to move the gun back toward Tabby, I tossed the medal towards her, just to her left. Instinctively, she grabbed for it with her left hand, taking her eyes off Tabby as she did.

This was it. Some of us might die, all of us might die, or none of us might die. When there was no choice, one reacted and acted.

Everything happened at once and so fast that, later, if I had to relate the details, I would have to close my eyes and mind-play it back in super slow motion.

I sprung forward, hands and arms out in front of me. I guess that was instinct, figuring it she swung the gun and shot at me, maybe a hand or arm might take, deflect or slow down the impact. As they say, "desperate times call for desperate actions," and this was an act of desperation.

I went up onto the coffee table, hoping the assassin would pull the gun away from Tabby and toward me. As soon as I'd launched myself toward Dragica Zorić, out of the corner of my eye I sensed movement from Nan, who was also in motion.

My eye was on Zorić's Sig Sauer when I heard an inhuman screech and the gun went off. Afterwards, I realized it was Tabby who Nan was after, not Zorić, hoping to tackle Aunt Tabby and move her out of the line of fire.

When the bullets started flying, it wasn't until after it was all over that I knew who lived, who was alive but wounded, and who was dead.

The explosion filled the room like the wump from a big gun on a Navy battleship.

I heard Tabby scream.

I took two steps across the top of the coffee table, launching myself headfirst at the assassin, my hand reaching for the Sig Sauer. For some reason, Zorić's head was thrown back, her mouth open, a sound emanating from her throat that I could only describe as part human, part feral.

Zorić had also thrown her left hand backward, behind her head, in an attempt to grab at something; what I couldn't tell. In the meantime, she'd swung her gun hand away from me, out of reach, and was firing blindly downward. Tabby was screaming like a banshee, so at least I knew she was still alive.

Then I heard Nan yell out words I'd never heard come out of her mouth and didn't know were a part of her vocabulary.

Unable to grab the gun, I did the next best thing. I lowered my head and rammed it into Dragica Zorić's face. I felt the bones in her nose give way as she pulled off two more rounds, then lost her balance and toppled over backwards.

There was one more shot before her elbow slammed against the floor and the weapon dropped from her hand. It was then I saw the cause of her struggle.

Where in the hell—

Basil!

He had a mouthful of hair and his claws were embedded in the back of Dragica Zorić's head.

Between Zorić's screeching and cursing in Serbian, Aunt Tabby's hysterical screaming, Nan's yelling, "You bitch! You bitch!" and Basil making noises like an angry tiger, it sounded like the inside of a asylum for the criminally insane.

I was on top of Zorić and pulled my right arm up to deliver a massive fist to her face when she brought a knee up and caught me between the legs.

Pain shot up into my head like a bolt of lightening and I rolled over onto my right side, drawing my knees up into a fetal position.

Once, when I was in Somalia, a old woman kicked me in the cobblestones while we were trying to clear a two-story house where a sniper had been firing at us from the roof. My testicles had ached for days. Dave "The Wave" Meekins laughed about it until one day, a few weeks later, it happened to him, this time by a twelve-year old girl. They didn't like us much when we were messing around in their country. I didn't like being there so much, either.

I saw Zorić reach for the Sig Sauer with her right hand. Nan was on hands and knees, scrambling across the floor, trying to get to it first.

At the same time, Zorić had reached behind her with her left hand and grabbed Basil by the scruff of his neck, trying to wrench him from the back of her head, but Basil held on, his claws deep in her scalp. He was growling, hissed and spitting like a little banshee.

Just as Zorić's fingers touched the gun, Nan dove forward and knocked it out of reach.

Instead of making another try for the weapon, Zorić brought her right hand back and grabbed Basil. Now she had two hands on him, both around his neck. In one final yank she pulled Basil away from the back of her head. Not only was Zorić's nose bleeding severely, but there was blood and bits of hair and skin torn from her scalp. Even so, she held on.

I had to move fast before she broke his neck or choked him to death.

Ignoring the pain, I moved my head toward Zorić's nearest arm and chomped down like an angry pit bull.

By then, Nan had scrambled past her, got the Sig Sauer in her hand, then turned and fired one round, hitting Zorić in the right hip.

Zorić let out another screech, letting go of Basil, one hand reaching for her hip, trying to shake me loose with the other one.

Once he was free, Basil let out what sounded like a croak. He jumped backward off Zorić's body, then turned and fled down the hall toward the bedrooms at the other end.

But Dragica Zorić wasn't finished. As soon as Basil was out of the way, she moved her hand from her hip, swinging it at me, punching me with her fist square in the forehead. It felt as if I'd been hit with a pile driver. Stunned, I released her left arm and fell back away from her.

I put my palms on the floor, attempting to steady myself, blinking my eyes and shaking my head, trying to clear my vision.

Suddenly, Zorić, growling, rolled toward me. I heard a *snick*, and saw a knife in her right hand — a Kubotan hidden-blade knife disguised as a key ring. Where it came from, I didn't know.

The growl was the last noise that Dragica Zorić uttered.

Two shots rang out and the Serbian assassin gasped once, then fell forward.

Later, Nan told me that the first shot she'd fired that hit Zorić in the hip was meant for the back of Zorić's shoulder, but the recoil startled her and she'd jerked the barrel to the right. She'd fired low, afraid that she might hit Basil or me by mistake.

She'd mentioned Basil first. I reminded her of that later, after we finally got home.

I struggled to my feet and, bent over, stumbled around the chair to check on Aunt Tabby, who was on her left side, facing me, sobbing, a hand clutching her right buttocks.

"Keep your eyes on the girl," I said to Nan, which was unnecessary, as she was dead.

While Nan tended to Aunt Tabby, I went into the kitchen and called 911. When I hung up with them, I called the sheriff's office direct and spoke to the weekend person who identified herself as Amy Murcheson, telling her what happened and asking her to notify Sheriff Grimes, Clyde Henderson and Detective Jenkins.

When I hung up with Amy, I went to Nan, knelt down, kissed her on the lips, then limped down the hall, looking for Basil.

Epilogue

RAIN SPLATTERED AGAINST the windows on the back porch, which was really the front porch, but who wants to argue about it. It faced the Croatan Sound. When my mother was alive (rest her soul) she declared that was the front of the place. Funny thing was, she never liked coming down here all that much and it had become a retreat for my dad (also resting in peace with Mother) and his fishing buddies.

The front porch, which was really the back porch, was open to the elements. It faced Blue Heron Marsh and the tree line separating me from Highway 12 — thank goodness for that. The Atlantic Ocean was another quarter mile or so east.

Nan and I sat on what I considered the back porch, sipping Jack Daniels Black Label on the rocks, watching the sun sinking in the west and the charter fishing boats heading for their berths after the day's outing. One of the boats and its captain I knew very well.

"There's *Happy Days II*," I said. The original *Happy Days* was blown to smithereens after my friend, Dave "The Wave" Meekins, lost it in a poker game, but, once again, that was yet another story.

"How's Dave been? Haven't seen him lately. Not even in the shop," Nan said. She called her restaurant at Shallowbag Bay "the shop."

"Haven't seen him in over six weeks," I said. "Guess he's been busy with the charters."

"When are you going to go back to see Aunt Tabby?" Nan asked.

I groaned. "You know I love her, but two weeks there was more than I could bear."

I'd stayed another week after the incident with Dragica Zorić. After they'd taken Nan's statement and we'd gone up to the hospital to see how Aunt Tabby was faring, Randy Fearing declared Zorić's death justifiable homicide (as in self defense) and Nan had returned home early the next day, Monday morning, Tabby had been stitched up and was in the recovery process after one of Zorić's wild shots had taken a chunk of flesh out of her behind.

"Since you've come back here, she's called every day at the shop to complain about how much her butt still hurts. She calls it her bummy." Nan chuckled. "Of course, she couches the call as wanting to see how you're doing. She hates that she can't call you direct," eye brows raising.

I knew that bugged Nan, too.

"I'll bet she asks when I'm coming back to Weeksville,"

"That, too. You know, she was disappointed that you didn't return for Betty Weeks' funeral."

Two weeks after I'd confronted Miss Betty about Erskine's so-called accident, they found her stretched out across her bed with a bullet hole between her eyes. She'd used one of Erskine's hunting rifles. Whether that was a statement or simply poetic justice, I didn't know. There was no note.

As it turned out, based on my report, Jenkins had gone to the NTSB and they'd taken another look. It didn't take long for them to find readable fingerprints on the connector link inside what remained of Yellow Bird's fuselage.

Apparently, the catalyst to her dire action was Detective Jenkins' and Clyde Henderson's appearance at her house with a search warrant, which included the right to take her fingerprints. Miss Betty knew she'd been found out and saved the state the cost of a trial and incarceration.

"That would have been very uncomfortable for the family, don't you think?"

"More like traumatic, I imagine," Nan said. "Even more traumatic than her death, I'm guessing.

Then, "You shouldn't feel guilty, you know. You did the right thing . . . for Erskine's sake."

I didn't answer. Even if Bobby and Patty Nixon never found out I was the instrument of Miss Betty's demise, it would be hard for me to look either of them in the eye. I hoped Aubrey and the rest of the people in the sheriff's office kept it to themselves, but figured that was too much to ask.

"One good thing out of it all. I'm glad the farmers made out with their new crop dusting contracts," I said.

"Nice trick you pulled to make that happen," Nan said.

Nan was correct on both counts. The price may have been high for the Weeks family and the community, but Erskine's murder didn't go unresolved, and the price I had to pay was worth it . . . to me, anyway.

That Chapman fell all over himself to be sure the Livermores didn't get the farmer's business gave me a warm and fuzzy feeling for them. And Bobby had negotiated the deals. He and Patty made out pretty well, too, although I did feel guilty when he thanked me for my part.

"Where's Basil?" Nan asked. "He was on my lap a minute ago," looking around.

I got up and looked in the great room, then came back and sat down. "He's on his favorite window sill, watching for visitors and friends . . . and enemies." Then, smirking, "I've noticed how every time you come over he gets on your lap for scratchies and kind words."

When I'd asked Nan how he'd suddenly showed up at Aunt Tabby's after four days, Nan told me that when she'd made the turn off Union Church onto Tyler Swamp, there he was, trotting down the side of the road, a cat on a mission, heading down to Tabby's.

"When I stopped, opened the door and called to him, he came running right over and hopped in. He knew it was me." Then, she added, "You know, it's a good thing I got impatient about seeing you, especially after I found out what was going on. Otherwise, you and Aunt Tabby would be dead and I'd be a sad and unhappy camper, not to mention what might have become of Basil."

"He's an ungrateful, double-dipping skunk," I said. "I know he probably took up with someone who was feeding him some over-priced brand of cat food. Then, when they got tired of him and threw him out, he decided to find his way back to Tabby's."

"Oh, stop," Nan said. "You know, darned well that you love that guy no matter what. Besides, that's the second time he's come to the rescue."

The first time was when Tico Carijona and three of his men came here to Blue Heron Marsh in the middle of the night to kill me while I was sleeping. It was Basil who saw them coming and alerted me.

"We should call him Supercat," Nan said.

I snorted. "When I saw him clawing at the back of Zorić's head, I was never so happy to see that four-legged critter in all my life."

Nan had told me that when she had knocked on Tabby's door and Tabby had called for her to come in, Basil had strutted inside like he owned the place.

"I thought Tabby sounded strange, but didn't think anything about it until I saw that woman standing behind her with a gun to the back of her head," Nan had said.

Basil had disappeared and Nan had been placed in the seat across from Tabby.

Nan told both me and the cops that the Serbian woman said they would wait for Mr. Webb Sawyer to arrive. Then she had talked incessantly about how I had assassinated her helpless uncle as he sat in a military cell, put there on trumped up charges by meddling Americans.

"Why did you think Mrs. Weeks killed her husband?" Nan asked, shifting subjects. "Didn't you say you thought he'd decided to stay with her and not go with that Cookie Goode woman?"

I shrugged. "Between being hung up over her long dead child and Erskine's betrayal, she went off the deep end." I thought for a moment. "Poor Miss

Betty," shaking my head. "She might have gotten off on an insanity plea. Who knows."

"Maybe, but she couldn't have handled the humiliation." Then, "You think the Goode woman killed her husband, like Betty did with hers?"

Again I shrugged. "I don't think so, but I'm wondering if Miss Betty didn't get the idea when she looked into Cookie."

"That Cookie seems kinda kookie," Nan said.

I laughed. "She was a drama queen, for sure. When she didn't create it, I think it found her. What Erskine saw in her is beyond me."

"And that damn Renner guy. He's got a lot of nerve suing you for assault when he was the one who threatened you with a rifle."

"The assault accusation is against his son," I reminded her. "And don't forget the destruction of property."

"What an idiot," Nan said.

"The one I feel sorry for is the wife, Jenine. Why do women get hooked up with such assholes? Are they that desperate?"

"Some of them are." Then, "Want another?" Nan asked, holding up her glass.

"Sure."

She was back in a few with refills, including extra ice for both of us.

When she sat back down, Nan said, "You know, Webb, considering all the lies, half truths and deceptions you experienced in your own quiet little home-town community, it's probably not a good time to bring this up, but I've been thinking."

"Um."

"Was that a sigh or a groan?" Nan chided.

Answering could be like stepping into a minefield. I just smiled.

When I didn't reply, she went on with, "I think I should move in with you."

Talk about being blind-sided.

"I ... uh ... move in with me?" I sputtered.

"You know. Pack up my clothes and personal belongings and move over here. Live with you. It's just that you're always doing your best to get yourself killed and I want to enjoy your company most of the time instead of just some of the time. You know, before some weirdo does you in."

"Well, that's a nice thought," trying to make light of it, buying time, trying to process what she'd said.

"No, I'm serious, Webb. I know you value your privacy, but I work a lot of hours over at the shop most of the time and wouldn't even be in your hair. And it won't bother me if you get up and decide you want to go fishing alone or with one of your fishing buddies . . . and that includes your trips down to Ocracoke to see Blythe," talking about my buddy from my high school days, Blythe Parsons.

"I . . . ah . . . really don't have room for all your furniture here and, besides, what would you do about your house?" It was a lame argument and I knew it but I was so nonplused by her statement that I was groping for something to say.

"No problem. I'll just leave the furniture there and rent the place furnished. Well, maybe I would bring over my dresser so I'll have a place for my clothes. I can even put it in your spare room. And there's a closet in there I can use so I'm not in your way. Make it sort of like a dressing room. Of course we'd have to straighten it up. It's kind of a mess in there, you know."

When I didn't reply, she kept rolling with, "In fact, you don't have to do anything in there. I'll straighten it up myself. Anyway, it needs a woman's touch." When I still didn't reply, she said, "Are you going to say anything? Yes? No? Maybe so?" Then, "You know I love you, Webb, but I don't want to get married anymore than you do. So if you decide it's not working out, you can send me packing back to Manteo."

"Can I have a few minutes to think about it?" I asked.

"Sure," Then, "You know, I think you need to relax first before you make a decision." When I looked at my glass of JD and took a long pull, she said, "I'm talking about bumping and grinding, not booze." She put on a leering grin with the up-and-down eyebrows, doing her best to make the elephant on the porch disappear.

"I . . . ah—"

"Your boys feeling okay?"

I snorted. "They've been through it before. They've learned to have a short memory."

"Want to go test them out, just to be sure?"

"You really are the Devil come to tempt me." It was all I could think of to say.

"Dat's me," Nan replied.

Douglas Quinn Presents

Eagle's Nest

The Next Book in the

Webb Sawyer Mystery Series

Turn the Page for a Preview of

Eagle's Nest . . .

Eagle's Nest
Prologue

A PAIR OF Zeiss 20x60-S Image Stabilization binoculars to his eyes, the man in the Ray-Ban Wayfarer sunglasses and the Atlanta Braves baseball cap watched from two blocks away. The binoculars were the best a person could buy. In this case, they were part of the payment from an affiliated group who didn't want to get their hands dirty. The Zeiss, along with $5,000 cash was his price for the action. The aluminum hard case for the glasses and his throw-away cell phone sat next to him on the passenger seat of the thirteen year old white Dodge Ram van. He'd used $2,500 of the cash for the van.

He swept the Zeiss from left to right, scanning the protesters. The lens could bring 1,000 yards up to 330 feet. From his 100 yards away he could see the hairs on the back of their necks.

Today, many of them would become fallen martyrs.

He saw Renata pull up in a silver 2005 silver Malibu that looked as if it had been in one too many demolition derbies. He stroked the hair of his full black beard, thinking, *but it got her to where she needed to be today.*

Renata was a full-figured girl, twenty-seven years old, shoulder length black hair, big on tits, short on brains and self esteem; totally depressed and high from shooting up heroin—just enough to keep her coherent but compliant. She was the perfect dupe.

It was midwinter, and even in Atlanta it was cold enough for a coat. She was told to wear one whether it was cold or not.

"You're just going to scare them," he'd told her. "It's not even real. They'll get the message. They're evil people doing evil things. We don't want them here and I know you don't either. Don't worry. As soon as you're being booked, our attorney will be there ready to bail you out. You won't even have to appear in court. You'll be back in Bogota before they know what happened. You can buy a lot of smack with $10,000. As soon as the attorney has you out, you'll collect the money and be on the next plane out."

Dumb bitch bought it.

Renata walked across the street and pushed her way through the crowd of protestors, ignoring their shouts and accusations, the filthy name calling, and the threats of eternal damnation.

Today there was a bonus. WATL had a TV production truck on site, hoping for something good to give their viewers—a thirty-second clip before moving on to the next thing.

The man laughed inwardly. *I think they'll have more than that for their fickle viewers today.*

Godless bastards!

Renata was almost through the protesters when someone from behind pushed her and she stumbled forward, lost her balance and fell to her hands and knees.

The crowd took up the chant, "Killer! Killer! Killer! Killer . . . !"

The man had told Renata, "No matter what they say or do to you, ignore them. Just think of that ten grand and the free ticket home and get into that building."

Someone came running out of the front door and grabbed Renata by the arms, pulling her to her feet, then, putting an arm around her, guided her into the building.

"Killer! Killer! Killer! Killer . . . !" the chants continued.

Once Renata was inside, the man breathed an audible sigh of relief. He reached over and picked up the phone, already thinking about the route back to the motel; about shaving off his facial hair; about getting rid of the Ray-Bans and Atlanta Braves baseball cap, just in case anyone spotted him and provided a description. The van he'd leave in a place where it surely would be stolen.

Then the only person he trusted would pick him up, drive him up Route 29 into the Chattahoochee National Forest, then onto Owltown Road and out to Owltown, where he'd meet with a man named Jed.

Jed would know him only by L.T., an alias, but Jed wouldn't know that. There was only one thing he would know. He was to provide L.T. with camping gear, food and water, a hunting knife with sheath, a Smithson .300 H&H hunting rifle with scope and three hundred rounds of ammunition, a compass, and maps of both the Chattahoochee National Forest and the Cherokee National Forest in North Carolina.

The man looked at his watch.

Time to rock and roll, he thought.

The man punched in a phone number on his cell.

Five seconds later, the Everton Family Planning Clinic exploded in a ball of fire, engulfing the whole building in seconds. The protesters were gone; blown away. The TV truck was on it's side and in flames.

He turned on the engine and calmly drove away, ready to begin the next phase of his crusade.

Made in the USA
Lexington, KY
17 August 2017